CATHERINE COOKSON

Beloved by readers on both sides of the Atlantic, Catherine Cookson is England's most popular and vibrant storyteller. Her unforgettable novels capture the very human passions of men and women who struggle and ultimately triumph over adversity, seeking strength or solace in love.

Now the bestselling author of *Katie Mulholland* and *The Dwelling Place* has created a memorable new series of novels about an English family—at the heart of which stands an irresistible and irrepressible young lady named Mary Ann.

THE DEVIL AND MARY ANN
The third novel in Catherine Cookson's engaging Mary Ann series

"A charming story . . . with a heroine of such human warmth as to be attractive to the young of all ages."

—*Publishers Weekly*

The Devil and Mary Ann

Catherine Cookson

BANTAM BOOKS · TORONTO · NEW YORK · LONDON

THE DEVIL AND MARY ANN

*A Bantam Book / published by arrangement with
William Morrow and Company, Inc.*

PRINTING HISTORY

*First published in Great Britain in 1958
Morrow edition published November 1975
2nd printing .... January 1976
Bantam edition / April 1977*

ISBN 0-553-02899-5

The Devil and Mary Ann

1

From her bedroom window in the farmhouse Mary Ann was surveying her kingdom almost for the last time. Below her lay a part of the garden. Late wallflowers were blooming in patches of red and yellow glory; but it was to the lank and drooping leaves of the daffodils that her eyes were drawn now, for they symbolised her feelings. She too was dying . . . she knew she was dying. Tomorrow when she left the farm and her da and her ma and their Michael she would die. How could she live without them? Well, without her da? The separation from her ma would be a dreadful wrench, but being parted from her da would drain from her all desire to live. Her nose gave a series of rapid twitches, and she admonished herself, "You'd better not start bubbling, your ma'll be up in a minute." Her large, brown eyes, that seemed to take up most of her elfin face, blinked and she moved her gaze over her kingdom. The huddle of the farm buildings making three sides of the courtyard; the foundations of the big, new barn to the right; the two farm cottages, one of which her own family had so lately occupied, bordering the road that ran past the farm gates; and away up the hill, behind the cottages, Mr. Lord's new house, standing as guardian and owner over all. Even this came into the realm of her kingdom. And it was her kingdom, bought for her da with her sacrifice.

Mary Ann's thoughts may not have literally taken this shape, but her feelings told her more plainly than anything else could have done that for love of her da she had sold herself to Mr. Lord, and the price he had demanded of her was—education, and that was to begin tomorrow. In return, her da had been made mana-

1

ger of the farm. But her da, of course, did not know of this deal. Eeh! no; and he must never know.

The fact that her da was now manager of the farm where, a month ago, he had been just a farm-hand, still had the aura of a miracle around it. And the miracle enlarged itself a thousandfold, when she thought back to the time, just a few months previously, when they had lived in Jarrow in two attics at the top of Mulhattans' Hall, and her da had worked in the shipyard and was forever on the booze. Eeh! fancy thinking that. She shook her head vigorously to throw off the memory. Her da never got drunk, not really; he got sick a bit but not drunk. Everybody knew he never got really drunk; it was Sarah Flannagan who had started that lie.

Oh, Sarah Flannagan! A little spark of joy forced itself into the gloom in her small chest. Today, when she went to Mulhattans' Hall to say goodbye to Mrs. McBride, she hoped that the big, lying, cheeky cat would be in the street and she'd show her. She'd be all got up in her new clothes—she wouldn't fight with her; no, that was strictly out now—but she'd go up to her and say, "So you see, Sarah Flannagan, every blessed thing I said has come true. Me da is a manager, and I'm going to be a lady and talk swanky. So get that out of your crop if you can." Yes, that's what she'd say to her, all swanky like. Then she'd walk away with her head in the air.

It was going to be a busy day. She must go and see Father Owen an' all and pay a last visit to the Holy Family. Sadness settled on her again on this thought, to be abruptly swept away on the sight of her da. He had just come out of the cowshed and was walking across the yard with Mr. Jones. Her heart swelled with pride. He looked grand did her da; even with only one hand he was better and bigger than any man in the world. The thought of his affliction brought a flame of tenderness into her body. But he was managing fine. She stressed this point to herself, for whenever she consciously thought of the accident that had taken off his hand a certain part of her mind was attacked by a fear, and this she would press away, making no effort to ask

2

the reason for its presence. Mike Shaughnessy had done a very good job in taking the blame of his accident from her young shoulders and placing it at the door of his own carelessness; in doing so he had sealed off effectively the remorse that would have surely turned her brain.

When her da got the hook for the end, he said his hand would be worth ten of any other man's. He had said that to her only yesterday, when she had gone to his office—oh yes; it was his office now—to tell him that dinner was ready. And he had stopped what he was doing with the books and suddenly lifted her on to his knee and held her close for a long time. Then Mr. Lord had come in, and her da had put her down and his face had gone all red. Neither of them had said anything, and this had left her with a certain uneasiness. Yet she couldn't somehow understand why she should feel uneasy. But she always did when Mr. Lord came on her when she was with her da. When she had Mr. Lord all to herself she never felt like that; she could talk to him, twenty-to-the-dozen, and make him laugh. But not when her da was there.

Her da was now making his way to the house, and Mr. Jones was going towards his cottage. Mr. Jones looked littler than ever. Mr. Jones didn't like her. He never spoke to her, not since the time she had thrown a One o'clock Gun under his bed on Guy Fawkes Day and he had run out of his house in his pants like a mad man. That was the day Mr. Lord had laughed and her da had got mad at her, madder than he had ever been, and he'd said she was to have a walloping and Mr. Lord said she wasn't. That was the first time she had felt that funny something between the two of them.

She knocked at the window now and waved to her da, and Mike waved back, a wide wave of his great arm. And he was almost at the side gate when round the outskirts of the house came Mrs. Polinski, and she called to him, "Good morning." And he said back to her, "Good morning." And he stopped at the gate as she hurried up, and Mary Ann looked down on them.

Mrs. Polinski was blonde, but her hair wasn't like her ma's in a great bun at the back of her head and of a lovely colour like looking into the sun; Mrs. Polinski's was—tousey, and she wore it cut like a lad's, all over the place. But she didn't look like a lad.

Mrs. Polinski was always very nice to her. Yet Mary Ann, as she somehow put it to herself, didn't know what was up with her; some part of the child wouldn't come to the fore and meet the new farm-hand's wife on the terms she so liberally offered . . . let's all be bairns together. Mary Ann sensed an unnatural-ness in this attitude. Mrs. Polinski was old; she was over twenty, and therefore past the age of acting the goat, and this included hop-scotch. Her da laughed at Mrs. Polinski when she played with her, but her ma said, if she was to go in and mend Mr. Polinski's coat and get a good dinner ready for him it would fit her better. And her da had said, "She'll learn."

Her da liked Mr. Polinski. He said that although a puff of wind would blow him over he could do double what Mr. Jones did, and he'd have a farm of his own some day and good luck to him. Mr. Polinski was from Poland but Mrs. Polinski just came from Dover.

She watched her now, laughing up at her da and her da laughing in return. Oh, her da did look grand. His red hair was rumpled and his shirt neck was open and she could see the curly hairs on the top of his chest.

"Haven't you got your things on yet?"

She swung round to the door, and there was Mi-chael, his expression this morning without its usual brooding seriousness and his voice unusually kind. Up to yesterday his greeting would have taken the form of, "Get a move on, you, or else you'll catch it," to which her retort would have been of the quality, "Aw, you! . . . nuts!" But on this last day of life her reply even touched on sweetness as she said, "I won't be a tick, Michael."

And she wasn't a tick, for she flung herself into her clothes—not her good ones; these wouldn't be donned until after breakfast and her usual scamper around the farm—and was downstairs in a matter of minutes.

As if she hadn't seen him for weeks she leapt from the doorway into Mike's arms. Mike had just turned from Lizzie, who was at the stove, and as Mary Ann pulled his face round to hers he finished saying to his

4

wife, "You could teach her a lot . . . Polinski has a thin time of it on the whole. Why don't you take her under your wing, Liz?"

"You know my views. Anyway, we'll talk of that later."

This hesitation on her mother's part to talk of Mrs. Polinski was, Mary Ann knew without any undue hurt to her feelings, because she was there. But from the little she had overheard, Mary Ann's opinion of her own judgment took on a heightened glow. Her mother didn't cotton on to Mrs. Polinski either.

"Sit up . . . come on." Lizzie turned from the stove and brought her hand in an affectionate slap on Mary Ann's bottom, and Mary Ann, grabbing at Mike's neck, yelled, "She's braying me, da, she's braying me."

This causing them all to laugh, even Michael, Mary Ann ascended into her seventh heaven, while tomorrow sprang into the far future, leaving her all the day. Her ma and da were happy and laughing, joined by a band of love that she could almost feel. Their Michael was nice, and there, with an egg on top of it, was a thick slice of Irish roll for her breakfast, not half a slice, as was usual, and that, too, only after she had pushed down a great bowl of porridge.

After they were all seated and the grace said, in which Mike did not join, and had started to eat, the chatter suddenly ceased, and Mary Ann, in the middle of chewing on and relishing the superb flavour of a mouthful of bacon, felt her mouth drop open as she watched her mother rise quickly from the table and go into the scullery. Was her ma crying? . . . And then her da, his eyes fixed on his plate, stopped eating. And then their Michael, his cheek full of fried bread, gulped down some tea, and her ma had told him, time without number, not to drink while he was eating. Then almost as quickly as she had gone, Lizzie came back into the room bringing bread with her, and there, before Mary Ann's eyes, was a plateful not touched already on the table.

The silence shrieked in Mary Ann's ears, becoming almost unbearable, and her innate sense of requirement told her that a diversion was needed, and a strong one. And without further thought she heard herself saying, "When I see Sarah Flannagan again I won't half tell her something. I'll say, 'Your da can't buy you clothes like this.' "

"And your da hasn't." Mike's tone was flat and held just a thread of bitterness.

Mary Ann looked across the table into Mike's eyes, then turned her gaze to her mother. Lizzie was busily eating and did not raise her head. She had said the wrong thing—her da hadn't bought her clothes, Mr. Lord had, boxes of them. Well, two big cases full, right from vests to one black felt school hat and one gray one for Sundays. And her name was on everything—Mary Ann Shaughnessy. Her ma had sewed and sewed at them for days. Everything she had had been given to her by Mr. Lord, and her da didn't like it. She was daft for saying such a thing . . . she was daft, she was. The lump, coming swiftly from nowhere, blocked her throat, but past it struggled the words: "I don't want to . . . I don't want t . . . to. Oh, Da!"

"There! See what you've started." Lizzie was on her feet, pulling Mary Ann to her and pressing her head into her waist.

Mike, rising from the table, went to the mantelpiece and, grabbing at his pipe, growled, "I'm sorry." And Michael, making the greatest effort of his life in an attempt at small talk, put out his hand and stabbed gently at his sister's shoulders, and in a not at all steady voice said, "Now I'll be able to get my own back on you, you were always chipping me about the Grammar School. But a Convent's worse. You'll be so swanky when you come back we won't know a word you're saying. You'll be all South Country."

Mary Ann's crying ceased, and with a shuddering sob she turned from her mother and answered Michael: "I won't then . . . so! Nobody'll make me swanky . . . will they? Will they, Da?"

Her voice brought Mike round to her, and over the distance of the long shining kitchen he smiled gently at her and moved his head slowly.

"No," he said. "No. Make up your mind finally on that, at any rate. Let nobody make you swanky. . . . You still want to go?" He asked this quietly, yet his voice filled the kitchen.

Now Lizzie's eyes darted between the two of them, and she brought Mary Ann's to hers. What Mary Ann saw there stilled the truth hovering on her lips and reminded her forcibly of the bargain with Mr. Lord, and she said, "Yes, Da."

"You sure?" said Mike.

"Yes, Da."

They looked at each other until Lizzie could bear it no longer, and grabbing up the dishes with a clatter and saying as she did so, "Well, this is a breakfast spoilt, I must say," she went into the scullery, and after depositing the crockery in the sink she leant against the table for a moment, one hand gripping the front of her blouse. What if the child had said no! He would, and like a shot, have put his foot down. And then, as like as not, the whole situation would have exploded.

Lizzie knew that Mr. Lord, thwarted of his ambition to educate Mary Ann, was not likely to treat Mike as he was doing now, even though Mike was carrying out the difficult task of managing the farm much better than she had imagined he could do. Both Mr. Lord and Mary Ann, she knew, were under the impression that they, and they alone, knew of the bargain between them, the bargain being that, if Mary Ann agreed to going away to school, her father would be given the chance to run the farm. How it had all come about she didn't know, but certain circumstances that led up to Mike's appointment showed only too plainly Mary Ann's finger guiding Mike's destiny. Any faint suspicion Mike might have felt had been lulled by Mary Ann herself. Mike did not know Mary Ann as she did. Somehow his very love for her blinded his vision, and should it ever come out that he owed all his present success not alone to his ability but to his child selling herself—and that is how he would put it—away would go the farm and their life of security. She could even see him making use of the six months' trial which he was now working to bring their life here to an end in order to keep his self-respect.

Tomorrow night, when she left the child all those miles away in the south, near St. Leonards, she would, she knew, leave part of her own life behind her. But even so, she was longing now for the moment to arrive when Mary Ann would be safely installed, when the worst part of this business would be over and the future of them all secure . . . well, as secure as anybody's future could be allowing for fate, in the form of the bottle which had dogged their married life. But, strangely enough, at this moment Mike's weakness was troubling her least. It was Mary Ann's strength that was worrying her. Would it carry the child through these final stages? After all, she was but a child, she was not yet nine. She had only recently, Lizzie thought fondly, been a baby. Wasn't it too much to expect of her that she should be parted from Mike, who was the very breath of her life, when she had only to make a sign and he would say, "To hell with education! She doesn't want to go and she's not going."

Lizzie let out a long painful breath. If only it was tomorrow morning and they were on their way. The thing to do was to keep her occupied today, and away from Mike as much as possible without arousing any comment from him. And so, going into the kitchen now, she said briskly, "Well, what are you going to do?"

"Who, me, Ma?"

"Yes, you. Who else? I generally know what the rest of my family are up to."

Lizzie laughed, and Mary Ann said, with just a touch of importance, "Eeh, well, I've got a lot of people to see. I must go and see Mrs. McBride, and say 'Tara' to Agnes and Mary. And, oh, I must go and see Father Owen and . . . and who else?" As she pondered with her head on one side, Mike and Michael looked from her to each other, and nodding they both said together, mimicking her voice and manner, "And, oh, that Sarah Flannagan."

Laughter filled the kitchen again, and Mary Ann dashed from her father to Michael, crying, "Oh, you! you! Go on, you cheeky things, you." And into Lizzie's worry came a thin thread of happiness. That little action of Michael in joining his father in this bit of teasing warmed her heart. Perhaps with Mary Ann gone Mike would turn more to the boy, and Michael's brooding nature would expand towards him, and he

8

would forget the past and look up to this man whom he so closely resembled.

"Well, that's settled, at least." Lizzie bustled about, while Michael took up his bag and after making brief goodbyes went off to school—his term had already started. And Mike, after kissing Lizzie, lifted Mary Ann up and looked at her hard for a moment, then held her close for another brief moment before going quickly out, leaving behind him a strained silence, into which Lizzie poured her words with an attempt at lightness.

"You needn't help me with the dishes this morning. Go on, put your good things on and then you can get off. And, oh, by the way—" her voice stopped Mary Ann at the kitchen door—"wasn't there somebody else you forgot to put on your visiting list?"

"Who, Ma?"

"Mr. Lord."

"Oh, but I'll see him in the morning."

"But only on the way to the station, and we'll all be in the car then. I would call in on your way back and have a word with him. Are you going to stay and have something at Mrs. McBride's?"

"No, Ma. I was coming back for me dinner."

"Very well, you can go to Mr. Lord's this afternoon then."

"But Ma, he might come here—he's been nearly every afternoon."

Lizzie turned her back on Mary Ann and went to the stove and said slowly, "Well, in that case I wouldn't bother him. He'll likely want to talk to your da, and they can never do business with people about. You understand?"

"Yes, Ma."

Soberly Mary Ann went upstairs, a weight pressing on her shoulders. She understood she wasn't to chatter and jump round Mr. Lord in front of her da. She understood all right; her ma needn't have told her.

2

Again Mary Ann was telling herself something for the very last time; she was sitting in the bus on her way to Jarrow. With newly awakened eyes, she looked out of the window. Never had she seen a field of rhubarb running in scarlet and green waves, nor the long, flat patches of land stretching away into the distance aboil with molten yellow. Even the great chimneys, sticking up like pipe shanks on the horizon, looked beautiful; and the gigantic, gear-bespangled gantries that reared up from the river were like fairy tracery edging and hemming in this beautiful world she was leaving.

A rainbow, actually appearing in the sky at that moment, filled her small chest with wonder. And when it stretched its magnet ends over Jarrow, Hebburn and Pelaw and lifted them clean up from the earth to suspend them in dazzling light, it was too much for her. Her nose started to run; she sniffed and choked and groped for her hankie in the band of her knickers, forgetting that she had on her best clothes. Then, retrieving the neatly folded handkerchief, one which bore her name, from her pocket, she was in the act of desecrating it when the real purpose of its presence on her person at all today came back to her, and gently she pushed it into its folds again, name up, and carried out the operation on her nose with her thumb, but covertly, for this procedure was most strictly forbidden.

On raising her eyes, she saw they were now passing the gates of Mr. Lord's house, and her head swung round to catch one last glimpse of them. They seemed to be guarding the entry to celestial bliss. Never more would she go up that drive . . . oh well, she might this afternoon, but that would be the last time, for when she came back for the summer holidays Mr. Lord would be living in his new house up at the farm.

The bus was now skimming past the grounds, past the hedge and the barbed wire through which she had once forced her way. But that was a long time ago, years and years—in fact, last summer.

The bus was moving now among the close-packed houses, and when she alighted at Ferry Street it was raining, pelting down, yet the sun was still shining, and the conductor said, "You'll have to run, hinny, or you'll be soaked."

Running had not been laid down in her plans at all for today; she was to walk to the top of Burton Street and then slow down, taking her time, until she came to Mulhattans' Hall, for everybody in Burton Street knew her, and they would stop her and exclaim in tones of admiration, that is, all except Mrs. Flannagan. "Oh, Mary Ann," they would say, "you do look lovely and I hear you're going away to a posh school. And your da's somebody now, isn't he? . . . eh? Manager of the farm and gives orders. Well, well." And here it was, raining cats and dogs.

She dashed from the bus into a shop doorway for shelter. But inactivity never being her strong point, she was soon out again and, hugging the walls, she ran as quickly as her legs could carry her along the street. This procedure she even had to carry out in Burton Street, where, but for three toddlers blocking up the water in the gutter with their feet and freshly compounded mud, there wasn't a soul to be seen.

She galloped up the steps of Mulhattans' Hall to the testy exclamations of, "Hang and bust it!" and as she stood shaking the rain from herself Mrs. McBride's door was pulled open and the aperture was almost filled by the great bulk of Fanny herself.

"Hullo there, hinny. This is nice weather to bring. Come on in, don't stand there dripping like a cheap umbrella. Come inside."

"I'm all wet, Mrs. McBride."

"Aye. Well, you've been wet afore. . . . But by, what a shame, and them your new things. Let me have a look at you." Stooping, Fanny held her at arm's length. "By! you look bonny, real bonny."

11

Mary Ann's soul was soothed. "Do I, Mrs. McBride?"

"You do, hinny. But there, get them off. It's a good job I've a bit fire on, for sun or no sun it's cold. And then we'll have a sup tea, eh?"

Taking Mary Ann's coat, Fanny hung it over a chair, exclaiming of its colour as she did so, "Never seen a bonnier blue—never. And your hat matches an' all. . . . Sit down and tell me all your news. How's Mike?"

"He's grand."

"Ah, that's it. There's a miracle for you, if ever. . . . And now for a cup of tea. And there's some griddle cake, I made it last night. . . . What's he got to say 'bout you going away?"

"Oh, he says——" Mary Ann stopped and looked at the enormous rump of Mrs. McBride as she bent over the fire, placing the kettle into its heart. There was no need to pretend here. Mrs. McBride was the only person in the world with whom she needn't pretend; that was, with the exception of Father Owen, yet he being a close relation of God's was not in the same category as Mrs. McBride. Like God, she felt, the priest had an unfair advantage; he knew what she was thinking and was going to say even before she started . . . at least, Father Owen had this power when in the confessional.

Fanny turned from the fire and, slowly straightening her creaking back, looked at Mary Ann.

"He doesn't want me to go."

"Well, that doesn't surprise me. It would only have surprised me if it had been t'other way round. What does he say?"

"Nothing much."

"That's bad. Always is with Mike. . . . And—and Mr. Lord. How does your da get on with him now?"

"All right. Fine . . . well. . . ."

"Aye. . . . Aye well, we'll leave it at that then, eh? And you're going away in the mornin'?"

"Yes."

Fanny sat down opposite to Mary Ann and, stretching her arm across the table, patted her young friend's hand. "I'll miss you, hinny. I missed you when you left here, but now it'll only be the holidays I'll see you."

A furious tickling came into Mary Ann's nose, worse

than in the bus, and with unblinking eyes she looked at Fanny and whispered, "I don't want to go, Mrs. McBride."

After a moment of staring at her, Fanny's fat seemed to flow back and forward above the area of the table. Then with a hitch to her bust she brought it to a standstill, and stated the fact that was already sealed in Mary Ann's mind: "You've got to—remember there's your da, and you're doing it for him. And you're going to be educated like you never dreamed. Just think what'd happen if you backed out now. Think of the old boy . . . he'd give everybody up there a hell of a time, because he thinks he's God Almighty himself, does that one. And you know who'd come in for the brunt of it, don't you?"

Their eyes held; then Fanny, after a significant nod, raised her encumbering body and went to the now spluttering kettle.

Yes, she knew all right. Mr. Lord would give her da hell. Eeh! she was swearing . . . but not really, only thinking. And if her da got upset he might go on the . . . get sick again; and then her mother would look like she used to, all tightened up; and their Michael wouldn't laugh, like he did a bit now. No, she knew her fate was sealed.

Fanny turned towards the table once again, the great brown teapot in her hand. And now her face was split by a wide beam and her voice sounded eager and full of interest as she said, "Is it true, what your ma was telling me? You're booked to learn languages?"

Mary Ann, quick to take the cue, forced a smile to match that of this virile old woman whose wisdom was tempered with the hard experience of life, and resurrecting herself from the abyss of despair into which she seemed bound to fall at any moment, she said, "Aye, I mean yes . . . French and German."

"French and German! My God! it's a scholar you're going to be. By, won't that be like a kick under the chin for our dear friends?" Fanny leant forward and thumbed the window indicating the Flannagans' house across the street, and Mary Ann, her face now springing into glee, poked her chin up and pursed her mouth as she articulated, "And el-e-cution an' all."

"El-e-cution?"

"Yes, talkin' properly you know."

"No!"

"Uh-huh!"

"My, wait till she hears that. That'll drive Nellie Flannagan up the lum."

"An' I'll be a lady." Now Mary Ann was getting warm. "A real one, and talk swanky, and look down me nose."

Principles were being swept away on a wave of pride when Fanny's fingers suddenly took up an admonishing position. "Ah, now! now!" The finger wagged. "You've got to watch out . . . you don't want this school to change you altogether, do you? For then you won't only turn your nose up at the Flannagans, you'll turn it up at me and your——"

"No, no. Oh! I won't. Oh! Mrs. McBride, no I won't. I won't ever turn me nose up at you." Mary Ann was deeply hurt by the suggestion.

"Ah well, time will tell." Fanny sighed and the smile sank from her face. "You want treacle on your griddle cake?"

"Yes, please."

Mary Ann, now on her feet, watched Fanny go into the scullery, and her thoughts once again slipped into despondency. The only consolation this going away to school offered was that she would learn to be a lady and talk swanky. But now, apparently, there were dangers even in that.

The rain had stopped, the sun was shining brightly, but a cloud had settled on Mary Ann's chest, bringing a feeling of sickness with it. She sat down and waited for Mrs. McBride's appearance, wondering if she could say she didn't want any griddle cake now because she was feeling sick. But she knew she mustn't say this, she mustn't hurt Mrs. McBride. She must eat the griddle cake, even if it choked her.

It was eleven o'clock when Mary Ann reached the church. She was "full up" in more ways than one. She wouldn't see Mrs. McBride again for ages and ages. Mrs. McBride had lifted her up and held her, and she had cried and pushed a whole half-crown into her hand, with strict orders to spend it, the lot. Her fingers now blindly picked out the half-crown from the coppers in her pocket. Mrs. McBride was kind, she was; and she liked her da, she did. Oh, she was going to miss Mrs. McBride.

The church was empty except for two cleaners, women with long pinnies on and their hair tied up with scarves. They were washing the walls round behind St. Anthony's altar. Some feeling told Mary Ann that cleaners were out of place in a church; the church should need no cleaning by mortal hand, some act of God should keep the dust down and the floor clean. Slowly she approached the altar of the Holy Family; then knelt down and glued her eyes on the group of statuary. For as long as she could remember she had come to the Holy Family with her troubles, and even, at times, remembered to come with her joys. And now for the last time she knelt before them, and as they gazed down on her they looked as sad as she expected them to be . . . they knew she was going all right. The Infant moved in His Mother's arms, and Mary hitched Him up closer to her and said softly, "Well, Mary Ann?" And Mary Ann replied, "Oh, Blessed Mother Mary, I don't want to go. Make something happen to stop me."

The Infant screwed round and looked down on Mary Ann, and Saint Joseph looked down on her, and Mother Mary herself. And they didn't say a word between them, until the silence yelled in Mary Ann's ears and she dropped her head.

Then the Virgin said, "Look at me, Mary Ann." And Mary Ann looked up into the sweet and serious face of the Mother, and Mary said, "You have given your word. Moreover, Mr. Lord has paid you in advance for your word. Do not let the Devil tempt you to break it, nor ask me to show him the way."

Mary Ann's head drooped still further now. They weren't nice a bit, and this was her last visit an' all. Eeh! what was she saying? Eeh! she was sorry. Eeh! it was a wonder Our Lady didn't strike her down dead. . . . She'd light a candle.

Still with her head bowed, she moved to the half-moon of candles that stood to the side of the altar rail and groping at the coins in her pocket she pulled out two, and, still with lowered eyes, dropped them into the box. But as the second one left her fingers a cry escaped her that rang through the empty church and brought the cleaners from behind the altar . . . she had put in her half-crown!

A long time ago she had done something similar, but that had been only a sixpence. This was a fortune, a whole half-crown. She turned her back on the cleaners and looked accusingly up at the group above her. They had let her go and do it, and they were laughing—Saint Joseph's beard was moving. It was nothing to laugh at; and she wasn't going to leave it in, she wasn't. She didn't care. No, she didn't! Candles were only twopence. She wanted her half-crown back, and then she'd light one—two perhaps—but she wanted her half-crown back first.

Her thoughts gabbled in her head as she looked back down the church. She could see no signs of the cleaners now, they were well behind the altar. There was nobody here but herself. She'd get her half-crown out of the box, she would.

The box, she saw, had only a little lock on the lid. Little or big, she knew she couldn't hope to open it, but she could . . . tip it up, couldn't she? Without further thought of the right or wrong of her actions and momentarily oblivious to the combined condemnation of the Holy Family, she lifted the box from its setting. And when she held it in her hand the cold iron burned her fingers. Anyway it set a spark to her conscience and she exclaimed, "Eeh!" And again, "Eeh!" But conscience or no conscience, and "Eeh" or no "Eeh!" she was going to get her half-crown out. She only had to turn it upside-down, like you did with a money box. But where would she do it?

She looked around her. If she went in one of the pews the women might hear her, even if they were behind the altar. This last brought a most helpful thought into her mind . . . why shouldn't she, too, go behind the altar? They wouldn't see her or hear her there. And she'd get her half-crown out and slip the box back and no one would be any the wiser, except

16

herself. And it would learn her to look at her money in future. Her ma was always telling her.

But even with the decision determinedly taken, she found it needed a great deal of courage to walk up the steps and go behind the altar of the Holy Family. And, once there, the purpose for her presence was temporarily swept aside by the forbidding aspect of the place. The back of the altar looked mucky; and there was just enough room between it and the wall to allow for the movement of her elbows.

Cautiously she knelt down and attacked the box by turning it sharply on its side. The sound of the coins filled the space and ricocheted off the walls upwards, and she followed its flight with startled eyes— the roof of the church, seen from this angle, appeared as far away as the sky—the sound eventually died away, and tensely she listened, with her teeth clamped down hard on her lip. But there was no other sound, of voices or footsteps. And so she again returned to her operation, but turning the box gently this time upside-down on the floor. After giving it a little shake she looked beneath it. There was nothing there. Slowly she raised it above her eyes . . . and yes, there it was! her half-crown. She could see it lying partly across the slot, its shine outdoing that of the penny which blocked the other half. . . . What she wanted was a knife—when her ma emptied her Post Office Savings' tin she used a knife. But she hadn't a knife. . . . Perhaps if she just tilted it slightly it would slide out. She tried this at some length, but holding the box above her head made her arms ache.

"Bust!" The exclamation of exasperation was whispered, and she sat back on her heels with the box on her lap and asked herself what she was going to do next.

But she was never to know, for the voice of God hit her on the back of the neck, knocking her on her face and sending the box spinning into the air. And as it clattered down again, almost braining her, she screamed, and the voice came thundering over her, crying, "Get up! get up! Come out of that!"

Being unable to turn, slowly, with jangling limbs,

she crawled backwards. Then God lifted her clean off the floor by the collar of her coat and swung her round to Him. And her hat fell off backwards and she was looking up into the startled face of Father Owen, whose mouth was agape and whose voice was so high that it came out of the top of his head as he cried, "For the love of God . . . Mary Ann!"

Mary Ann tried to swallow, but she found the process impossible, for here, one on each side of the priest, stood the cleaners. And it was the look in their eyes that was restricting her breath as much as the shock she had just experienced.

"I told you, Father, it was the way she came in. We watched her, didn't we?" one woman enquired of the other across Father Owen. "And all the bairns at school . . . we thought it was funny, didn't we?"

"Aye. And I said, 'Go and get Father Owen,' didn't I? Because if anything goes we'll get the blame, I've had some."

"Be quiet!" The priest held up his hand, silencing the women. Then still holding Mary Ann by the shoulder, he said, "Tell me, Mary Ann."

"Me . . . me. . . ." The lump moved but wouldn't go, and she gasped and coughed. And the priest, thumping her on the back, said, "There, there. Now tell me."

"Me half-crown, Father . . . I—I dropped it in—instead of a penny . . . I was only trying to get it out."

The priest's hold slackened and he straightened his long, thin length, looked almost furtively from one woman to the other, coughed and blew his nose so loudly that the noise re-echoed off the back of the altar and filled the church again before he said, "Why didn't you come and tell me?"

"I—I didn't know where to find you afore dinner time. You're always out."

"Yes, yes. Well, go in there and bring me that box, we'll get your half-crown out." He pushed her towards the back of the altar again, and as she disappeared he turned to the women and said, "You did quite right, quite right. But you see it has been explained."

18

The women, as if both worked by the same string, put their heads slightly on one side and surveyed the priest, as if seeing someone who called forth their pity. Then the same string turned them about and they went slowly up the church back to their work.

Father Owen, sighing and looking once more down on Mary Ann where she stood, the picture of guilt, with the box in her hand, said, "You'll be the death of me one of these days, child. Of that I'm as sure as I am of being alive at this moment, and also of being taken for a dopey old imbecile by certain ladies I won't give a name to. Come along."

In the vestry Father Owen did not immediately open the box but, sitting himself down, he looked gravely on Mary Ann, which added much to her already heavy sense of sin.

"You realise, Mary Ann, you've done a very serious thing?"

"But, Father . . ." It was a small protest.

"Never mind, 'But Father . . .'" The priest's hand was raised now, his fingers spread wide, an action, Mary Ann recognised instantly, that was kept only for bad hats, them that broke windows in the school and, deadly sickening thought, stole.

"Was it such a sacrifice to give half-a-crown to the Holy Family?" The priest stared hard at her. "If I'm to believe all I hear, they've done a lot for you. Just think of all the wonderful things that have happened in the past few months . . . think."

The last was a command, and Mary Ann thought. She thought hard. But the only thing that came to her mind was the event of her da losing his hand. They had let that happen, hadn't they? And then they had got her into this trouble now. Eeh! what was the matter with her . . . she'd go to hell. This thought, added to the misery of her impending departure, and the expression on the face of her beloved priest, was too much. She burst into a storm of tears.

Quickly, Father Owen brought her to his knee, all sternness gone. "There, there! Now, don't cry. Come on . . . come on."

But Mary Ann's head was pressed into his waistcoat, and it was some time, however, before he could induce her to stop. When finally, sniffing and sobbing, she drew away from him, he said, "Aw! look at your face now. Here, let me wipe it."

As he plied his handkerchief round her face Mary Ann gazed up at him and jerked out, on recurrent sobs, "I didn't meant it, Father. I didn't mean it."

"No, no, of course you didn't. It was the Devil tempting you and you weren't ready for him. That's how it was."

Yes, that's how it must have been. For Mary Ann, looking back, couldn't see herself doing anything so awful as to take the candle box behind the altar and try to empty it. Not for all the half-crowns in the world could she have done it on her own. It was the Devil all right that had pushed her into that.

"I don't want the half-crown, Father, not now."

"Oh, you'll have your half-crown. . . . The Holy Family would be the last to want to make on you. Come and sit down, child." He drew her up on to the bench and to his side. "There now." He looked her over. "I see you've got on your fine clothes already for tomorrow. But look at the bottom of your coat, it's all dust." He brushed it off; then, without looking at her, said, "You'll be starting a new life tomorrow, Mary Ann." He went on brushing lightly with his hand, and when there was no answer to his comment he added, "Are you excited?"

"No, Father."

"No?" He stopped his brushing.

"No, Father. I don't want to go."

Now the priest's head turned quickly, and they confronted each other. "Have you told your mother this . . . or . . . or your da?"

"No, Father."

The priest stretched himself upwards before saying, "That's a good girl, because this time next week things'll look different altogether. Believe me, they will. And just think where you're going . . . one of the finest Convents in the country, and Mr. Lord's own sister Mother Superior. Why, you're a very lucky girl. Not many get your chance, Mary Ann."

"No, Father."

"And it will all work out beautifully."

20

"Yes, Father."

Would it? It was undoubtedly a chance of a life-time, and would have very favourable results on nine-ty-nine children out of a hundred, but the priest had a fear in him that this child would be the hundredth. Old Lord had a bee in his bonnet where she was concerned, and if she pleased him her future was as sure as anything on this earth could be. But he was counting without Mike. . . . But no, that was wrong; it was because the old fellow had counted Mike and saw him as an opponent to his plans that he had picked on this convent so far away. The fact that it was run by his sister was merely an excuse, for he hadn't spoken to her since she had come over into the Faith thirty years ago. If it was education alone he was after for the child, there were fine schools and convents near that would have answered his purpose just as well. Father Owen shook his head at his thoughts. It was diabolical but he felt, nevertheless, true that old Lord's idea was to separate the child from her father for as long as possible, hoping that a different environment would estrange her from her present surroundings . . . and, through it, lift her affection and loyalty, not for-getting love, away from Mike and on to the higher plane of himself. Oh, he knew Peter Lord, and he knew that this was the substance of his scheme. Yet nothing could be done about it, for if the child didn't comply there would be a heap of trouble for that family again. And the awkward part was that the mite was fully aware of this. Oh dear, yes . . . yes, she was aware of it all right.

"Well, Mary Ann—" Father Owen pulled down his slack waistcoat—"I envy you I do, going to the South of England. I was back there meself many years ago —at both Bexhill and Hastings I stayed—and, as I remember, the air was so fine it went to my head like wine and put me to sleep. I couldn't keep meself awake night or day . . . I was properly doped. I just couldn't keep awake."

"Couldn't you, Father?"

"No, I couldn't. And now, my child—" he took her two hands in his—"you won't forget us all in this fine school?"

21

"Oh no, Father—never." Her head moved slowly from side to side with the truth of this statement.

"Nor your ma, and, of course, your da."

"Forget me ma and da!" Her voice was full of incredulity, and a little smile that could have held pity touched her lips. "Forget me da!"

"Of course you won't!" The priest's voice was hearty. "But you mustn't underestimate our friend." He bent above her with a thumb in each ear and his fingers splayed outwards as he said, "You know, old Nick. Not that he's any friend of mine although he's tried to take up with me for years." He laughed down on her now. "The Devil, Mary Ann, let me tell you, has many guises . . . do you know that?"

"No, Father."

"Well, he has. He gets dressed up like so many different people that you don't know who he's going to take off next. He's the unfairest specimen that ever walked. For instance. . . ." The priest looked up at the vestry ceiling as if searching for some case with which to demonstrate his point. "Well, for instance, should you ever meet a nice man whom you don't know and he offers you some sweets and asks you to go for a walk—" down dropped his eyes to Mary Ann, and his voice dropped too, as he ended—"Rest assured, Mary Ann, that will be the Devil."

"It will, Father?"

"It will. . . . Or he may be driving a car and want to give you a ride. That will be him again. As sure as life that will be him. Or he may not be dressed as a man at all, he may be got up as a woman; or a girl even; but whatever guise he puts on, as soon as he opens his mouth and starts to tempt you to do something that your heart tells you isn't right you can be sure it's him, no matter what he's wearing."

Mary Ann's world suddenly became peopled with devils, with an easily recognised one right in the forefront, and she helped the priest in his illustration by saying somewhat eagerly, "I know, like Sarah Flannagan, Father."

"Not at all, not at all." The priest stood up quickly, his voice brusque now. "Sarah's got no more of the Devil in her than you have. There's fifty-fifty twixt

22

you and her, believe me." He nodded sharply down at her.

This assault, unfair as it surely was, obliterated even the candle-box incident and made her think, "Well, would you believe it!"

Father Owen's hand descended on her head, and at the look on her face his mirth rang out, and he cried, "Come along with you, or else I'll never get any work done today. And here—" he put his hand in his pocket—"here's your half-crown; I'll settle with the Holy Family later. How's that?"

"Oh, thank you, Father." She was slightly mollified. "Come on then."

They went out of the vestry together, and after genuflecting side by side to the main altar they went up the aisle, Mary Ann keeping her eyes strictly turned from the altar of Saint Anthony where the women were. But when at the church door she looked up for the last time on her true friend the tears welled again.

Bending to her, the priest took her kiss on his cheek, and when, with her arms about his thin neck, she cried, "Father! Oh, Father!" he answered somewhat thickly, "There, there. Go on now, and may God bless you and take care of you."

With a push that was almost rough he thrust her away and quickly re-entered the church, and she was left with her world, for the moment, desolate.

The sun was shining with dazzling brightness on the wet pavement and made her eyes blink, and she stood sniffing and at a loss, considering the next step in the order of good-byes. It was nearly twelve o'clock by the big clock in Harry Siddon's, the watchmaker. Should she stay at the corner of Dee Street and wait for Agnes and Mary, or go right to the school gates? Her self-esteem at a very low ebb and crying out urgently for support immediately suggested the school gate, but also told her she'd have to run! So with no more debating she ran, and just reached the main gate as the bell rang.

Almost, it would seem, as if shot from both sides of the building there came two racing, widening streams of screaming children. Not being part of either, the noise to her seemed terrific, and it brought with it a feeling that puzzled her, for she could not recognise that she was envious of their rights of the moment for lung expansion.

The sight of her checked fragments of the avalanche, and they came to her side, crying "Hello, Mary Ann."

"Hello, Mary Ann."

"Eeh! Mary Ann. Hello."

"Hello," she said. "I've come to say good-bye to Agnes and Mary."

"Mary's off bad, she's got the mumps, and Agnes brought a note yesterday 'cos she's not comin' the day, she's goin' with her ma to Durham. Eeh! you do look nice, Mary Ann . . . doesn't she?"

The chorus of "Eehs!" applied a little salve to the acute feeling of disappointment at not seeing her friends for the last time, or, to be more correct, that they were not having the pleasure of seeing her dressed in her splendour, nor the opportunity of pouring their ever-ready admiration over her head.

"When you goin', Mary Ann?"

"The morrer."

"Are you going in a train?"

"Yes, and in a car." She had brightened visibly; the pain of partings was forgotten; there was nothing but the present, for she had an audience. "Mr. Lord . . . he's coming for us at eight o'clock and takin' me ma and da and our Michael and me to Newcastle. Me ma's goin' with me all the way, and I've got dozens of boxes of clothes . . . cases, all new. And me name's on everything, full length—Mary Ann Shaughnessy."

"It would be, Milady Bug."

Mary Ann swung round, new clothes and prestige forgotten. There, standing not a foot from her and not apparently impressed in the slightest by her splendours, stood Sarah Flannagan.

They glared at each other, Mary Ann having to thrust her head back to keep her eyes fixed on the taller girl. This was the old battle ground.

"What do you want round here, anyway . . . showing off as usual? . . . 'I'm going in a big car!' " Sarah

24

gave an impression of Mary Ann, which drew a titter from the fickle spectators. "And you'll come back, likely as not, in the Black Maria . . . or the muck cart."

Mary Ann's chin was out; her lips were out; and her eyes were popping. "You! . . . You're jealous . . . that's what you are."

"Huh! Listen to her. Jealous! What have I got to be jealous of? An upstart? For that's all you are. Me ma says you're nothing but an upstart. And what's more, my da hadn't to be dooled out with a job to keep him quiet. Me ma says if old Lord hadn't given your da the job on the farm, he would have had to fork out thousands and thousands for his lost hand. He's made a fool of him, and everybody knows it's only charity your da's on."

"You! . . . How dare you! Oh!" Mary Ann was lost for words. "You! you! and your ma," she managed to splutter. "You and your ma, there's a pair of you. And you'll end up in hell for the lies you tell. As for your da, he's so hen-pecked he can't wipe his nose afore he gets permission."

This last eloquent thrust was remembered from a little eavesdropping; it was a statement her father had laughingly made to her mother. Now it penetrated Sarah's superior guard, causing her fury to erupt. And this brought her even nearer to Mary Ann. Whereupon, Mary Ann, having no known supporter, retreated just the slightest, but not ignobly, for she brought to her face a tantalising sneer that seemed to make Sarah swell.

"You, you to talk about anybody . . . you've got some nerve with a da like yours, you have. A big drunken, fightin' no-good, and it's only a few weeks back that you had to come right up to our street and fetch him, and him singing with the street out. . . . Your da!" Sarah's scorn was searing, "Ten a penny."

The financial significance of the last remark subtly reduced Mike's standard, socially, morally and physically, to the lowest denomination. It was an insult not to be borne . . . it had to be repudiated right away. Mary Ann needed words, fighting words, words of scorn and fire. They were all there, milling around inside of her but finding an outlet impossible owing to

25

the barrier of indignation blocking their path somewhere in the region of her upper ribs. But there
were no impeding thoughts standing in the way of
her right hand, and guided by, of course, nothing but
right it raised itself and contacted Sarah's face full on
with a resounding slap.

Sarah choked and gasped, and the "eehs" that filled
the air told Mary Ann, if the pain in her hand had not
done so, that that was a whopper. But Sarah's swift retaliation cut short the glow of conquest, all that Mary
Ann was aware of in the next moment was that her
head was ringing and that she was falling backward.
Preservation of her new clothes forbade this in-
dignity, and she told herself frantically that whatever
she did she mustn't fall, so she reeled on her heels
into the roadway, her arms waving in an endeavour
to regain her balance. And she might have done so
but for a shining puddle of water. It was just a small
puddle, but one seeming to possess impish and mag-
netic qualities, for it drew her small buttocks towards
it, and as they made contact with the muddy water,
it flew away in sprays, that is, all that did not fall back
on her.

Tears of fright and mortification ran from her eyes.
Her onetime audience were now laughing their heads
off, and Sarah's voice came to her, as if from a
distance, crying, "Look at who's going to be a lady!
I'm going to a posh school, I am, I'm going to be a
lady. Lady Muck of Clarty Hall!"

Suddenly there was a scurrying of feet, and as
Mary Ann turned herself tearfully over she saw them
racing away in all directions. And when she was erect
once more she was standing alone except for Miss
Johnson, who was facing her from the gate.

"Oh, it's you."

"Yes, Miss."

Miss Johnson slowly advanced to the edge of the
pavement, then vented her spleen on the child she
had never liked.

"It doesn't look as if your glowing prospects have
altered you much," she said. "Get yourself away
home. I am sure your mother will be pleased to see
you."

Turning slowly about, Mary Ann walked somewhat drunkenly away. She hated Miss Johnson, she did. And eeh! her clothes. Eeh! her ma would go mad. Eeh! what was the back like? Look at the front of her coat . . . and her hands and her cuffs. Eeh! what was she to do? . . . And all through her. At this moment she prayed through her feelings for every catastrophe, calamity, disaster, and mortification to fall on that—that . . . ! She could find no words as a fitting pseudonym for the hated name of Sarah Flannagan.

Her legs, without any directions from her, took her towards the bus stop, where, a bus arriving at the same moment, she was on it before her mind cried at her, "You should have gone back to Mrs. McBride, she would have cleaned you up."

The conductor stood over her, grinning, and his heartening remark, "By! your ma's goin' to be pleased to see you," seemed to endorse that of her teacher and suggested to her again that she should get off and go back to her friend, who had on many other occasions cleaned her up. But a deadness had descended on her, the result mostly of a morning that had not gone at all according to plan. It had been such a morning which her mother would have referred to as . . . something having got into it.

Father Owen's discourse on the Devil coming back to her mind, caused her head to move impatiently, a sure sign of her inward disbelief. According to him the Devil took up only half of Sarah Flannagan. Her critical faculty told her with authority that there were some things even a priest didn't know. But what was she to do now? These were her going away clothes, she just couldn't go home like this.

They were leaving the town, and it was the sight of the first tree that connected her harassed thoughts with Mr. Lord's house. He'd be out, at the farm, or in Newcastle or some place, and there'd only be old Ben in. Old Ben wasn't bad; in fact, he had been nice to her lately . . . well, not nice exactly but not awful, like on her first visit when he tried to throw her out of the house. She would go to him and ask him to clean her up.

The conductor's grin followed her when she

27

alighted, but with as much defiant dignity as she could muster she ignored him and the departing bus, and, crossing the deserted road, made for the great open iron gates.

This position of the gates, even after some months, had failed to make them look at ease, for the burden of twenty years of locks and chains needed some throwing off, even by gates, and by their forbidding aspect it would seem that they did not thank their liberator as she ran past them and up the drive.

She hadn't even reached the turn of the drive before she heard the hum of the car. Unmistakably Mr. Lord's car, and if she had been able to think of anything it would have been that Father Owen was right after all—the Devil was certainly out this morning. Wildly she looked towards the hedges on each side of her, but, not being a ferret she saw there was no escape that way; she was trapped by the last person on earth she wished to meet at this moment. It wasn't fair, it wasn't . . . the last time she'd had a row with Sarah Flannagan he had to come on the scene, and she had a feeling that Mr. Lord got one up on her da when she was in this kind of a mess.

In another second they were face to face; Mr. Lord, with narrowed eyes beneath his white, bristling brows, was looking through the windscreen at her. Standing as if struck, in the middle of the drive she returned his scrutiny.

After suffering a long survey by Mr. Lord, during which he uttered no command of "Come here!" she walked slowly to the side of the car and, not with head bent in contrition, but with chin lifted to his scowling countenance, she muttered, "I fell down."

"You fell down?" The voice held neither anger nor pity, but what it did hold confirmed her earlier feelings.

"Yes."

"I don't suppose this could be the result of another fight, could it?"

She remained silent, and he went on, "And what are you doing here? Now—" he raised his finger— "don't tell me you've called to see how I am."

"I wasn't going to." Her chin jerked.

"Well?"

"I was going to ask Ben—Mr. Ben to clean me up."

"You were, were you! Well, Mr. Ben has something better to do . . . your mother will see to that. Get in."

Dodging under his arm that held open the door, she climbed on to the seat. The door crashed closed, making her jump as it always did, and Mr. Lord, without looking at her and in the process of starting up the car, exclaimed, "I'm right, I imagine, when I think that you are wearing your new clothes, those in which you are to travel tomorrow?"

There was no need to answer this, and she sat upright on the edge of the seat, her eyes saddened by the unfair trials of the morning, but her pursed lips showing the spirit that still defied them.

The car leapt over the road, and almost, it would seem, within seconds the fields of the farm came into view, and with them retribution of some sort came nearer. . . . Mean, he was . . . that's what he was . . . mean. He could have let her go to Mr. Ben, he could. She hated him. . . . Eeh! no, she didn't. Well, he could have——

Her thoughts were checked by the car being turned up a side lane and brought to a stop. This, for the first time during the drive, brought her head round to him, and she looked up at the forbidding profile of "The Lord" as she thought of him. Only once before had he stopped the car like this, and that was when he told her he would give her da the farm manager's job if she would promise to go away to school and not let on that he had asked her. Perhaps he was going to say it didn't matter and she needn't go. No. Hope of such wholesale reprieve fled on the thought of "don't be daft", for he would, she felt, send her away to this school if she were dying. She had a swift mental picture of being carried on a stretcher to the train and being received at the convent by rows and rows of sympathetic nuns. Yet hope was never really dead in her, and it rose with its false voice and suggested that he might be going to say that she could go some place nearer, where she could come back at the weekends and see her da.

The car ceased its throbbing, and she watched him lean back, draw in a long breath, then let it out again, and as he did so he turned his head and looked at her. And then he smiled, just a little bit, with his mouth.

Quickly she responded to his mood. He could be nice . . . she liked him, she did. She would like to make him laugh. But at the moment she didn't feel like laughing.

"Tomorrow morning there will be no time to talk, Mary Ann." His voice was kind, and he was looking at her as if he didn't mind the mess she was in . . . but, still, he was talking about tomorrow morning. "Now, child, listen to me." He had taken her hands into his long bony ones. "Now listen to what I'm saying. Tomorrow you begin a new life. From tomorrow you have the opportunity to become—well—" his shoulders moved; his moustache was pressed outwards and he released one hand and spread his fingers wide, and they seemed to encompass the world—"you can be anything you want to be, Mary Ann. Do you understand?"

Her eyes were fixed tight on his, and her head moved once.

"Anything. You must forget about—about all this." He waved his hand around the car, but the indication took in the farm and all it held.

The light in her eyes faded somewhat, and he was quick to add, "Until the holidays; they'll soon come round. And you must learn. Apply yourself to your lessons—think of nothing else but learning when you are there. And if you play your part at school, I'll play my part here. You understand?"

"Yes."

Yes, she understood the implications, and the knowledge of her understanding pressed like a weight on her heart.

"You have a head on your shoulders, Mary Ann." He nodded slowly at her. "You are older than your years . . . you can lap up knowledge quickly if you have the mind. Pay attention . . . above all things, pay attention to your English, then languages will follow as easily as——" He snapped his fingers. "I will

30

know of your progress from your letters. . . . You will write to me?"

This last was not put as an order, but as a request, and she said, "Yes. Yes, I'll write to you."

After one look that took her in from her muddied hat to her shoes, he turned back to the wheel, and his next words tugged at and brought to the surface the affection she had for him. "You'll write . . . but you won't think of me until you have to do that irksome duty; you'll forget me."

Now she could respond, for below the brusqueness of his voice lay the buried loneliness that she had discovered on their first meeting. This was the part of him that she liked . . . loved. This was the part of him she used all her efforts to make laugh. All the benefits she and the family had received from his hands rushed before her, and she knew that but for him they would still be in Mulhattans' Hall . . . perhaps not even there, but some place worse.

She was kneeling on the seat now, close to his side, his bony, blue-veined hands gripped by her two small ones. "No, I won't! I won't forget you ever, I won't! And I'll try to learn for you, I will." She nearly added, "If you'll see to me da." But wisdom forbade this and prompted a more soothing balm to the old man's feelings, so swiftly she reached up, and, with her arms about his neck, she planted a kiss on the close-shaved wrinkled cheek. His eyes, now a few inches from hers, appeared pale and misty as they enveloped her, and with his hands cupping her small elfin face, he said, "Don't fail me, Mary Ann, will you?"

This softly spoken demand brought a damper to this nice part of the proceedings, and, after a somewhat doubtful sounding "No," she slid down to the seat. The car started and they were out on the main road again; then before you could say "Jack Robinson" they had turned into the lane which led to the farm, swept past the cottages where only a few weeks ago she had lived, right through the mud that the cattle made in the dip and into the actual farmyard.

Her eyes darted up at him. Why hadn't he put her off at their door, she'd only have to walk back? Then the sight of Mike, coming out of the cow byres at that moment gave her the reason. Yet again she couldn't fully explain it, she only knew that he wanted her da to see her all messed up. Oh! he was mean, he was.

Mike came swiftly towards the car, his eyes darting from one to the other, and he greeted Mr. Lord before he could alight. "Morning, Sir. Anything wrong?"

It was evident that Mike was surprised to see his master.

"No; nothing particularly." Mr. Lord eased himself out of the car. "When I phoned you to say I wouldn't be over until tomorrow morning, with this meeting coming up, I didn't know I was going to run into . . . this." He inclined his head slowly back into the car; then added, "Come on, get out." His voice certainly held no tone of endearment now, conveying only that Mary Ann and all her works were a source of annoyance to him.

Legs first, and with a good display of knickers, she slid from the seat and presented herself to her da, whereupon the wind was drawn in so thinly through Mike's teeth as to make a whistling sound, which spoke of exasperation and caused her heart to sink. He was mad at her; and it was her last day. Oh! it was mean of Mr. Lord, it was.

"Sarah Flannagan again." There was no sign of the laughter in Mike's voice that had accompanied the name earlier in the morning. "And your new things!"

From her eye level she was looking at the arm where it finished at the end of the sleeve. She wanted to grab it and cry, "Oh, Da! It was because she was saying nasty things . . . bad things about you that I hit her." But Mike's voice forbade any explanation whatever as he said, "Go on home, and see what your mother has to say."

Without looking at either of them she walked away to the sound of Mike's voice saying gruffly, "I'm sorry she put you out, Sir."

The world was all wrong; nothing was right, or ever would be again. Didn't they know it was her last day?

Dismally she took the path to the back door. The only consolation for her now was that things couldn't get worse, anyway not today, for whatever her ma said or did wouldn't be as bad as the way her da had looked at her.

But that there were differing degrees of trouble and that a large portion of the very worst kind awaited her was to be proved within the next minute, for she had hardly entered the scullery before the voice of her grannie hit her ear and brought to her face a wide-eyed look of incredulity. Not her grannie! Not the day, oh, no! She had never been near since they had come to live in the farmhouse, so she couldn't be here today. No, it couldn't be her grannie!

But it was her grannie. Only too true it was, and the sound of her told Mary Ann to escape, and quickly, for if her grannie saw her like this she would never hear the last of it.

Lifting her feet most cautiously now, she was about to turn and flee when the kitchen door, from being ajar, was pulled wide open, so that her grannie's voice came to her, saying, "Stone floors like these are a death trap. You'll be crippled with rheumatism afore you're here a——" The voice trailed off and Mrs. McMullen's eyes became fixed on Mary Ann's body caught in the stance of flight. "Well! So it's you. What are you up too?"

Mary Ann slumped; then closed her eyes as a gasp came from both her grannie and her mother, who, too, was now standing in the doorway.

"Oh! Mary Ann."

If her mother had gone for her it wouldn't have been so bad, but to sound sad like that, and in front of her grannie.

Mrs. McMullen's round, black eyes were moving over her grand-daughter with righteous satisfaction. "Well, you look a mess I must say. But it doesn't surprise me."

Mary Ann moved to her mother.

"How did it happen?"

"I fell, Ma."

"I fell, Ma!" As they stood looking at each other,

33

Mrs. McMullen gave a "Huh!" of a laugh. "You fell all right; and, of course, you weren't fighting and acting the hooligan."

Lizzie's face became tight, as she turned her back on her mother. But her voice held no reprimand as she said to Mary Ann, "Get your things off and I'll see to them."

Mary Ann got her things off, watched silently by Mrs. McMullen, and when she turned to the sink to wash, her grannie went into the kitchen, but she sent her voice back into the scullery, saying, "If you expect any silk purses to be made out of sows' ears, then I'm afraid you're in for a disappointment. Money down the drain. The man must be in his dotage."

That there wasn't a hair's difference between her grannie and Sarah Flannagan, Mary Ann had always been sure, and now it was confirmed. Silk purses . . . that's what Sarah Flannagan had said.

She saw her mother's hands gripping her coat, and she knew it was because of her grannie. She turned from the sink and tiptoed to her, and with a most pained countenance whispered, "Oh, ma!"

"Shush!" Lizzie's finger was on her lips, and when she wagged it warningly Mary Ann, with a hopeless sigh, went back to the sink again.

It was awful . . . awful. How long would her grannie stop? Hours and hours. . . . This was her day; everything should have been lovely; everybody should have been lovely to her; and what had happened? Something had got into it. . . . The Devil. She stopped rolling the soap between her hands. But why should he pick on her, and all at once? . . .

Mike's surprise equalled Mary Ann's when he came in and saw his mother-in-law already seated at the dinner table. There were no greetings exchanged between these two; enemies they had been from the beginning and enemies they would remain until the end.

A swift look that held pleading passed from Lizzie to Mike, for Mike's entry had not caused even a pause in Mrs. McMullen's discourse. He might have been a figment of Lizzie's and Mary Ann's imagination, so little impression did his presence apparently make on her.

That her grannie's cheap thrusts were now prodding her da, Mary Ann was well aware, and when Lizzie said to her, "Come and sit up," she thought. And if she says any more, I'll say to her, "Shut up, you!" I will . . . I don't care.

"Chicken? Things are looking up!" Mrs. McMullen's fuzzy head was bent over her plate. "Ah, well, you can afford them when you get them for nothing, I suppose."

"We didn't get it for nothing; me ma bought it cos it's a special dinner the day, for——"

"Mary Ann!" Both Mike and Lizzie spoke together, and Mary Ann slowly drew her eyes away from her grandmother. And Mrs. McMullen, with her high, tight, neat bosom swelling, exclaimed, "You should've been a dog, you've got the bark of one!"

"That's enough." Mike's voice was deep and quiet; it rolled over Mary Ann's head like distant thunder. He was standing behind her chair and his hand slid to her shoulder. What was in his eyes she could not see, but whatever it was it quelled the retort on her grannie's lips, and at the same time narrowed her eyes and tightened her face. Yet it did not effectively still her tongue, for she continued to talk, addressing herself solely to her daughter, yet all the while aiming her darts at both her son-in-law and grand-daughter.

"Will I help you?" she called to Lizzie in the scullery. And when Lizzie's reply of, "No, thank you, I can manage," came back to her, she called again, "These floors will be the death of you . . . cold stone. Wait till the winter comes. And the distance you've got to walk! Frying pan into the fire, if you ask me. You were nearly killed by worry afore, now you'll be just as effectively polished off in this place. . . . Like a barracks."

"Start, will you?" Lizzie came hurrying into the kitchen. "Say your grace, Mary Ann. Don't wait for me, anyone, just start. Gravy, Mother?"

"When do you think you'll get all these rooms furnished?"

"Oh, gradually. Gravy, Mike?" Lizzie was seated now, a fixed smile on her face.

Silently Mike took the tureen, and Mary Ann said painfully, "You've given me sprouts, Ma, and you know I don't like them."

"Oh, have I? Well just leave them on the side of your plate."

"Huh! I never did."

There was no need to enquire as to what Mrs. McMullen never did, they all knew it was connected with sprouts and eating them whether you liked them or not. And from the look that the old lady bestowed on her grandchild, it was evident that it would have given her the greatest pleasure to ram the sprouts singly down Mary Ann's gullet.

"It's either all or nothing . . . eight rooms!" Mrs. McMullen had returned to the matter of furnishings. "You'll be ready for your old-age pension by the time you get them fixed."

"I don't think so." Lizzie's voice was even. "I'm going to the sales. . . . At sales you can often pick up bargains."

Mrs. McMullen's hands paused while conveying a piece of the breast of chicken to her mouth. "Bargains! Don't be silly; those auctioneer fellows are crooks and fakers. Just read what they are up to in the papers. Faking pictures and furniture."

"Well, as I won't be wanting that kind of thing, it won't trouble me." Lizzie still wore her smile. "Do you want some more stuffing, Mary Ann? And you can pick your bone up in your fingers."

Mary Ann picked up the chicken bone and proceeded to strip it. It was nice and sweet. She loved chicken wing, especially where the skin stuck to the bone at the end. She was dissecting the last piece of anatomy when she gave an unintentional suck, loud enough to bring all eyes on her and, of course, her grannie's voice.

"Well, it's to be hoped they show you how to eat, if nothing else!"

Mike's eyes, like flashes of fire, darted to the old woman. But Mrs. McMullen's eyes were lowered to her plate and she continued her discourse regarding

36

the furnishing of rooms. "Well, even if you get them furnished, what'll they be for, she's going?" This was accompanied by a bland nod towards Mary Ann. "And once she gets a taste of a fancy school, you needn't think this place'll hold her after a few years. And if I know Michael he'll be off as soon as he can, and there you'll be left, eight rooms for two of you. That's if you're here, of course."

As she spoke the last words Mike's chair scraped loudly on the stone floor, and almost at the same time, Lizzie, the armour of her smile now gone, jumped to her feet, saying, hurriedly, "I'll bring the pudding in. Mike . . . Mike!" She had to repeat his name to draw his eyes away from her mother's bent head. "Mike, come and give me a hand . . . Mike!"

Slowly Mike turned from the table and went into the scullery, and Lizzie, close behind him, shut the door and, going to him, took him by the arm.

"Oh! Mike, why do you let her get at you? You know she's doing it on purpose. Why don't you laugh at her?"

"Laugh at her!" Mike's teeth ground each other, setting Lizzie's on edge, and his voice rumbled in his throat, "Strangle her, more like!"

"Mike! don't say that. Can't you see? She's mad because we're set and comfortable."

"Why didn't you tell me she was here?"

"I couldn't; she had just got in when Mary Ann came in, all mud and——"

"I know. He brought her back."

"Mr. Lord?"

"Aye."

"Oh! no." Lizzie's fingers went to her mouth. "And in her new things an' all!"

"Don't worry, he got a great deal of satisfaction out of it. I don't know whether he takes me for a complete fool or not where she's concerned, but he got a kick out of showing me just what he was taking her away from."

"Oh, Mike! Don't look at it like that, he's not taking her away."

"Isn't he?" Mike reached for his coat, and as Lizzie moved to help his maimed arm into it, he thrust

37

her aside almost roughly; then turning swiftly to her again, he grabbed her hand into his and, gripping it, he said, urgently, "Liz, I want to talk to you. I've been thinking all morning . . . and then that old——" His eyes flicked towards the kitchen door. "Liz, if we let her go we've lost her. I've never agreed with your mother in me life, but she's right there. This fancy place is bound to change her . . . it can't but help it. I'm frightened, Liz, frightened inside."

His hand was almost cracking her knuckles, and Lizzie was now filled with a feeling akin to terror. "Mike . . . she's got to go."

"Got to?"

"I mean she's—she wants to. She'll—she'll break her heart if she doesn't go."

"You really think so?" Mike's gaze was penetrating into her, and Lizzie willed her eyes not to fall before it. Then he ended rapidly, "Anyway, how does she know what she wants, she's only a bairn?"

"She's old for her years, you know she is, and it's a chance in a lifetime. You said yourself many a time you wished you'd had the chance of education."

His grip on her hand slackened and his head drooped. "It's sending her so damned far away that's getting me."

Lizzie looked at him with love and pity in her eyes, but she continued to press Mr. Lord's case. "He thought with his sister being Mother Superior she'd likely be better looked after there."

Her voice trailed off, and Mike turned away and picked up his cap. "I wonder. I wonder a lot of things. Sometimes I think . . . Oh!" he pulled the cap firmly on to his head and made for the door; but there he turned back quickly, and, coming to her again, he pulled her to him, and with his one arm about her, he kissed her roughly, "I'm sorry about the dinner, Liz, but you know how it is."

After holding him close for a moment, she let him go and, moving to the window, she watched him walk down the path and into the lane. And, as ever, pride of him rose in her, but it did not swamp the fear, and as she braced herself to go into the kitchen again the fear came flooding over her. But it was not of her

38

mother—the feeling her mother aroused was simply acute irritation—no, the fear was of her daughter, and she prayed for tomorrow to come and be gone, and Mary Ann with it.

3

It was four o'clock and never had an afternoon seemed so long and empty to Mary Ann. After changing her clothes, right through, her mother had sent her out in her old things; and, glad to escape, she had immediately sought out her da. But to her surprise and inner hurt, Mike had said he was up to the eyes in work and that she must keep out of the way. He was a bit mad, she could see—that was her grannie. Oh, she hated her grannie, she did. But this was her last day; surely he hadn't forgotten that. Tomorrow she wouldn't be here, even if he had heaps of time to spare.

In the cowshed, Mr. Jones, too, had no use for her presence. He didn't even have to say so, he just looked. Len was up the long field mending a fence. Mr. Polinski only was available. But conversation was difficult at any time with him, and today doubly so, as he was working under a machine in the open barn. Not even the dogs were to be seen.

Completely at a loose end, she decided to go and say a lengthy goodbye to Mrs. Jones. But after three knocks on the cottage door she realised that even this doubtful pleasure was to be denied her. She was in the act of turning away when the back door of "their house"—she still thought of the next cottage as "their house"—was pulled open, and Mrs. Polinski stood there. She wasn't laughing now as she did when speaking to her da, her face was straight, and Mary

Ann's discerning eyes told her that Mrs. Polinski had been crying, for in spite of her being all done up, her eyes were red and swollen.

When she saw Mary Ann the young woman's expression changed, and, smiling now, she said, "Hello there."

"Hello," said Mary Ann, politely. "I've come to say goodbye to Mrs. Jones, but I think she's out."

"Yes, she is. But aren't you going to say goodbye to me?" The young woman paused, waiting for Mary Ann to say, "Yes." And when she did so Mrs. Polinski stepped aside, saying, "Come in and see if I've got any sweets left. Come on."

Mary Ann went in, and was immediately arrested by the change in the cottage. She had known the kitchen as a colourful place, all bright and shiny, but now it looked awful. There was a red carpet on the floor. Whoever heard of a carpet in the kitchen! No wonder it was mucky. And a red suite, all greasy at the back where the heads had been. And dust . . . the mantelpiece was thick with it. Even the ashes hadn't been taken out for days . . . anybody could see that.

"Look, have a chocolate. You're lucky, for they're nearly finished."

Mary Ann stared down at the box offered to her. You only had boxes of chocolates at Christmas. "Oh, ta . . . thank you." She took one, a silver-papered one.

"Take two."

"Oh, can I? Ta."

"You're going in the morning then?"

"Yes." The wonderful taste of the chocolate was taking even the sting out of this admission.

"You're lucky."

Mary Ann paused in her chewing, but remained mute to this.

"You don't know how lucky . . . with a man like Mr. Lord at your back." Mrs. Polinski shook her head slowly, as if at the wonder of it.

Again Mary Ann found nothing to say; so she ate the second chocolate.

"Do you know it's only four and a half years ago since I left school?"

Mary Ann stopped munching. "Only four and a half?"

"Yes, and oh, how I wish I was back." Mrs. Polinski sat down heavily; then leant towards Mary Ann. "Make school last as long as possible."

Her voice sounded hard, and Mary Ann said, "I don't want to; I don't like school."

"No, not now you don't, no one ever does, but one day you'll look back and long for school again. How old do you think I am?" She pressed herself back against the couch, giving Mary Ann room for scrutiny.

Mary Ann looked at the round, smooth face, the blonde hair that wasn't like her ma's, and she thought, I don't know; but she's married so she must be old. "Twenty," she said.

"You're nearly right."

Mary Ann gave no congratulatory exclamation at this, and Mrs. Polinski sighed and, pulling a bundle of sewing towards her, said somewhat dispiritedly, "I'm making myself a frock. Do you like the colour?" She held the dress up.

Politely Mary Ann looked at the dress, and politely she said, "Yes, it's nice." But in her head she was saying, quite distinctly, "I don't like it. Why does she have everything red?"

"Your mother's going to miss you."

"Yes," Mary Ann nodded. "So's me da."

"Your da." The hands became still on the material, and Mrs. Polinski looked at Mary Ann, a smile on her lips now. "You like your da, don't you?"

"Yes."

"Yes." Again Mrs. Polinski sighed; and her hands began to move once more. "Who'd blame you; he's a fine man is your father—your da." She laughed softly now, as if to herself.

As Mary Ann stared at the girl aimlessly fumbling with the material, she had a strong and urgent desire to get up from the couch and run away, to fly away. This was odd, for anyone who spoke highly of her da commanded her whole attention. Yet this feeling urged her not to listen to Mrs. Polinski, but to dash off and not to her da, but to her mother. And she knew what she'd say to her mother . . . she'd say, "I don't like Mrs. Polinski, I don't." And if her mother asked why, she'd say, " 'Cos she wants to go back to school." But she knew that wasn't really why she didn't like her. Then, why didn't she? She shook her head. Swiftly she rose now, saying, "Eeh! I've got to go, I forgot something. Thanks for the sweets."

"Oh." Mrs. Polinski pulled herself out of her reverie. "Oh, all right. . . . Well, goodbye, Mary Ann. Be a good girl, and remember what I told you."

There was no interest in her tone at all now, and its lack was expressed finally, when she added, "You can let yourself out. Bye-bye."

"Bye-bye."

Once outside, Mary Ann began to run, not caring very much where she was bound for; and her thoughts ran with her, jumping when she jumped. Mrs. Polinski was awful. The thought was high in her head. Look at her house, all red and dirty. She skipped over the grass verge. She didn't like her, she didn't. On and on she ran, her thoughts swirling around Mrs. Polinski until, when in sight of the main road, she was brought to a sudden stop by a stitch in her side.

She stood groaning. "Oh! . . . Oh! By gum . . . Ooh! Crikey Moses!" It was the worst of the many stitches she had experienced, it brought her over double. "Oh! Lordy! Lordy!"

"Are you hurt?"

She glanced up sideways at the young man bending above her.

"Oh! I've got a stitch. Oh! it's awful."

"Rub it." His face was serious and a little twisted, as if he, too, was feeling the stitch, and she did as he bid her, and rubbed her side vigorously.

Phew! As she straightened up she was actually sweating, and the young man's voice was sympathetic as he said, "Yes, I know what that is. It can be awful."

Mary Ann looked at him. "It's gone now."

"Good."

She continued to stare at the stranger as she rubbed her side. Who was he? He looked nice, and he talked swanky. Like Mr. Lord, only different. He was look-

42

ing now across the field, to where stood the skeleton of the new barn.

"That barn," he said. "Whose is it?"

"Me da's."

When his eyes quickly came to hers, she added quickly and in a somewhat offended tone, "Well, he's manager, it's the same thing."

"I'm looking for Mr. Lord's farm."

She blinked twice, before saying, "That's it."

He was turning his gaze to the field again, when he hesitated and looked down at her once more, and there was the faintest trace of a smile on his sombre countenance, and it told Mary Ann that he understood things without a lot of explaining, and she thought again, He's nice.

"What's your name?"

"Mary Ann Shaughnessy; and me da's Mike Shaughnessy. He's a grand farmer, me da."

"Yes, I'm sure he is."

"He knows everything." She stressed this point, smiling broadly up at him.

"Does he? I'm glad of that."

"What's your name?"

"Tony. Tony Brown."

She didn't think much of Brown as a name, but he was nice, and not old—well, not very. She did not ask, "How old are you?" because her mother had said she hadn't to ask people that. But she tried to gain her information by putting her question on a more friendly basis: "I'm eight, goin' on for nine. Are you very old?"

"Yes, pretty old."

The admission was sad, and she said, comfortingly, "Well, it doesn't matter. And you going to our farm?"

He nodded. "I suppose I'm going to see your father."

"Oh, are you?" Her smile spread into a great welcoming beam. "Oh, I'll take you."

"Thanks."

Tomorrow was again forgotten. Hopping and jumping over the puddles and on and off the grass verge, she led the way back to the farm, chattering to her new, sober-looking acquaintance all the while.

But when, within a short distance of the yard, she found he wasn't following her, she stopped and turned to see him standing staring toward the farmhouse, whereupon she offered proudly: "That's our house."

He looked at her, then asked slowly, "Doesn't . . . doesn't Mr. Lord live here?"

"No, not yet. His house isn't ready, but it soon will be. Look, there it is, on the hill . . . look!"

He followed her finger, and then said briefly, "Show me where I'll find your father."

"Come on then; he'll be here somewhere."

She went dashing off ahead now, crying loudly, "Da! Da! . . . Oh, Mr. Polinski!" She pulled up as a short, dark man, in his late thirties, came from behind a rick, carrying a cart shaft on his shoulder. "Where's me da? Do you know?"

"In office—" he nodded towards the old diary that the late manager had converted into an office— "wit old man."

Mr. Polinski's "old man" meant Mr. Lord. She hadn't known he was here again. He must have come by when she was in Mrs. Polinski's house. She turned round now and waited for the young man to come up.

"He's in his office," she said. "And Mr. Lord's there an' all, so I can't go in."

She saw the young man stop in his stride, and then he did a funny thing. He turned completely round towards the entrance to the farmyard, as if he was going back that way, and she said hastily, pointing, "The office is over there . . . that door."

Slowly he turned again, and then, without saying "Ta" or "Thanks", he went across the yard, and she stood watching him, standing with her finger-nail between her teeth, in sudden troubled perplexity. She knew she hadn't seen him before, and yet she felt she had. Perhaps she had seen him in Jarrow somewhere, or perhaps in church. And this feeling of recognition seemed to be connected with his walk, with his back?

Out of a million backs she could have picked her da's or her ma's, and somehow she knew she could have picked this young man's, too. It was funny. She bit on her finger as if trying to tear off the nail.

44

Before the young man reached the office the door opened and Mr. Lord came out, followed by Mike, and they both looked enquiringly at the young man, who had now come to a stop a few yards away from them.

Mary Ann now moved cautiously forward, and as she came up to them her da was saying, "Oh, yes, of course; you're Brown, aren't you?"

"Yes, sir." The young man was looking directly at her father, and Mary Ann's chest swelled with pride . . . he had called her da, "Sir."

"It's the young fellow from the Agricultural College, sir." Mike had turned to Mr. Lord, and when Mr. Lord did not answer, he added, "Remember? I told you he had written."

Mr. Lord's eyes, narrowed behind his beetling brows, were fixed on the visitor. And now the young man was returning his stare, hard, almost it seemed to Mary Ann with dislike, like she looked at Sarah Flannagan.

"Why do you particularly want to get experience here? It's only a small farm." Mr. Lord's mouth was at its grimmest.

"I don't." The words were shot out, and Mr. Brown bit his lip as if regretting them; then added, with slightly lowered head, "I mean, I don't mind, I would rather start on a small farm."

Mary Ann looked from one to the other, and she saw that the dislike was in Mr. Lord's eyes now, and she thought, Aw! he won't take him on; not when he looks like that he won't. Aw! And she felt a great sense of disappointment.

She saw her da give a hitch to his trousers, and his chin go up as he turned to Mr. Lord and said, "We'll have to have an extra hand, anyway, sir. What about a trail, we can't go far wrong in that?" He spoke as if the young man wasn't present. And Mr. Lord, moving his head restlessly, replied in much the same way, "I suppose it's up to you. But I'm warning you, we're carrying no dead-weight, Agricultural College or not, the milk comes out the same way; and they cannot alter the seasons."

Mr. Lord now walked away, but he had not gone

far when he turned and called Mike to him. And when Mike, with a glance at the young fellow, went towards him, he said, "You've got a free hand as you know, but I'm not sure whether it would be wise to take him on; he looks all head and no hands, and you don't want that kind. It's labour you want."

For Mike's part, he had instinctively taken to the young fellow, but he was wise not to make this too evident. Moreover, he did not despise men with headpieces on a farm, for he was finding his self-imposed study at night more tiring than the work of the day. And so, hitching at his belt again, he sighed and said, "You're right there, sir, only too true. But what do you say if I give him a trial—that is, if it's all the same to you?"

Mr. Lord looked past Mike's head to the young man again, and his eyes stayed on him for a moment before he said, "Well, don't start complaining to me about him, that's all." And on this he walked away.

Mike stood for a moment watching his master before turning and going back to the boy, and immediately he saw that the young fellow's back was up, and his sympathy went out to him, for he knew only too well how the old man could draw out a temper. The antagonism between the two had been the swiftest thing he had ever seen, except perhaps his own feelings for Ratcliffe, his late boss.

"Well, now—" he confronted the boy—"we'll have to talk, I suppose; but first of all, what about a cup of tea? Come on over to the house."

"Da." All this time Mary Ann had stood in the background, keeping her tongue quiet, but now she realised that her father had clearly forgotten about her grannie, for he was walking away towards the house, talking as he went. "Where are you living?" he was asking the young man.

"At present, in Newcastle. I have a room there."

"Da."

"Yes? Come on." Mike held out his hand, but went on, "You're not from these parts then?"

"No, sir." The young man did not seem of a communicative nature, and Mike said, "Well, you'll have to come nearer than Newcastle. Newcastle's a long way

46

when the dawn rises early. Yes, we'll have to see about that."

"Da!" She tugged at his hand. He must be daft, she told herself, if he was going to take a stranger into their house, and her grannie there, for she would soon give him a picture of their life, and especially her da's, which would be awful, to say the very least. "Da!" she tugged again and whispered urgently, "Da! me grannie."

"Oh!" Mike stopped abruptly and looked down on her, and his colour rising just the slightest he said, "Yes, your grannie." But as he turned to his companion with a laughing apology on his lips, the need for it was taken away, for there, going along the road past the farm entrance were Lizzie and her mother, and Lizzie, looking in his direction, called, "Mary Ann!"

"Oh! bust."

"Go on." Her da was speaking under his breath, and reluctantly, with slow measured steps, she went towards the gate.

"Your grannie's just going . . . are you coming to the bus with us?"

The true and natural retort would have been "No!" but something in Lizzie's tone and the way she held out her hand asked for obedience, and so, taking her mother's hand, she walked reluctantly back along the road, trying to shut her ears to her grandmother's vicious chatter.

"Nothing ever stays put—get that into your head— we're here today and gone tomorrow, and that applies to worldly goods. And jobs an' all, a lot can happen in a six months' trial, so don't bank your hopes on a golden future. You won't take to it kindly when you find yourself on the dung heap again."

Mary Ann felt her mother's fingers suddenly stiffen, and her voice came harsh when she demanded, "Who told you he was on a six months' trial?"

"Ah, I have me little birds."

Mary Ann saw them, hordes of them, fighting, screeching little birds, and she willed them to swoop down on her grannie and peck her eyes out. She even saw her grannie being borne to the ground by them,

47

and with deep satisfaction she gazed down on her, pecked to death by her little birds.

Oh! her grannie. She wished she was dead, she did. Eeh! . . . well, she did.

"Well, you can tell your little birds that the six months' trial is only a figure of speech, he's set for life."

"Huh!" It was a small laugh that spoke volumes. "I'm glad you think so. But you were always one to fool yourself. You mark my words, if it isn't one thing it will be another."

"You hope it will be like that." Lizzie's voice was very low and came tightly from between her teeth.

"I've no need to hope. If I didn't know the man it'd be different. The first time you let him off the lead it'll be hi-ho for the pubs and 'Get the cans on John Michael'."

Mary Ann's fingers were hurting, so tightly crushed were they in her mother's hand. There was silence now, but as they neared the main road the sound of the approaching bus came to them, and Mrs. McMullen exclaimed in exasperation, "It's early, there's another five minutes yet."

Lizzie said nothing, not even when the bus stopped and she assisted her mother on to it.

From the platform, Mrs. McMullen turned, and now in a pathetic tone, that immediately caught the sympathy of the listeners in the bus, she said, "That's it, go and leave me in a huff. When are you coming down to see me?"

"I don't know."

"Well!"

The bus moved off, and Lizzie turned quickly away from the sight of her mother's pained countenance. But once in the shelter of the lane she stopped, and stood biting hard on her lip.

When Mary Ann edged close to her she put her arms about her and pressed her head into her waist for a moment, then easing her away again, she stooped and kissed her and looking deep into her eyes she spoke, not of her mother, or of what she had said, but to Mary Ann's surprise, she used the same words as Mr. Lord had done. "There won't be much time to

48

talk tomorrow, Mary Ann," she said. "Now promise me you'll be a good girl at this school, and you'll learn and make us proud of you."

The weight of the world was on her again, and more heavily now.

"Promise . . . so much depends on you, Mary Ann."

Mary Ann stared up at her mother, and the look of anxiety she saw deep in Lizzie's eyes forced her to smile wistfully and promise, "All right, Ma, I will."

Lizzie kissed her again, and Mary Ann clung to her in an effort to stop the tears from spurting, and when, blinking rapidly, she looked up at her mother, Lizzie laughed and said, "That bus saved you, it was your turn next. You would have learned of all the things you aren't going to be in that school."

Mary Ann gave a sniffling, cackling, laugh, and Lizzie, catching hold of her hand again, cried, "Come on; let's go home."

So together, like two girls released from a tyrant, they sped down the road, laughing and shouting to each other as they leapt over the puddles.

It was over an extra wide puddle that it happened. Lizzie, with a lift of her arm, was assisting Mary Ann in a flying leap when she fell. Having been pulled down beside her mother, Mary Ann lay laughing into her hands for a moment. This was mainly to save herself from crying, for the stones had grazed both her legs and the palms of her hands. But she was brought quickly out of her simulated laughter by the sound of a groan from her mother. Lizzie was sitting on the road holding on to her ankle with both hands; her lips were apart, and her teeth were tightly pressed together.

"What's the matter, Ma? Oh! Ma."

"I—I've hurt my ankle. Help me up."

Mary Ann, with all her small strength, helped her mother on to her good foot; then watched the colour drain from her face. Terrified, she helped her to hop to the grass verge, and when Lizzie dropped down on to it and gasped, "Go—go and get your da," she replied in a daze, "Me da?"

"Yes."

"Oh!" After one last look at her mother Mary Ann bounded away, calling, "Da! Da!"

She had reached the farmyard when she pulled herself up, and turning, made for the house. Her da would be in the house with the new man. But Mike wasn't in the house. Dashing back into the yard again she ran full tilt into Len, and to her garbled question of, "Where's me da?" he said, "In the new barn. But mind, the old boy's there. What's up with you?"

She was gone before he had finished, and when, still yelling, she rounded the outbuildings and came to the front of the new barn, she was confronted by three pairs of eyes and Mr. Lord's voice.

"Stop that noise this moment!"

For once, she took no notice whatever of him, or his orders, but flew to Mike, crying, "Oh, Da! Da!" The necessity to breathe checked her words, and Mike put in sharply, "Behave yourself!"

"It's me ma . . . she's hurt herself . . . she's lying on the road and she's white!"

After just one second's pause while he stared down at her, Mike was away, and he was out of the gate before her flying legs had carried her half-way across the yard. When the young man caught up with her he called, "What is it?"

She was so out of puff that she didn't even try to answer. They were on the road now, and in the distance she saw her da raising her ma up with his one good arm. The young man sprinted ahead, and when, panting loudly, she reached the group, he was linking his hand to Mike's to make a seat for her mother.

Lizzie's face was drawn, and she was near tears, and when she exclaimed bitterly, "For this to happen!" Mary Ann felt, somehow, that she wasn't referring to the pain she was in but the accident's bearing on the morrow.

Walking now behind the two men, the meaning of what her mother's accident meant to her filled her with guilty-conscience-streaked joy: They wouldn't be able to send her the morrow. They couldn't if her ma couldn't walk, could they?

From its beginning, it had undoubtedly been a day during which the Devil had certainly been master. But once more he had been vanquished; her secret prayers had been answered. What was his power to compare with that of the Holy Family? Hadn't they even brought her grannie here to bring things about? Likely, her grannie had been in the middle of her washing, or some such, and they had said, "Get your things on and go and see Lizzie," because her mother would never have gone up the road if it hadn't been to see her grannie to the bus, would she?

Realising the advantage of possessing such allies as the Holy Family had unconsciously brought to Mary Ann's face an expression which was not in keeping with the events of the moment, and she was not aware that the relief she was feeling had slipped through, until her eyes met Mr. Lord's, where he stood by the gate.

The joy was wiped from her face; she even stopped dead for a moment, brought to a halt, it would seem, by the knowledge in the eyes regarding her. Then as she stared at him an odd thing happened, for out of his head sprouted two horns, and between his thin legs came flicking a tail, a forked tail. Her joy sank; she could feel it draining from her chest, right through her stomach and down her legs. Dread reality was on her again. It was as Father Owen said, the Devil had many guises. And now he had gone into . . . The Lord, and she knew that there was going to be a fight on between him and her amalgamated company of the Holy Family, and for the life of her at this moment she didn't know which side to back.

4

And now it was her da saying, "There won't be any time in the morning to talk." He was sitting on her bed and his voice was very low. He looked tired, weary.

"If you're not happy there, you'll tell me, won't you? You'll write? Very likely they'll read your letters. I think they do—but if you're not happy get a letter to me somehow. . . . Look . . . look at me." He brought her face to his again. "You really want to go to this school? Tell me the truth now."

No power of hers brought her head to a sharp nod, nor her voice to say, "Yes, Da"; it was the combined voices of her ma and Mr. Lord inside which did it. She could still hear Mr. Lord saying airily to her da, "She'll be all right. She'll be in the care of the guard to London, and a nun will meet the train. I've arranged everything. This is a very unfortunate happening. I would take her myself, but I hate trains and—" his voice had dropped to a note of regret—"and, of course, it's a pity you can't be spared." Then on again it had gone, lightly, airily, "Oh, she'll be all right. Anyway, she must be there for the beginning of term." And then her mother, holding her hand tightly until the bones hurt, and saying, "Mr. Lord has made all arrangements. And, darling, if your da should ask you if you still want to go, you'll say yes, won't you? You'll say yes."

She had said it.

Mike stared at her; then shook his head in a bewildered fashion. "Then why aren't you more happy about it?"

"Well. . . . Well, I don't want to leave you."

Pulling her to him, he held her tightly, and as he stroked her hair, he murmured, "Don't worry about me, I'll be all right."

Although he had not put it into definite words, she knew he was telling her he wouldn't get . . . sick. She clung to him silently, until, laying her down he pulled the clothes about her; then kissing her gently and saying, "Sleep now," he went swiftly out, forgetting to switch off the light.

She wanted to cry, a loud crying, that would bring him hurrying back, but instead, she lay staring up at the beam which started in the centre of the room and sloped down over her head, to disappear into the wall at the side of the bed. Methodically, she counted the holes in it, as many as she could see, and when she had reached seventy-two Michael came in. Awkward and shy, he stood at the foot of her bed and said, "Hello."

"Hello," she said.

This polite exchange was too much, and turning swiftly over she buried her head in the pillow, and Michael, moving quickly to her, whispered, "What is it?" He touched her shoulder, and when her sobs rose he went hastily and closed the door; then coming back to the bed, and going down on his hunkers, he whispered again, "What is it? Don't you want to go?"

Slowly she twisted round, and raising herself on her elbow and with the corner of the sheet pressed tightly over her mouth, she shook her head vigorously.

"Good Lord!" It was the lowest of whispers. But he did not ask, "Then why are you going?" The small sister who could madden him in so many ways had always remained outside his understanding. When he thought of the things she did and got off with, in his imagination they made her appear older than himself, quite grown-up in fact, different altogether from her appearance. Sometimes, looking at her in exasperation, he couldn't associate her doings with the look of her at all. She should have just been . . . his little sister, but "her!" and "she!" and "that little beast!" as he sometimes was justifiably brought to think of her, never had any connection in his mind with her small and fragile make-up. Grudgingly, he was aware that she had powers which he himself was without. Cheek, he sometimes named them—he had not reached the stage where he could pinpoint them simply as facets of character.

Now he looked into her eyes, all streaming with tears, and although he couldn't fathom it all out, he knew that she was not going to this school, as he had thought, partly to display her sense of showing off, but she was going solely to please Mr. Lord. And in pleasing Mr. Lord. . . . His thoughts would go no further; he would not allow himself to think. This is all mixed up with me da, for in that thought lay fear and insecurity. The wonder of his father being manager of a farm still lay on the surface of his mind—it had not yet weight enough to sink in—and made a reassuring pattern of life that held no fear . . . no fear of drink and unemployment and a broken home, and no fear of death that he had so nearly reached, when he put his head in the gas oven. . . . So, going so far as to take hold of her hand, which was a long way for him, he said, "You'll like it. And—and I'll write to you."

"Will—will you?" Unconsciously she blew her nose on the end of the sheet, and as he watched her he did not say, as he surely would have done under any other circumstances, "Stop that. Use your handkerchief, you dirty thing!" but "Yes, I will, and I'll tell you how things are going."

"You will?" She looked up, her face eager under her tears as she whispered, "Will you tell me about me da, and if everything's all right with him?"

They looked at each other in silence for a moment, and then he said, briefly, "Yes."

"Promise?"

"Yes."

"And of course about me ma and her foot . . . and the farm an' all. And everything."

"I promise I'll write you once a week."

In this moment, such a promise seemed a very small price to pay for what she was doing, and, quite suddenly, he knew that he didn't want her to go, and a fear came on him that with her going the bond that held them all together would be broken, and they would drift. The fear was not so much for his mother but for his father, yet he was only too well aware that what touched one touched the other.

Rising, he said, "Go on, get to sleep now, it's late. I'll put the light out for you. . . . I'm going to the station with you in the morning. Good-night."

The light went out and the door was gently closed, and slowly she slid down, and turning her face once more into the pillow she started to cry again, but softly, so that no one should hear.

It was the first time she had been "over the bridge", in Newcastle Central station, and never before had she seen a train as grand as this one, with places all set for breakfast and everything. And she was to have milk and biscuits at ten o'clock and her dinner at twelve—it was all arranged—and the guard was to look after her.

She had four comics and a real box of chocolates, and a pile of money, one pound, seventeen and fourpence. The excitement of all this splendour and wealth had taken a slight edge off the coming wrench, until Michael said, "Just another five minutes."

This statement, while it sent her heart tumbling heavily into her shoes, seemed to arouse a nerve of energy in both her da and Mr. Lord. Mike moved quickly and went inside the compartment and looked up at the cases on the rack; then, turning to the elderly couple, the only other occupants of the carriage and interested spectators, he said thickly, "Would you— would you give an eye to her?"

The old man, hitching himself to the front of the seat, said, "Aye, lad, don't you worry—we're going right through. The missis and me'll see she comes to no harm."

The voice was thick Geordie, and, a little reassured, Mike nodded and said, "Thanks. Thanks very much. It's her first trip alone."

"Poor wee thing." The woman, too, was sitting forward now, and she emphasised her statement by adding, "She looks so small."

"Aye—" Mike turned away and the words were lost in his throat—"she's small." Why the hell had he let this happen! Why had he stood for it! He should have put his foot down and said, "A school near, or none at all."

As he stepped down on to the platform, even his breathing was checked. Mr. Lord was bending over Mary Ann and tying a watch on her wrist. A flame of searing jealousy shot through him, making him fighting mad, as if he'd had a belly-full of booze. Buying her again . . . at the last minute like this . . . with a watch that looked all gold. And what had he himself given her? Some comics and a few chocolates. And now the old fellow was pushing an envelope into her pocket. God! he wished he could get over this feeling against him. He had tried, and he thought he had succeeded. Then last night when he had insisted on her going, he had hated him.

"Da! Da, look what Mr. Lord's given me. Isn't it lovely?" She was holding her wrist high.

The doors along the train began to bang, and Mr. Lord said quietly, "Come now." On this she turned from Mike again and stared up at the face that seemed, in the last few minutes, to have suddenly become very, very old, and in her impetuous way she rushed at him and held up her arms and face.

Mike turned towards Michael, and he did not look round again until her voice cried, "Oh! Da . . . it's going!" Swiftly now he lifted her into his arms, and cupping her face with his good hand he held it still, drawing her on his mind.

"Oh! Mary Ann."

"Da . . . Da."

"Don't cry." His voice was unsteady, and he went on, low and hurriedly, "But remember what I told you last night—if you don't like it, tell me."

"Oh! Da."

"All aboard!"

"Oh! Da." Panic was now welling in her, and as Mike's arms crushed her close to him she became filled with terror, consumed by it, terror of the train . . . the school . . . the unknown.

"Da! Da! Oh! Da."

"There now. Ssh! There now. Say goodbye to Michael."

"Goodbye." There was no sound of the word, and when Michael put his lips to her cheek the tears spurted, and she was blind. She felt herself lifted into the carriage; she heard the door bang and the window pulled down; she felt her da's face close to hers again. Then Mr. Lord's voice, saying, "Goodbye, child. Learn——" was cut abruptly off. But the wheels took up his words and chanted, "Learn, learn, learn, learn— learny, learn, learny, learn." Faster and faster they went, and her da was still beside the window, running with the train.

"Oh! Da."

"Be careful, hinny." The woman had hold of her.

"God bless you, my love."

"Careful! Oh! be careful."

He was gone, left standing alone on the very end of the platform, and she struggled from the woman's hands and tried to lean her head out of the window. But she couldn't reach, and so she put out both her hands and waved them frantically.

"There, there. Come on," coaxed the old woman.

Limply she sat down on the edge of the seat, and blinking through the rain of tears she stared dazedly at the blurred outline of the old couple.

"My! you're a clever lass to go all this way on your own. Come and sit aside me, and tell me your name."

The old man drew her over to his knee, and with a "Ups-a-daisy!" lifted her on to the seat. "There now," he said, "dry your eyes and tell me what they call you."

"Mary—Ann."

"Mary Ann." He smiled, and the old woman said, "That's a good old-fashioned name. And it's funny you know, we've got two grand-daughters, and one's called Mary Elizabeth, and the other's called Ann Elizabeth."

Mary Ann sniffed and rubbed at her eyes with her handkerchief. "Me ma's name's Elizabeth. She was c-coming with me, but she f-fell down last night and put her ankle out."

"Oh!" They nodded at each other, and the old man said, "By! he's a fine-looking fellow is your da. I've never seen a mass of red hair like he's got, not for years, I haven't."

Still emitting shivering sobs, she looked from one to the other. They were nice. The man was like Mrs. McBride, the way he talked, only he was a man; and the woman was very little, but she had a nice face.

She sobbed a great sob, and licked at her tears; then asked brokenly, "Would you like a sweet—a chocolate? They're real chocolates. It's a pound box—me da bought it for me."

Without waiting for their reply she slipped off the seat to fetch the chocolates, and when she was settled again the old woman said, "My! what a grand box. . . . And who was the old man? Your granda?"

"No, he's Mr. Lord. He owns the farm; he's sending me to school."

"Oh." Over her head, the couple looked at each other again, and the old man said, "This school where you are going—where is it?"

"It's in the country, outside of a place called St. Leonards. It's the Convent of the Holy Child of Bethlehem."

"A convent?"

The horror in the old man's voice brought her attention sharply from the unwrapping of the Cellophane around the box, and she looked up at him. His brows were now gathered and his chin jutted as he repeated, "A convent?"

"Yes." Her voice was very small, as if she was admitting to some personal misdemeanour.

"God in heaven! all that way and to a convent. It isn't right."

"George!" The little woman's voice was stern now.

But George did not seem to hear it. "You a Catholic then?" he demanded.

"Yes."

"George!"

"Aren't there no schools near? Have you been in a convent afore?"

"George! Do you hear me?"

"No—I mean yes, there are some near." Mary Ann looked in bewilderment from one to the other. "But I haven't been in a convent afore."

"Come on, dear, open your chocolates." The old woman, greatly agitated, began to assist with the opening of the box, while the old man, leaning back against the seat with a soft thud, fumbled in his pocket for his pipe.

"Oh, they're lovely!" The woman gazed down on the top layer of chocolates, and Mary Ann said, "You have one."

"Thank you."

"Will you have one, Mi-mister?" Mary Ann turned to the old man. But once again he was obscured by the tears she could not stop.

"No, thanks, I'm having me pipe, hinny. . . . Ah well, all right, I will. There, I'll have that one." He picked a small chocolate from the corner of the box. "Our name's Wilson. How old are you?"

"Eight, nearly nine."

"Eight. My God!"

For no reason Mary Ann could see her age seemed to

annoy the old man, for he stuffed the chocolate into his pocket, shook his head sharply, then glared at his wife. But Mrs. Wilson was occupied in extracting some knitting from her bag in the corner of the seat; so once again Mr. Wilson lay back. And as he filled his pipe he began to mutter to himself.

Mary Ann looked from one to the other questioningly, but neither of them looked at her, and she was puzzled. She liked them, they represented, through their voices and kindly manner, all the people she was leaving behind. If she hadn't felt so utterly miserable she would have talked to them and told them all about the farm and her da. They liked her da.

"Will you have another chocolate?"

"No, thanks, hinny," Mrs. Wilson smiled down on her. "You eat them, or save them for school; it's always nice to have some taffy or something as a stand-by at school."

Mary Ann sat staring down at the box on her lap. She had never seen such lovely chocolates, but she didn't want to eat them. Da. Oh! Da. Oh! Ma. Oh! Ma, I'm frightened. Panic was rising in her again, when her attention was brought from herself by Mr. Wilson's mutterings becoming louder.

"Them places! . . . Traps . . . no schooling . . . I know what I know."

"George! That's enough." This was not said as a command but as a plea, and the gentle words seemed to have a strange power over Mr. Wilson, for they changed his attitude. After taking only one deep breath, he said brightly, "Would you like to go and sit in the corner, hinny, and look out of the window?"

"Yes, please."

"Go on then."

Heavily Mary Ann went across to the other seat and knelt up into the corner; then tucking her legs under her, she turned almost completely around so that in this position she could pretend she was looking out of the window and cry and they wouldn't know it.

The old people looked at each other; then Mrs. Wilson concentrated her attention on her knitting, while he gave himself up to his pipe and his mutterings, but kept the latter well below his breath.

The eternity of the journey was nearly over and Mary Ann was feeling tired—and different. The farm and all she loved seemed far away in time like last Christmas, and when she tried to think about them a funny thing happened—everything became blurred and ran into one; even her da's face wouldn't stay put, and she couldn't see what he looked like. But Mr. and Mrs. Wilson seemed to have been in her life for ever and she felt that she knew all about them, about Mary Elizabeth and Ann Elizabeth, and even about their other grand-daughter. But when Mr. Wilson started to talk of her, Mrs. Wilson had shut him up by saying, "George!" Yet at intervals during the endless journey he had kept coming back to her. Her name was Teresa. Teresa was in a convent, too, but they hadn't seen her for years, nor her father. Without being told, Mary Ann knew why this was . . . he had "turned". When people turned it did something, caused rows and things. She wished her da would turn. She prayed that he would, every night she prayed, because as everybody knew all Protestants were destined for hell. . . .

At times during the journey Father Owen's words came into her mind, and she had wondered if Mr. Wilson was the Devil dressed up again. But then she had discarded that idea, for there was Mrs. Wilson, and she couldn't see the Devil being married.

But now she was having grave doubts as to Mr. Wilson's true identity, for after buttoning up his coat and adjusting his cap he sat down again on the edge of his seat and, leaning towards her, he said, solemnly, "Now, me bairn, listen to what I'm saying; you've a sensible head on your little shoulders." He paused before going on. "Now, if they do anything to frighten you at that place you write straight away to your da. They'll likely watch you like a prisoner, but you——"

"George!" Mrs. Wilson, gathering her belongings together, spoke urgently and sharply under her breath. "It's you who's doing the frightening. You'll have her scared to death."

"I'm only doing me duty." Mr. Wilson was on his feet again. "And if I'd done it years ago and been firm with our Jimmy things wouldn't have been as they are today . . . family divided and——"

"Be quiet!"

Mary Ann looked quickly at Mrs. Wilson. She sounded just like her ma when her patience was being tried by her grannie.

"You're as much to blame as anybody. Talk about them being bigoted, they've got some way to go to catch up to you."

"Well!" Mr. Wilson's tone, besides being surprised, held all the hurt and misunderstanding in the world. He stared at his wife, then, stretching his scraggy neck out of his collar, he turned and looked out of the window, and Mary Ann yet once again divided her gaze between them. They were fighting, and about the convent. But why should they? Convent's, although she had never been in one, held no terrors for her, rather the reverse. She had always wanted to go to one. The only terror lay in the distance that this one was from Newcastle—if it had been "round about", this first day would have been one of joy, for then she could have gone home for the night and told her da all about it.

"Are you all ready, my dear?" Mrs. Wilson was smiling now as if nothing had happened. "You've got all your things together? That's right, put your coat on. Can you feel the train slowing? Aye, it's been a long run, even it's tired."

After Mary Ann had put on her coat, her hands automatically went to her pockets, and coming in contact with the envelope for the first time, she drew it out and gasped her surprise. "Look!" she cried. "Look what I've found in me pocket!"

"Didn't you know it was there? We saw him put it in —the old man—didn't we, George?"

George, apparently forgiven, turned from the window, and said, "Aye. Yes, we saw him. Go on, open it."

Mary Ann, opening the envelope, drew out two sheets of paper. Between them was a folded pound note. Her eyes flicked up at the old people. Then slowly she read out the few words written on the paper:

"My dear child,
   If you want to please me pay great attention to your lessons and learn—learn everything you can. I know

61

you won't disappoint me. You are a brave little girl, and when you think of me, think of me by the name you once called me—Your Granda."

There was a lump in her throat again. Oh! he was nice. Oh, he was. And to write her a letter. If her da, too, had thought of writing her a letter it would have been wonderful, better even than this. But he had bought her comics, hadn't he, and chocolates.

"By! some more money. By, you're lucky." Mrs. Wilson was enthusiastic, but the sight of the pound note returned Mr. Wilson to his natural aversion which centred around anything Catholic. "If you want to keep it," he said, "you hide it. Have you any place to put it?"

"Me purse."

"Oh, they'll look through that."

"I've got me locket." From beneath her dress she pulled out a narrow chain, from which hung a locket, with a holy picture painted on each side, and when she sprung it open to reveal a small rosary Mr. Wilson made a sound in his throat which was too deep for interpretation. Then, with an evident effort towards calmness, he said, "Put them things in your bag, and put your note in there, and the other one an' all from your purse."

Not only did Mr. Wilson give her advice on the expedience of storage, but to his seeming satisfaction he also carried out the operation, and when the locket was once more reposing under cover on Mary Ann's chest, he said, "Well, that's that." Doubtless he felt he had gained a victory over all convents and their iron rules, and the Catholic Church in particular.

As the train came to a jolting stop, which nearly knocked Mary Ann off her seat, Mr. Wilson exclaimed, "Well, now, it's goodbye, me bairn, but we'll likely come across each other again; it's a small world when all's said and done. And when we go back at the end of the month I'll call and see your da, I will that."

"Oh, will you? Oh! ta."

"I will. Goodbye now, hinny, and be a good lass."

"Goodbye, me bairn."

"Goodbye, Mrs. Wilson." Mary Ann looked up at the old woman; then slowly turned her eyes to the old man. These were the very last links with home, and she was loath to let them go. Her voice shook slightly as she said, "I wish I was coming with you."

Mrs. Wilson tapped her cheek, then stooped and kissed her hastily, saying, "Well, you are in a way. We'll likely be on the same train all the way down, and when we get to St. Leonards, we'll look out for you getting off. There now. Now, now, you mustn't cry. Be a brave lass. Come on, let's get these things out, the guard'll be along in a minute."

Almost before Mrs. Wilson had finished speaking there appeared beyond the corridor window the guard, accompanied by two black-robed nuns.

"Go on, hinny, there they are. Go on. Goodbye. The porter will come and get your things."

Mrs. Wilson seemed suddenly anxious that Mary Ann should be gone, and so, manoeuvring herself to block her husband's exit into the corridor, she pushed her away, and Mary Ann, coming to the door, looked straight into the face of the nun and knew her first disappointment.

Nuns were merely angels walking the earth, they were young and beautiful and holy and always smiling. The face before her was youngish, but it was bespectacled and unsmiling and possessed the largest set of buck teeth that Mary Ann had ever seen.

On the journey from London to St. Leonards Mary Ann discovered only one pleasing thing about her escorts: the one that spoke to her spoke nice—swanky, but nice—but she never smiled. The other nun smiled but didn't speak, and Mary Ann sat looking out of the window lost and alone. Really alone now.

From time to time she fervently wished that Mr. Wilson was sitting opposite. She wouldn't even mind if he went on about the convent. She wasn't interested in the passing scenery—she had seen too much scenery today. Her only impression of it was that it was greener, and the hills went up and down, and on and on. Her mind became a confused maze, whirling round her da, Mr. Lord, Mr. Wilson, her watch, her ma, their Michael, and, for some reason or other, the nice young man who had come to work on the farm. Then the rhythm of the wheels churned them altogether until only one filled her weary mind and tear-filled heart, and it went, "Diddle-de-da, diddle-de-da, diddle-de-da, diddle-de-da," then filed itself down into, "Me da, me da . . . me da, me da . . . me da, me da . . . me da, me da . . ." and to this chant her head drooped sideways on to the nun's arm, and she went fast asleep.

When she awoke exactly an hour later she didn't know where she was. She looked up at the nun, who was bending over her.

"Come along, we're there."

Drunkenly she got to her feet, and the nun, with deft fingers, straightened her hair and adjusted her hat, and then the train stopped, and she was on the platform. She had forgotten about Mr. and Mrs. Wilson until their bright faces and waving hands drew her attention, and she had only time to give one wave in return before the train ran into the tunnel.

"Hallo, there! Well, you've arrived." She turned to face another nun who seemed to have descended from the roof, so quickly had she made her appearance. "You look tired. Are you tired?"

"Yes, Miss."

"Yes, Miss. Ha! ha!" The laugh ran down the empty platform. "Sister, child. I'm Sister Agnes Mary." The voice was deep, not unlike a man's.

"Sister!" It was the escort speaking, and there was a strong breath of reprimand in the word.

Mary Ann, eyes slightly wider now, moved under the propulsion of the guiding hand of her escort towards the entrance, and ahead of them, carrying both her cases, strode Sister Agnes Mary. Fascinated, Mary Ann watched her make straight for a car, an old car, a very old car, and after dumping the cases into the boot pull open the door, squeeze herself in, and start up the engine.

Nothing at that moment could have surprised her more. Never had she seen a nun in a car, let alone driving one. All her preconceived ideas about nuns were being knocked to smithereens with sledge-hammer force.

"In you get." This from Sister Agnes. "Push that

box along, do it gently. You're not afraid of hamsters, are you?"

Mary Ann, in a stooped position on the step, stood riveted, gazing at the wire box full of mice, as she thought of them.

"Oh, well, all right, I'll bring them over here. . . . Here." She lifted the box over the back seat. "Hold it, Sister."

Sister Catherine took the box with no great show of pleasure, then putting Mary Ann into the back of the car, and indicating her silent companion to follow, she closed the door and without a word seated herself in the front next to Sister Agnes.

There was a grating somewhere under Mary Ann's seat, then, with a jerk that knocked her backwards, they were off. The young nun steadied her and smiled.

She had been in Mr. Lord's car when he drove fast, but it hadn't been this kind of fast, nor had it made all this noise and rattle. That the noise was even affecting the imperturbable driver was made evident when her voice, above the din, came to Mary Ann, crying, "Have to take His Eminence's inside out tonight."

"I thought you were going to do it this afternoon." Sister Catherine's voice, although loud, was still prim.

"Couldn't. Just got my Office in when I had to go to the laundry. Sister Teresa's got toothache. You'd think it would be rheumatics she'd get, not toothache, wouldn't you?" A pause. "She's small—what's her name?"

"Mary Ann Shaughnessy."

"Huh! 'Just a little bit of heaven'." The words were sung in a full contralto. "That should make the hearts of Sisters Alvis and Monica glad."

"Sister!" again the tone of reprimand, and then. . . . Could Mary Ann believe her ears, or was it the jingling of the car that made Sister Agnes Mary's reply sound like, "Oh, stow it!"

It must have been the jingling of the car, no nun could ever say such a thing, nuns couldn't know words like "stow it", they were angels. At this point, and so early in her acquaintance of the celestial beings, Mary Ann had to remind herself of this fact, which im-

65

mediately placed her further acquaintance with the heavenly overflow on a very insecure footing. Matters such as nuns being angels, as everybody knew, should be accepted without question, like the sun coming up and the rain coming down.

The town was left behind now, and the car was rocketing through the narrow, high-hedged lanes. Then, with startling suddenness, that seemed to be the main facet of its character, or was it its driver, it was out of the narrow lane and thundering up a broad drive. And the next minute it had stopped, and Mary Ann was once again lying back in the seat with her legs in the air.

"Come on, out you get, Miss Mary Ann Shaughnessy."

Sister Agnes Mary was holding open the door and laughing. "It's a big name for such a little soul, eh?"

"Yes, Miss—Sister."

Mary Ann stepped out of the car, and recognised immediately that she had dropped, or been thrown, into a new world. Before her were wide steps leading up to a house which was so big that the wall on either side seemed to stretch endlessly away, and all about, in front of the house, people—girls of all ages and grownups, and nuns, and over all she felt the canopy of excitement.

Before Sister Catherine's hand descended on her she glimpsed behind her a balustrade and, through its grey stone pillars, terraces falling away in a glory of colour.

Sister Catherine's hand firmly on her head now, she was directed up the steps and through the wide-open doors into a huge hall, with broad oak stairs leading from its farthest end.

Only two impressions touched her whirling mind here. One was that the floor was so highly polished that she could see her white socks in it, and the other that the school was a funny place to have big pictures. In her ascent of the main staircase she glanced up in some awe at the gigantic old paintings covering the walls. But, arrived on the first floor, even these were thrust into the background by the maze of corridors branching from the long gallery. Like an appendage to the silent nun, she turned and twisted and dodged the

66

scurrying figures of girls, and eventually arrived in a corridor away to the right, and at its end went through a door and into a dormitory full of beds. And the impression she had on arrival here was that nobody, nobody had taken the slightest notice of her. She could have been in her own school for all the curiosity she had aroused. And this, strangely enough, added to the weight of her loneliness.

Beside all the beds but one there were cases, and beside each case a child knelt or stood, and with the exception of two of them they were all chattering and laughing across to each other. Of the two, one was kneeling silently by her case and the other was crying by hers, and it was to the bed between these two that Sister Catherine took her. And from there she called imperiously to a girl at the end of the room: "Beatrice!"

Beatrice, a thin, lanky girl of about eleven, came running down the room. "Yes, Sister?"

"Must I remind you about running in the dormitory? Walk—I think we had all this out last term."

"Yes, Sister. I forgot."

To Mary Ann the voice sounded high, swanky and cheeky.

"This is Mary Ann Shaughnessy. Show her what is necessary, then take her down to tea."

"Yes, Sister."

Sister Catherine now turned to Mary Ann, saying, "When your cases come up Beatrice will show you what to do. After tea Reverend Mother wishes to see you; report to Mother St. Francis."

"Yes, Mi—Sister."

The Sister walked out, the door closed after her, and then to Mary Ann's open-mouthed horror, and it was horror, she saw Beatrice's face pucker up until her upper lip exposed in a half moon her top teeth, and her eyes screw up as if she were peering through glasses, and with her arms hanging like penguins' wings she took a few steps towards the door, saying, through her distorted mouth, "Catty Cathie! Catty Cathie!"

There were some apprehensive giggles, there were some laughs, there were also some murmurs of disapproval, but these were low, timid and covert.

"Did she bring you?" Beatrice was fronting Mary Ann now.

"Yes."

"Poor you; you should have had Aggie. Where are you from?"

"From Jarrow. No, I mean in the country outside—near Pelaw."

"Make up your mind."

Mary Ann stared at the girl. A moment ago she had stood in awe at her daring; a moment prior to that she had been made uneasy by her swanky voice and manner; now the voice and manner only annoyed her, and simply caused her to think, I don't like her, she's cheeky. Moreover, there was something familiar about the girl that puzzled her.

"What do you think you're doing?" Beatrice had turned from Mary Ann to the girl on her right who had lifted one of her cases on to the bed. "Get that off there—you know they haven't to be put on the bed."

The girl, who was nearly as tall as Beatrice, straightened her back and looked at her; then in a voice of a kind which Mary Ann had never heard before, she said, slowly, "Eef you do not like eet, then leeft it hoff, or go and run to teel Sister."

The two girls faced each other across the bed, then Beatrice, nodding slowly, said, "All right, you wait till tomorrow when the marks start." With this she walked away, and an oppressive silence fell on the room for a few seconds. Then it was broken by the sound of a bell and a number of voices calling together excitedly, "Tea! tea! tea! Come on."

There was a scrambling round the cases, and Mary Ann watched the legs flying down the dormitory. The girls were all running now, but at the door Beatrice stopped for a moment and called back to Mary Ann, "Come on." But she did not wait for her, and as Mary Ann made to walk away from her bed the girl from the next bed said, "Take hoff your coat and hat."

The tone was kindly, and Mary Ann took her things off, then looked at the girl. And the girl held out her hand and said, "Come."

With her hand in the strange girl's Mary Ann walked up the empty dormitory, and she had the feeling she was with someone "grown-up." Before the girl opened the door she paused and said, "My name is Lola, and yours ees Mary Han?"

"Yes."

The girl nodded, and a little smile lighted up her grave face. Outside the door they surprised the girl from the other bed. She was rubbing vigorously at her face, and Lola said, off-handedly, "You make hit worse, Marian. You are not the honly one who cry today. Come on."

Marian, walking on the other side of Mary Ann, sniffed a number of times, then spoke across her to Lola. "I wasn't crying about coming back . . . I wasn't really. It was when Sister Alvis told me I was in Beatrice's dorm. She's awful. She's hateful, I wish I wasn't nine."

Mary Ann, perhaps in an effort to comfort someone who looked and sounded as sad as she felt, said, "I'm only eight."

Now she had the attention of them both.

"Height?" said Lola. "But you should be down in zee Lower School. Thees is Middle School, nine to thirteen."

"But I'll soon be nine—in August."

They did not remark on this, but turning in the opposite direction from the main staircase they joined a mass of girls hurrying, but not running now, towards a narrower stairway at the end of the gallery.

Mary Ann could see nothing but gym-slips and white blouses until, reaching level ground again, she had her first glimpse of the dining-hall. Tables jutted out from the walls all round a great room, except for a space at the bottom end, which was taken up by a long table running lengthwise. Still attached to Lola, she was guided to a table some way down the room and pushed into a seat. And there before her was a plate holding three slices of bread and butter, a square of cake and a dob of jam, and, leaning against it, a card which bore the words "Mary Ann Shaughnessy".

She was staring at the card when all shuffling was suddenly cut off. So quick did the silence fall, that she turned round to see the cause, and just as she glimpsed it her head was brought to the front again by a shove from Lola. But by straining her eyes sideways she could see, filing through a side door and into the centre of the hall down towards the long table, a stream of nuns. She thought of them as a stream: she counted ten black-robed figures with white collars, and following these ten more in unrelieved black, and then, slightly behind, a small figure, so small that Mary Ann had the funny impression that the clothes were walking by themselves. She watched fascinated as they all filed into their seats, and towards the seat in the exact centre, facing the room, went the little black-encased figure.

"Bless us, O Lord, and these Thy gifts which we receive through Thy bounty. Through Jesus Christ, Our Lord. Amen."

"Amen."

The echo by the school to the Reverend Mother's voice seemed to be the signal for activity. Six of the white-collared Sisters left the table, and going, one after the other, to a lift in the wall, reached into the depths and brought out great enamel teapots and proceeded to supply the tables.

The grace that had just been said was at this moment giving Mary Ann a faint trace of comfort, for was it not the very same grace that she and their Michael said every day? After all, apart from its bigness, this school might be just like the one at Jarrow. That the grace was the only thing in common that the convent had with her late school was mercifully withheld from her.

"Eat your tea." A Sister was standing over her.

She looked up. "I'm not hungry, Sister."

"Nevertheless, eat your tea." The voice was low, thickened with an Irish twang, and the tone brooked no discussion.

Many of the plates about her were quickly emptied. Yet it was heartening to note that a number, like hers, still held a quantity of bread. So intriguing to her were the actions of the Sisters who were serving, and also the apparent immobility of all the black-robed figures at the top table, that when a little bell tinkled and the thin voice came again, saying the grace, the fifteen minutes the tea had taken seemed like one to her.

In silence, the top table was vacated, but as soon as the last nun had disappeared through the side door the

70

room became a hive of bustle, but, strangely, no chatter.

As Mary Ann went to move from her place, the Sister who had told her to eat her tea appeared again, but with a smile splitting her face now, and dropping to her hunkers, which in itself was a surprise, as Mary Ann had always been in some indecision whether or not there really were real legs beneath the skirts of nuns, she took Mary Ann's hands and said in a voice gurgling with laughter, "Mary Ann Shaughnessy. What a name! Are you from Ireland, child?"

"No. No, Sister." Who, even with all the sadness of the world on their shoulders, could help but smile back into this round, beaming face.

"No? But your father was?"

"No. Well, yes. . . ." There had always been a doubt about this, but how could she say, "Me da was an orphan without any name and the name Shaughnessy was just given him. They took it from the porter who picked him up at the gate." She had never said, even to herself, "Workhouse gate."

"Ah, ha! Now don't try and tell me you're Welsh or something with a name like Shaughnessy. . . . Shaughnessy. Oh! what a lovely mouthful. And what a North Country voice it is." She patted Mary Ann's cheek as she got to her feet. "Well, there, off you go. . . . Oh, you're with Lola? That's grand; Lola'll look after you."

The Sister patted Lola's cheek now, and for the first time Lola really smiled, and Mary Ann thought, She's nice, I like her, which could have meant, in this case, either or both of them.

"I'll take you to Mother St. Francis."

"Will you?" They were now in the Lower Hall. "What do they call that Sister?"

"Sister Alvis."

"Oh." A question arose in Mary Ann's mind. "Why do they call some Mother and some Sister?" she asked.

"The Mothers har mostly teachers, the Sisters do the work. They har the ones who wear the white collars."

"Oh. . . . Is the Reverend Mother nice?"

"She ees all right. You weel not see much of her. Come this way."

More corridors.

71

"Will you wait for me? I'll get lost comin' back."

"Yes."

"And will you show me what to do? I don't want that Beatrice to show me."

"She wouldn't, hin any case."

"But the Sister told her." Mary Ann's eyes widened.

"Sister Catherine is always telling her. She tries to punish her by geeving her duties, but it makes no deefference. You will see has time goes on."

"Are you from a foreign country?"

"Yes." Lola now smiled down on her. "France and Germany."

"Two!"

"Yes, my mother is French and my father German. But you, too, are from a foreign country."

"Me!" Mary Ann stopped, slightly indignant. "Me! No, I'm not, I'm from England, Jarrow."

"Oh. Ha! ha!" It was a small laugh and did not annoy Mary Ann in the least, nor did the insult to her beloved North which followed. "It is, nevertheless, odd how you talk—very guttural. Some people in France speak like thees. You will soon mend it here. I am only three terms, and I am mending mine very much."

Mary Ann didn't know now whether she wanted her voice mended—mending it, she understood, would make it sound swanky. And yet, that's what she was here for, that's why Mr. Lord had sent her.

"Here is Mother St. Francis."

They were approaching a nun. She had a round, fat face and, not to be disguised by her habit, a round, fat body. She looked about sixty, but appeared like a hundred to Mary Ann.

"Mother, this is Mary Ann Shaughnessy. She ees to see Reverend Mother."

"Ah, yes. Hello, my child."

"Hallo, Sister—Mother."

"You are small. You're in Middle House, aren't you? Yes— I remember. I'm the bursar, I look after your money." She laughed. "And your letters and everything—and everything. You see? Come along this way. From the Tyne, are you? I know the Tyne. . . . Ah, yes, this way. You wait, Lola."

It was evident to Mary Ann that Mother St. Francis

didn't need any answers, she gave them all to herself. She talked quickly as she waddled along.

"Now when Reverend Mother asks you a question, you answer 'Yes,' or 'No, Reverend Mother', you see? And don't speak unless you are spoken to. You see? There now, here we are."

A tap on a door, to which a small voice replied, and they were inside the room. And there was the little woman, sitting behind a big desk. As Mary Ann was pressed nearer she could see less and less of her, until, standing right close up to the desk, there seemed only the head and shoulders left.

"And you are Mary Ann?"

"Yes, Sis—Reverend Mother."

"And you've come a long journey by yourself?"

"Yes, Reverend Mother."

"And do you think you will like being here?"

"No, Reverend Mother."

There, it had dropped out before she could stop it. And on its heels came a little gasp from herself and a loud one from somewhere behind her, but from across the table came a laugh, a little tinkling laugh that reminded her somehow of the bells that went just before you had Communion.

"Come here."

She followed the beckoning finger and went round the side of the desk, and there two small, dry hands took hers.

"Let me look at you."

The Reverend Mother looked at Mary Ann, and Mary Ann looked back at her, wondering that anybody so small could be in such a position of majesty—she didn't, at close quarters, seem much bigger than herself.

"Tell me, child, how is my brother?"

Her brother? Mary Ann's mouth fell open in perplexity, and then snapped quickly closed as she remembered that this person before her was Mr. Lord's sister. How this could be she didn't rightly know for Mr. Lord wasn't a Catholic and he didn't, she felt, like Catholics. She didn't connect "turning" with the woman before her—no one could "turn" into a Reverend Mother.

"He's all right."

"He's well?"

"He gets cold now and then, but that's because he lives in that big old house and he's only got Ben to see to him. When he comes to live at the farm, me ma. . . ."

"Ahem!"

The sound was behind her again, and she finished lamely, "She'll see he's all right—Reverend Mother."

"He is very interested in you, my child."

She gave no answer to this, for didn't she know it. Look where it had landed her. She was forgetting again where it had also landed her father and mother and Michael.

"And he desires that you learn, and learn well. Are you going to do that?"

"Yes—Reverend Mother."

"That's a good child. Now go with Mother St. Francis, and God bless you and make you happy here."

Her hands were released, she was turned about by her guide and the next minute she was in the corridor being handed over to Lola.

"There you are then. There you are, that's over. You see? Now, up to the dormitory. Get your necessary things put in your drawers, then bring all the rest down to the stores. Leave your cases empty. Away now, then come to me and bring your money to be looked after. Off you go."

Not until they had reached the corridor leading to the dormitory did Mary Ann speak, and then she asked, "Do you really get your money back?"

"Yes, of course, when we go out on half-day, or to the beach."

Mary Ann was again silent—she didn't want to part with her money, any of it. She was glad now that Mr. Wilson had stuffed the notes in her locket. She touched her chest and felt a sense of comfort.

Her hand was still flat on her chest when she entered the dormitory, but it was immediately doubled into a fist as Beatrice's voice, which, at this moment, sounded strangely like her own, hit her, saying, "I'm from Jarr . . . aa . . . no, in the coun . . . tree. Pee . . . laa."

Beatrice was standing in the middle of the dormitory and causing a great deal of amusement with her imitation, but as Mary Ann slowly advanced towards her the laughter died away leaving a strained silence.

By her own bed and within a yard of Beatrice, Mary Ann stopped. Her face screwed up to a button, she glared at Beatrice. She knew now who she reminded her of—it was Sarah Flannagan.

Schools may be housed in elaborate country mansions with extensive grounds and terraces and playing fields; awe-inspiring nuns and Sisters might float through their richly-furnished interiors; rich men's daughters could be packed in dozens in air-conditioned dormitories; yet what were these girls after all but exactly the same types that filled the schools in Jarrow and such like towns. The only difference was they talked swanky. This would have summed up Mary Ann's thoughts had she been able to define them, but all she was aware of at the moment was the feeling that had ousted both loneliness and fear. It was a feeling that was not uncommon to her, and now it was telling her that this Beatrice was a cheeky thing, a cheeky beast—even a cheeky bitch!

"Who you makin' game of?"

Was there anything awe-inspiring or electrifying in that question? It would undoubtedly seem so, for never before had anything happened in the school lives of the ten spectators to call for such expressions as were now very much apparent on their faces. This new girl had dared to cheek a prefect, and such a prefect. She must be mad. The mouths were agape and hanging, the eyes stretched wide and bulging. Had Sister Alvis been present she would have supposed that nothing short of the second Pentecost, which alone she was for ever prophesying would be required to arouse them, had actually taken place. It is almost certain to say that to them something of equal importance had happened, for only a visitation by the Deity Himself could possibly have called forth the gasp that rose to the ceiling.

"You're a cheeky beast! And if you keep on I'll write and tell me da about you, so I will!"

The situation was quite beyond all recognized bounds. It was undoubtedly the first of such that had happened to Beatrice, and, as smart as she was, she could call up no move to counter it. All the unwritten rules on behaviour between prefects—although her real power would not begin until 6.45 a.m. tomorrow morning—and the crawling subservient sycophants known as pupils had been swept away by this—this —— The word "common" leapt to Beatrice's rescue, and using it in a way that would turn defeat into victory, she lifted her nose as if detecting a vile smell, slowly raised her head on high, and turning away gave her authoritative sentence to the audience: "Common individual!"

The spring Mary Ann was about to make was abruptly checked by Lola's hand, and so painful was the grip on her arm that sanity returned to her, and with it deflation. Shrugging off the guiding hand of Lola she went to her bedside and, kneeling down with a thud beside her cases, she turned the key in the lock of the largest one and lifted up the lid. Then sitting back on her heels, she gazed through misted eyes at the neatly folded clothes her mother had packed away only yesterday, and, her head drooping lower to hide her raining tears, she cried silently, "Oh! Ma, Ma, I want to come home. Oh! Ma."

5

Was it seven days or seven years or seven lifetimes that Mary Ann had been in the Convent of the Holy Child of Bethlehem? If you had asked her she would have pondered, refusing to believe that all the many different things that had been pushed into her head had taken only seven days to accomplish.

This time last week she had been a small creature of another world, but now the doings of that world had become vague, and to remind her that it had ever existed there remained only a few people. Her da—always her da; her ma—when she was in bed at night; their Michael at odd times; Mr. Lord, when she was in class; Father Owen when she was in church; Mrs. McBride rather funnily enough when she saw Sister Alvis; and Sarah Flannagan whenever her eyes alighted on Beatrice, which unfortunately even with the disparity in their ages, was often, for Beatrice was the allocator of marks—black ones. If nothing else had stuck in her mind the sources from which these were derived were firmly fixed. Dearly was she paying for cheeking a prefect. Although you acquired only one mark for being late, already her score in this section was four. But if you were skilfully manoeuvred to the last wash basin, and even there were the last to use it, what could you do? Only finish your dressing running along the corridor. Well, she had done that twice. The first time, encountering Mother St. Bede, she had been helped into her things, but the second time Mother St. Bede had not only sent her back to dress but had added two to her score. Then this same Mother St. Bede, who took English, a language quite different from any Mary Ann had previously listened to, had yesterday yelled at her, right at the top of her voice which was of some surprising height. "Child! child! child!" she had yelled, "it is not the BOO . . . CHER, it is the BUT . . . CHER. Say after me, the BUT-CHER, the BAY-KER, the CANDLE-STICK MAY-KER."

Dutifully she had repeated the butcher, the baker, the candlestick maker, and the laughter this oration in her own language had evoked had aroused her fighting spirit, yet at the same time made her want to cry. The whole place, in her estimation, was daft, with a daftness that went on in an intermittent never-ceasing whirl from seven-thirty a.m. till eight forty-five p.m.

On Mondays and Wednesdays the daftness was, if anything, intensified, for these were early Mass days when you were hoiked out of bed at a quarter to seven by Sister Monica, who slept behind a curtain at the end of the dormitory, and who brought you to life by slapping your bottom, and not just a little slap either, and at the same time calling, in a surprisingly cheerful voice at that unearthly hour, "Arise, arise. Arise to the glory of God. Come on now, up with yous."

77

Mary Ann was of the opinion that Sister Monica never slept. How could she, when even before that time she had said an hour's Office.

Having experienced as yet only one Monday and Wednesday, Mary Ann had already decided that she hated Mondays and Wednesdays. Back home she had liked going to Communion on a Friday and church at any time, but here church was different. It was inside the grounds, and the four houses, comprising children of seven to young ladies of seventeen, marched there in straggling, silent crocodiles. If you dared to open your mouth it was ten-to-one that somebody would pounce on you and up would go your score. You wouldn't think they would have bothered at that time in the morning, but they did.

This scoring of marks was not an individual thing either. Through them you apparently carried on your shoulders the honour of your house, for one girl's misdemeanours could prevent her house from getting the cup, and already Mary Ann knew just to what pitch of fervour each house could reach in their struggle to obtain this cup. Only yesterday it had been made clear to her by a spontaneous deputation, surrounding her on the playing field, that the attainment of the prize did not lie with her, but the loss of it did, and she had to stop getting black marks—or else.

For once in her life she had found nothing to say, but had stood near to tears in the corner of the field thinking, Oh! Da. Oh! Da. Then an odd thing had happened which took her mind off her troubles for a few moments. Over the railings in another field where the big girls were playing hockey she saw a strange sight. Her mind seemed to suggest that it was even a sacrilegious sight, for there, with her gown tucked up, was Mother St. Jude, and she was running, flying and shouting as she bashed out with a hockey stick as if she were throwing the hammer. Mary Ann knew very well now that nuns had legs, but this was the first time she had ever seen them, even a bit of them, and it didn't seem right. She was sure that none of the nuns in the North would ever run like that. Nuns should walk— and walk slowly.

Then there was Sister Agnes Mary. She couldn't get

over Sister Agnes Mary. Sister Agnes Mary could take a car right to bits—she had seen her doing it yesterday in the yard—and she bred mice, called hamsters; and she laughed. She was laughing all the time, except when she said her Office; and when saying that she would go round muttering to herself with a very straight face, being sorry, Mary Ann supposed, for all the laughing she had done.

This saying of "the Office" business both interested and puzzled Mary Ann. In all odd places she would come across a nun saying this Office. Sister Alvis had really startled her one day, for when passing her, and she apparently deeply engrossed in her reading, she had suddenly heard her exclaim, and loudly, "Jesus!" It had sounded so like Mrs. McBride that she had looked at the Sister and exclaimed, "Eeh!" before being pushed in the back by Lola.

And then there was the timetable. Oh! the timetable. It was the axis of the daftness. Tuesdays, Thursdays, Fridays and Saturdays, you rose at seven-thirty, washed and dressed, and got down to breakfast, if no impediment, by eight o'clock, and not until after the meal were you allowed to open your mouth. This compulsory silence was a great trial to Mary Ann. Between eight-twenty and nine o'clock you were expected to do various things, which included making your bed, going to Mother St. Francis for your letters, toothpaste, soap, and salts if you couldn't go to the lavatory, and to Sister Catherine if you had buttons off or things like that. Then nine o'clock was upon you before you knew where you were. From nine o'clock till half-past you had religious instruction. It was like the Bible history she used to have in Jarrow, and she didn't mind that in the least. But from nine-thirty to ten it was science.

Now Mary Ann knew nothing whatever about science and she didn't want to know, for science was all about frogs and tadpoles and she was repulsed by both, even before they were cut up. From frogs she went into French and Mother St. Matthew. Un, deux, trois, quatre. . . . The first four she could remember quite easily, for she resorted to a little unconscious Pelmanism and thought of the four figures as "under two cats". Le and la were another business entirely. Did it matter whether you knew they were males or females as long as you said Mr. or Mrs. That's all that mattered, surely. But apparently not to Mother St. Matthew.

Then followed milk; then gym. She liked gym—she could jump and skip better than some of the bigger girls, and "cowp her creels". This statement for turning a somersault had caused quite a diversion, but nobody was going to make her believe it should be "head over heels" . . . they were daft, all of them. Following gym, innocently arranged, was the visit to the infirmary and Matron who dealt with toothache, spots, and blisters. If you didn't have any of these things you had fifteen minutes to yourself.

From the infirmary you were pitchforked into history. Mary Ann thought of it as being pitchforked. She knew the word for her da used it a lot at one time. "I was pitchforked into the shipyard," he used to say, and now it seemed to describe the entry into the room where they took history. The room was at the end of a long corridor, and to Mary Ann that particular corridor was lined with prefects who pushed you along if you were speaking and pushed you along if you weren't, and at the classroom door, a week's experience had taught Mary Ann, Mother St. Bede would be waiting—as if she didn't have enough of her in English—to fling you into your seats. The only consolation she felt was that here she wasn't the only one to experience the nun's treatment for tardiness.

Mother St. Bede was identified to Mary Ann by three things. She yelled in her English class, she pushed in her history class, and, thirdly, she was known privately as "Mother Fear-o'-God," for at the height of exasperation she was known to fling her arms wide and cry, "Nothing but the fear of God will knock it into you. It's past me, it's past me!"

The only thing to be remembered during history was that it would be followed by geography and Mother Mary Divine. Oh, Mother Mary Divine was nice . . . she was lovely. She loved Mother Mary Divine. Mother Mary Divine patted her cheek and called her "Dear child", and she had won Mary Ann's heart forever by asking, and in the proper voice, "And how is canny Jarrow?"

At twelve-fifteen she reluctantly left Mother Mary Divine and went tearing with the rest of her class in the scramble for letters. If you were lucky and there was one for you you took it into the General Study and there devoured it. If you weren't you went out into the playground or into the fields where Sister Agnes Mary usually was. But you couldn't get near her, everybody wanted to be with Sister Agnes Mary 'cos she made you laugh. If you liked you could go and feed the rabbits or the mice, or the budgerigars. These latter were bred by an old Sister, so old that Mary Ann was fascinated by her wrinkles. She had little apples on her cheeks and her eyes were blue and sunk far into her head. Her name was Sister Prudence, but she was known, even to her face, as Sister Gran-Gran.

Dinner was a further trial to Mary Ann, for whether you liked it or not you had to eat it; if you didn't one of the Sisters stood over you until you did. Mary Ann didn't like cabbage. She hated cabbage and she had said so. This was another thing that had caused a diversion and, indeed, even some smothered chortling from the servers.

The afternoons hadn't been too bad at first. There was art and botany and games, followed three times a week by a bath. And no fire to sit at after you were dry either.

Then yesterday she had been told that one lesson had to be missed every afternoon to be replaced by elocution. At first she had been excited and thought, Now I'll show Sarah Flannagan, but that was before the lesson. Bas—kets . . . bill-iards . . . bat—ter—ies, and bluebot—tles. . . . Cas—kets, cam—els and castles, and sticking her tongue all over the place to try and talk swanky.

Following tea at four-fifteen there was twenty minutes' recreation, before the most trying part of the day. Whereas at home after school she could, and had, run wild, now she had to go and sit with her house in the study, and after the first ten minutes a bell would ring which meant "no talking". This was a foretaste of purgatory. It was no use trying to slip a word in, for at the high desk near the window sat first one study mistress and then another. Every half-hour they changed, and no matter who they were silence was the order of the day. The only diversion was the signal to leave the room, but even her courage failed at anything more than two requests.

From six-thirty to seven you could write your letter, that is if you had done all your homework, but they didn't call it homework. At seven o'clock you knelt and said the Angelus, and it was always wonderful to Mary Ann to hear the sound of her own voice again. Yet when, following this, they went to supper, she seemed to have very little to say to anyone—the inactivity of sitting always seemed to dry her up. After the meal, for one full hour the time was her own, to go out to play, weather permitting, or to write or read. The only thing you couldn't do was—moon. Nuns seemed to drop from the ceiling, appear through the walls, or up through the floorboards should you show the least suspicion of mooning.

Following on this hour was chapel for fifteen minutes. And here began another trial, because from the moment you stepped into line you were as good as gagged until breakfast the following morning. You could talk, oh! yes, if you were one of those people who were clever enough not to be caught, but Mary Ann had not yet learned the trick, so she was as good as dumb.

But tonight, the beginning of this particular trial was a good half-hour away. It was only eight o'clock and she was hugging three letters to her breast. They had all come at once, one each from her da, her ma and their Michael. This was only the second letter she'd had from her da, and it wasn't very long, but it was lovely, all about the farm. And then he said he missed her and was ticking off the days to the summer holiday. Her ma's letter was nice, but her ma's letters and everything about her ma were always nice. Her ma brought no worry to her mind, she could always be relied upon to be the same. She laughed at their Michael's letter. It was the first he'd written to her and it was funny, so different from when he talked. He said such things as "Up the school!" and "Miss La-de-da Mary Ann Shaughnessy". Then he had told her some bits of news that made her homesick in a different way. "You should have been home," he said, "on Wednesday.

82

Mr. Polinski hit Mrs. Polinski and she came running to our house, and there was a to-do. And what do you know? The new hand is going to stay with us. I like him, so does me da—my father. Sorry, Miss Shaughnessy." Oh, their Michael was funny.

As it was raining the recreation room, if not crowded, was well filled and Mary Ann, lucky for once, had bagged a little table near the window and was busy, between chews at her pen and glances out of the window on to a view whose beauty was entirely lost on her, writing to her ma and da. Only the heading on the paper did not say "Ma and Da," it said, "Dear Mother and Father." Her first letter had been confiscated not only for beginning with "Ma and Da" but because she had gone on to give graphic details of meals, at which there was cabbage, marks, of which she was acquiring a burden, Mother St. Bede, who was awful, and last but by no means least Beatrice. Now her gazing out of the window was a concentrated effort to formulate her news in such a way that it would get through. As the time was beginning to ebb away and her mind would suggest nothing in the nature of a code, she continued her letter by saying, "I am lerning to talk proply every afternoon and say bas—kets, bil—li—ards, bat—ter—ies and bluebottles. Cas—kets, cam—els and castles. Tell Mr. Lord and I will write him the morr—tomorrow. I had a pain in me stomach this morning cos I had a pill, and oh it was awful, and then I had to eat——" She had been going to say cabbage, but remembering that this slip might mean the rewriting of the whole letter she substituted instead a kindness she had received from the very Sister who had stood over her and made her stuff the cabbage down her throat, thereby bringing censure on the poor woman who had been trained to show no discrimination among the children. She scratched out "I had to eat" and wrote "Sister Mary Martha slipped me three sweets cos I ate me dinner. I wish I could see you. I have got to go to bed now. I think of you in bed and say Hail Marys for you. The Holy Family in the church here isn't like ours in Jarrow, they are cut out of wood and haven't any colours on them, and haven't got nice faces. It's confession tomorrow, I wish Father Owen was here. Will our

Michael tell him about me on Sunday? I've got to go, they're clearing up. Oh Ma. Goodnight Mother and Father and our Michael, and twenty million kisses, Mary Ann."

There, that was done. Just as she folded up the letter and placed it on top of the envelope ready for Mother St. Francis's inspection Marian came up and sat on the window seat.

"You writing again? You are always writing." She sounded slightly offended, and Mary Ann said, "Well, I like to write to me ma and da."

"Why do you always say ma and da?"

"Well, cos they are."

"You're funny." This statement was given as a criticism, but Mary Ann took it in good part and looked at her new friend, whose face was very straight and whose mouth was tight and who, Mary Ann knew from a week's experience, could burst into tears at any moment.

"Why don't you write to your da . . . father?"

Marian turned away, breathed on the window and drew a pattern with the point of her finger. "He's always travelling, he'd never get my letters."

"Then why don't you write to your ma then?"

"I do, every week."

"But why don't you every day?"

"Oh, that would be silly." With a swift movement of her hand Marian wiped out the pattern. "What's your father like?"

This was the first time anyone had asked after her da. Mary Ann closed her eyes for a moment, then opened them wide as she began on the subject that forever filled her heart. "He's wonderful. He's big—oh, ever so big, and he's got a lovely face." At this point, before she had even got warmed up, her discourse was broken into by Marian's voice saying abruptly, "Oh, all right. What's your mother like?"

Mary Ann blinked. "Oh, me ma? She's lovely an' all. Her hair's like gold and she's got masses and masses of it." Then, looking at Marian's tight face, she asked, merely out of politeness and not because she wanted to know, "Is your ma nice?"

"Yes, she's lovely, she's wonderful." Quite lively

now, Marian gave Mary Ann all her attention and described for her in glowing detail the wonder that went to make up her mother, and this description of a most glamorous being went on until Mother St. Francis's inspection interrupted it.

Mary Ann's letter having been passed with only her English at fault, which was nothing to worry about, at least in her opinion, the bell alone brought Marian's oration to a final stop. But she went to the chapel with her face aglow, and even later, when she was finishing her undressing under her nightie, as they all did, she smiled brightly across at Mary Ann. So it was surprising that some time later Mary Ann should wake in the faintly illuminated dark to hear the sound of muffled sobbing coming from Marian's bed. As she lay listening to it, it saddened her and made her want to join in, and she thought, Oh! Da. Oh! Ma.

When, after what seemed to her a long, long time, Marian was still crying, she raised herself up and peered towards her.

In the glow from the night-light at the end of the dormitory all she could make out was a contorted heap, and so it was the most natural thing in the world that she should get out of bed and creep over to Marian.

"Marian, what's the matter?"

Marian raised her head. "I—I want my—my Mummy and Daddy."

It was only a whisper, and Mary Ann whispered back, "So do I."

"Nobody loves me."

This statement stumped Mary Ann for a moment, then putting her arm around Marian's shoulder, she whispered, "Yes they do—I do, and Lola."

"Do you?" Their faces were close, their breaths fanned each other.

Mary Ann, shivering with the cold, at this point said, "Move over, and I'll come in with you."

Within a second she was well under the clothes and lying close to Marian, and, as if she were the elder, she put her arms about her and comforted her, saying, "Don't cry, Marian."

"I've no one to talk to," said Marian. "Lola won't listen, she says I'm to forget it."

Mary Ann did not enquire what she had to forget, but said, "Why don't you talk to the priest? I used to tell Father Owen everything."

"Did you?"

"Yes."

"I don't like to."

"Why not? They don't know who's telling them."

"They don't know?" There was a sound of amazed enquiry in Marian's voice; and after a couple of sniffs, she asked, "What do you mean?"

"Why, cos priests are blind when they are hearing confessions." Mary Ann spoke with authority. "I know cos Father Owen is in Jarrow; I used to tell him everything and he never knew it was me, cos God strikes them all blind once they get in the box. But they're all right when they come out again."

"That's silly!"

" 'Tisn't, Marian, honest."

"Who told you?"

"I've always known."

"Is it the truth, honest? I've never heard it before."

"Yes, it's the truth. Honest. . . . You go and tell everything to the priest—Father Hickey, he's not bad. But he's not like Father Owen. Oh, Father Owen was lovely. . . . Will you go and tell him what you're crying for?"

"Yes."

"Well, what are you crying for?" This was diplomacy at its worst.

There was a silence, during which Mary Ann became aware that she was being nearly smothered beneath the quilt, and she came up for air. And as she did so she had the terrifying impression that someone was moving about at the end of the dormitory. Then Marian said, "It's about my Mummy—my Mummy and Daddy don't live together."

"What!" Mary Ann brought her attention back to her bedmate.

"They're separated. . . . I—I've only seen Daddy once in—oh, once in a long, long time."

This admission threw everything else out of Mary Ann's mind, and bringing her head under the clothes again she whispered in deepest sympathy, "Oh!

Marian." Her arms tightened around the bigger girl. "Oh, poor Marian! . . . Look—" she had an idea— "when I go back home you can come with me. You'll love me da, and he'll——"

What Mike was to do in the way of giving Marian comfort died in Mary Ann's mind almost in the act of its conception, for was it up from Hell or down from Heaven that the hands came. She didn't know, but come they did, two great powerful hands, and she was lifted sky high, swung through the air and plumped into her bed, and it stone cold. And a voice, which had certainly not been nurtured in Heaven, hissed over her, "Move out of there again if you dare! I'll see you in the morning, you wicked child!"

Terror filled the night. What had she done? Only got into Marian's bed cos she was crying. . . . Oh! Ma . . . Ma. . . . I want to come home. . . . Why was she a wicked child? and what would happen in the morning? She wished she was dead. This was a surprising thought, for up to now nothing but the trouble between her ma and da had power to evoke a wish for her own demise. Her feet were cold and she was shivering. She began to cry, and to the chant of "Oh! Ma. Oh! Da", which went round and round in her head, she went to sleep.

The outcome of the bed episode had an effect on the occupants of the dormitory equal in Mary Ann's opinion to that of someone swearing at a priest or hitting a teacher, or some such earth-shaking catastrophe. She was gaped at, talked at, talked about, and pushed around, and, what was more, she received five discipline marks and six more for discourtesy. This latter injustice because she had dared to speak back to Sister Mary Martha, when all she had said was that she didn't know it was forbidden to get into another girl's bed. What was more, everybody in the house was laughing about priests being blind in confession, and this hadn't come about by Marian talking, but by Beatrice, who, seeing an opportunity to work for the cause of discipline marks, had risen stealthily and listened to the comforting advice Mary Ann was giving to Marian, and solely, let it be understood, in the cause of discipline had gone and informed the Sister.

And now Mary Ann was learning the deep science of comparative values of behaviour. Outside a convent you could sleep in a bed with somebody else, inside you couldn't. Sister Monica said so; Sister Agnes Mary said so; and Sister Catherine said so. Of course, Sister Catherine would! She said it a number of times, and in a number of different ways, as she took Mary Ann along to Mother St. Francis—who also said it. So, by ten o'clock, Mary Ann was left in no doubt as to the procedure of sleeping in a convent. And finally she awaited the order to appear before the Reverend Mother. But this threat did not materialise; instead, she was sent to Mother St. Bede—and English. And so unnerving had been the events of the morning that her stomach felt sick, and she wanted to go to the lavatory all the time; but such was the power of Mother St. Bede that her internal organs sympathetically understood the impossibility of a request to be relieved and did the only thing that was left to them, they swelled.

Half-way through the lesson Mother St. Bede banged the flat of her hand on the desk and called out loudly, "Mary Ann Shaughnessy! will you stop wriggling. Are you sitting on a pin?"

"No, Mother."

"Then don't act as if you were. Did you leave the room before you came in?"

This Irishism was fully understood by Mary Ann, and she said, "Yes, Mother," but had not the face to add, "but I want to leave again."

"Then sit still. Better still, stand up and read page fourteen."

Mary Ann turned the pages of her book, and to her relief she saw that the poem was one of Longfellow's. Oh, she could do him, she knew yards of Hiawatha—if only she didn't want to leave the room.

"What does it say?"

"Musins, by Longfellow."

"What does it say?"

"Musins. . . ."

"It does not say 'Musins', it says 'Musings'. Repeat . . . 'Musings.' . . . And who by?"

"Longfellow."

"It does not say Longfellow."

"Henry Wadsworth Longfellow."

"Begin."

"I sat by my window one night
And watched how the stars grew bright.
And the earth and the skies were a splendid sight
To a sober and musin' eye."

"Mus . . . inge . . . inge. Musing . . . eye."

"Musing eye." Oh dear! she felt sick.

"Go on."

"From Heaven the silver moon shone down,
With gentle and mella ray . . ."

"Stop! What's a mella ray? . . . Mellow, child."

". . . mellow ray,
And beneath the crowded roofs of the town
In broad light and shadda lay."

Bang! bang! bang! Mother St. Bede's hand bounced on the desk.

"Shadda! shadda! shadda! . . . shad—ow—ow—ow —dow. . . . Shadow!"

Mother St. Bede's lips were so far out that her mouth resembled a snout, and her "ow—ow—ow" sounded like the wailing of a screech owl.

"Shadow."

It was hot, she felt sick, her stomach was bursting. . . . Oh! Ma. . . .

"Go on."

But Mary Ann did not go on. To the amazement and surprise of both Mother St. Bede and the whole class she sat down with a plop. As she saw the great black figure of the English mistress looming towards her all the self-control, of which she had shown a great deal, fled. She was sick, right over her desk and on to the back of the girl in front of her. This was disgusting enough, but, what was more disgusting to her, for it was happening for the first time in her life that she could remember, she wet her knickers. This act released a wave of homesickness, and it was set free on a flood of crying and gabbling, which mounted as she was led from the room, and the gist of it which fell on the tortured ears of Mother St. Bede was, "Oh! Ma, Oh! Da. . . . Aa wanna go hoom."

6

All trials have their end, and after five weeks of them Mary Ann was now sailing along in the stream of school life. She remembered to sound her g's and draw out her a's; she was even beginning to take an interest in English, so much so, that she talked swanky to herself in bed, and even, by mistake, did it once in class, which did not annoy Mother St. Bede, but on the contrary seemed to please her.

She could now count up to fifty in French, and also ask in that language, "Is that the pen of your sister, and the house of your brother?" and other such profound questions. She had also begun to learn German. But she hadn't any real fancy for German, because her mouth filled up with spit when she tried to say the words. She was good at catechism, and exceptionally good at P.T., and she was learning to swim.

This last feat had developed a joyful anticipation in her, and she lived for Monday afternoons and the visit to the baths. And when, as was happening this week, the Wednesday afternoon walk was to be turned into two hours on the beach, life, when she didn't think of her da, was bearable. At least it had been until she received the letter from Michael.

Michael had never missed writing to her once a week, and his letters were a source of constant surprise to her, for in them there was more news than in either her da's or her ma's letters. Michael told her about the farm, the new hand, whom Mr. Lord didn't like, Mr. Polinski and Mrs. Polinski. He told her a lot about Mrs. Polinski, and because of this, Mary Ann was puzzled. Sometimes, as she read, she would say to herself, "What's he got to keep on about her for?" and then last week he had said, "I don't like Mrs. Polinski, and don't blame Mr. Polinski for hitting her. And you know something? me ma doesn't like her either. She's never out of our house, and always comes at mealtimes. Me ma was stiff with her last week, and she hasn't been back since." And then he had finished quite abruptly, "I wish you were here."

Never before had Michael ever expressed a need of her. At home he had been wont to push her away from himself and his concerns, but now through his letters she felt him very close to her. It could be said that she looked for his letters even more than those of her da, for only through his letters did she sense the real feeling at present in her home. Her mother's letters were all about what she must do and be a good girl, and her father said mostly how he missed her, and Mr. Lord's—one arrived every Monday morning, as if to set the tone for the week—were, in their briefness, all about learning, her learning. So it was Michael's letters she really looked forward to.

What does our Michael mean? she had asked herself for nearly two whole days. Somehow it seemed mixed up with Mrs. Polinski. And then she had a funny letter from her da that made her laugh. They had got a new bull and it had chased Mr. Jones up a drainpipe. Her da had added a postscript that nearly made her roll up; he had said, briefly, "Outside the drainpipe."

She had laughed and laughed as she imagined Mr. Jones clinging on to the drainpipe. And so Mr. Jones and the bull had dispelled the vague fear that Michael's letter had aroused. Until this morning, when she had received another one from him, and again he was on about Mrs. Polinski. After saying that Mr. Lord had gone for Tony in front of the men, he said, "It was all through that Mrs. Polinski; she was standing talking to him and making him waste his time. She's always talk-

91

ing to somebody. She's always waylaying me da. She's a brazen thing, paints and everything. There's only five more weeks to the holidays, but I wish you were here now."

Again Mary Ann experienced a disturbed feeling, and it overshadowed the day. She had been so excited when she knew they were going to the beach this afternoon, even if it were all pebbles and not sandy like it was at home, but now all she could think of was, I wonder what's up with our Michael, keeping on about Mrs. Polinski. I wish I was home. She had consulted the picture calendar in the corridor on which days were marked off delegated to various causes, such as Our Lady of Calvary, Our Lady of Sorrows, Blessed Mother of Bethlehem, The Precious Blood, The Blessed Sacrament, The Sacred Heart, Blessed Michael the Archangel—and, of course, the Saints; it seemed to Mary Ann the whole lot of them. After she had mentally replaced them all by dates, she worked out that there were not only five whole weeks but also three more days before they broke up, and only then would she know what their Michael meant.

In the scramble after lunch for bathing costumes, towels and their tent bags, under which they undressed, and then the arranging of herself in the crocodile so as to be next to Marian, she forgot, or at least pushed to the back of her mind, Michael and his letter.

The sun was fierce, the sky high and blue, and although she was wearing one of her outdoor dresses which was cool and light, she still felt hot and longed for the moment when the waves would splash over her.

The nuns in charge of the company of fifteen were Sister Alvis and Sister Agnes Mary, and no two Sisters could have been more suited for the job in hand, for they enjoyed the beach as much as did the children, and their broad smiles and rejoinders to the continual stream of questions flung at them on the bus journey caused surprised glances from the other passengers. When Sister Agnes Mary's hoarse laugh rang out there were raised eyebrows, and small, surprised smiles from various quarters, and when the company alighted, before entering St. Leonards in order to take a short cut to the beach, the eyes of the passengers followed them,

92

the Sisters in particular, as if they had witnessed for the first time two laughing bears.

Mary Ann had hold of Sister Alvis's hand. She liked Sister Alvis, for although she wasn't as old as Mrs. Mc-Bride, she was the nearest thing in looks and sound to her, particularly when she said, "Jesus", that could be found in this polite part of the world. And now Mary Ann, in an effort to draw the nun's attention, informed her of her prowess in swimming of which Sister Alvis, having helped with her coaching, was already well aware. "I can swim six breast strokes, Sister."

"Can you, my child? Glory be to God."

"I'll soon be able to swim the length of the bath."

"You will, you will. With God's help, you will."

"I wish me da could see me."

Ah, we were on a very delicate subject here. Sister Alvis had had her instructions of how to deal with the da complex, and she now threw her attention to the front of the disordered ranks and found diversion as a small figure leaped away, in answer to the call of her first glimpse of water, and she cried, "Oh! Sweet Jesus in Heaven, there's Anna Maria off again. Come back here this instant. . . . Sister—" she turned to where Sister Agnes Mary was walking with the bigger girls— "look, Anna Maria has started again."

"Oh, she has—Anna Maria!" Sister Agnes Mary was after the enthusiast, running over the dunes, leaving the rest of them laughing. Everybody loved to see Sister Agnes Mary run, for she did so with a strong, almost masculine galloping gait, doubtless occasioned by the bulky habit, of which, as she watched the Sister running, Mary Ann became consciously aware for the first time. Oh! poor Sister Agnes Mary, she must be hot in all those clothes. And poor Sister Alvis—and all the Sisters and Mothers. She knew a sudden pity for them. Why couldn't they take some of them off? She had an overpowering desire to put this question to Sister Alvis, but already she had learnt one thing at the convent—painfully she had acquired a quality of restraint —so she turned her question into a statement. "Isn't it hot, Sister?" she said.

"It is, child—lovely. God be thanked for such a lovely day and may He send many more this summer."

Without asking, Mary Ann had been given her answer. Sisters and nuns didn't feel the heat.

The water was beautiful, even if you weren't allowed to go out past the sentries, the sentries being Lola and Beatrice and another girl. At first she lay at the edge and let the waves, which were gentle today, roll over her; then, enough of that, she kicked the water and yelled, and, taking Marian by surprise, pushed her face forward into a wave, only to be concerned when Marian, having recovered herself, looked on the point of crying.

"Oh! Marian, I was only playing." Her contrition was equal to a misdeed of far greater magnitude. "Push me—come on, I'll let you. Come on!" Marian pushed, and Mary Ann, letting herself go, fell over backwards with a great deal of spluttering and not a bad performance of drowning, and then turning over she cried, "Look, watch me, I can swim seven now. Look!"

Marian watched her. She, after four years of learning, could swim about as much as Mary Ann was doing after as many weeks. But she didn't like the water; the baths were bad enough, but the sea was frightening to her.

Spluttering and squeezing the water down herself, Mary Ann stood beside her friend. . . . "Can't—can't I do it!"

"Yes, you're doing fine. But come on out; let's go and pick shells."

"But we've just come in; and, anyway, Sister won't let us."

"She will if we don't go far, just to where the rock comes out. If she'll let us, will you come?"

"Oh, all right."

This was indeed a sacrifice, and in case permission should be given, she plunged into the water again to make the most of her time, but almost before she had completed her six strokes, Marian was back, and pulling her up by the costume.

"She says we can, just as far as the rock, but not round it. We must keep in sight."

"Oh, all right." Mary Ann stood puffing and blowing. "But—but let's plodge along at the edge; we'll find a lot then."

94

So they paddled slowly to where the rock, jutting out, formed the cove, and when they reached it they sat down on one of the sandy patches and sorted out their shells.

At what point Mary Ann became aware of the voices from the other side of the rock she didn't know. She was lost for the moment in the wonder of the shells and her senses dulled somewhat by the heat, and perhaps she had forgotten she wasn't on the sands at Shields, and so the voices that came to her at intervals were not from another world but the everyday sounds she was used to. And then she was brought upright by a long-drawn sigh, and a voice saying, "Eeh by! it's hot."

She stared at Marian, but Marian was engrossed in grading her shells. And when the voice came again, saying, "Giz a drink, lass," she rose to her feet and carefully paddling to the point of the rock she craned round it and saw two people seated in the shade of the cliff. As she recognised them her mouth fell open and everything else was forgotten.

"Mr. Wilson!" She was scrambling round the small promontory and over the shingle to the couple who had now risen to their feet.

"Well! hinny." Mr. Wilson greeted her as if she were his own child. "Well! me bairn, where've you sprung from?"

"Hallo, hinny."

"Hallo, Mrs. Wilson." Mary Ann thrust out a hand to each of them, and they hung over her, exclaiming their wonder at her sudden appearance.

"I'm from round the bend . . . I'm with me house. It's Wednesday, we have it off, an' I was picking shells an' I heard you. . . . Oh!"

Her joy at being among her own kind again was something she as yet could not formulate into words, but Mr. Wilson did it for her. "An' you heard our voices, and it was like home again, eh?" he said laughing.

"Yes," she nodded.

"Well, come and sit doon—" he made his voice broader for her benefit—"and hev a drop tea. Well, hinny, we've often spoke of you. How you getting on?"

"Oh, all right, Mr. Wilson."

"You like it?"

Mary Ann did not answer immediately, but looked up at Mrs. Wilson who was handing her the top of the Thermos flask, brimful of milky tea.

"Ta." She slipped back as naturally as breathing into the old idiom. And then she answered Mr. Wilson. "Sometimes . . . but—" her face suddenly lost its brightness—"I wish I was home, everything's different here."

"You're telling me, hinny; we've had 'bout enough an' all, haven't we, lass?" He looked at his wife, and Mrs. Wilson said, "Well, it isn't like home . . . though, mind, everybody's been more than kind. We came to stay for three months with me daughter, but we think we'll be making a move back soon. But it's a problem —we've let our house."

"Oh, we've been into that—" Mr. Wilson waved the house question aside—"we'll get fixed somewhere. But, hinny—" he took Mary Ann by the shoulders—"you're not as bonny as when I saw you last . . . thinner. Do they gi' ye enough to eat?"

"Oh, yes, heaps—and they make you stuff it down, cabbage an' all. And——"

"They treat you all right?" Mr. Wilson, finding nothing to get at in having too much food, altered his approach.

"Yes."

"Hit you or anything? Lock you up?"

Mary Ann's eyes widened. "No. No, they don't."

"Look, have a bit cake." Mrs. Wilson thrust a paper plate towards Mary Ann.

"Oh, ta, Mrs. Wilson."

"Mary Ann! Mary Ann!" The almost hysterical shouting coming from behind the rock startled them all, and Mary Ann, springing up and remembering that she wasn't on the sands, said, "Eeh! I'll catch it, I'm not supposed to be round here. That's Marian, my friend."

"Well, bring her round, hinny."

"It's out of bounds. Eeh! I'd better go."

"Mary Ann! Mary Ann! Oh, Mary Ann!" Now

Marian's screams were hysterical, and to her voice others were joined, a chorus of them.

"Eeh!" Mary Ann looked from one to the other, her eyes large and startled. "Eeh! Ta-ra, Mr. Wilson. Ta-ra, Mrs. Wilson; it was lovely seeing you."

She turned and ran down to the water's edge, and as she plodged wildly in she imagined somehow that the end of the rock had moved out into the water, for the shingle, sloping steeply at that point, brought the water round her waist. It was still calm and sunny water, but when three steps from the end of the rock it came up to her armpits, the world suddenly became a mass of water and she knew a tiny tremor of fear, and just as she heard Mr. Wilson's anxious voice, calling, "Come on back here, hinny!" around the bend rushed Sister Agnes Mary, with the bottom of her habit, although tucked up a little, trailing in the water.

"Child! you'll be punished for this. . . . You will! you will!"

Voice and manner were so unlike those of Sister Agnes Mary that all Mary Ann could do was to stare up at her, and when she was hoisted out of the water and into the Sister's arms, she saw that she was really flaming mad.

Sister Agnes Mary was flaming mad, but it was with fright. Like a distraught mother seeking relief from her fear in action and heedless of the shingle crippling Mary Ann's bare feet, she pulled her along the beach. At the assembling point from where, only ten minutes before, Mary Ann had departed, Sister Agnes Mary took her hands and slapped them; then did the same to her bottom, and sent her, crying now, to get dressed, while Marian stood by sniffling and saying, "I thought she was drowned when I didn't see her—I thought she was drowned."

During all this Mr. Wilson had been standing by the point of the rock, his trousers rolled up well above the knees, sending an angry commentary back to his wife.

"What did I tell you! Nun clouting her . . . and in the open. If they do that with folks lookin', what'll they do when they can't be seen. . . . It's as I've always said . . . for two pins I'd——"

97

"George! you'll do no such thing. Come on, it's none of your business. Perhaps the woman was worried."

"Worried? and belting her like that! She looks as big as a house and as mad as a hatter. . . . Convents! By, if I had my way."

He stood taking in the proceedings of the group, now being hustled into their clothes until the rising tide threatened to engulf him, when he retreated, telling his only listener what he thought about convents—as if she didn't already know—and that he'd give that bairn's da an earful of what went on when he saw him.

Dating from the beach incident, life became a problem to Mary Ann, one large, painful problem made up of lesser problems, one of which, the honour of her house, rated highly. Not that she cared too much for the honour of her house, but the ten black marks she had received for just going round the bend put her away ahead of the worst culprit in the convent, and was bound, she was assured from all sides, which included Lola, to place their house bottom in the running for the cup. She had lain awake at nights thinking along such entwined lines as "Bust the cup!" and "Oh! Da," and "What's our Michael mean? He's always keeping on"; then, during this particular week, fourteen days after the fateful Wednesday and still three weeks and three days from the holidays, she had asked herself each night not "What does our Michael mean?" but "Why didn't he write last week?" It was now eleven days altogether since she had heard from him, and during that time she'd had two letters from her da but only one from her ma, and all three letters had been short, telling her nothing, only to be a good girl and learn her lessons—as if Mr. Lord didn't tell her that every Monday morning.

Leaving out her home worries and returning to her school ones, there remained one ray of hope on her horizon, a ray that might be the means of her getting twenty-five whole marks and so erasing some of the blackness from her sheet. In each house, every year, was held a competition for the best written essay and the best sonnet. Now Mary Ann wasn't as yet much good at the essay, but as to sonnets—she knew them as poetry—she thought she was the tops. She was good at poetry, she told herself with conviction. Hadn't even Mother St. Bede praised her for her efforts—although she had added she must not misconstrue things, like the way she had when asked to write a twelve-line poem on "Flag Day", and she wrote:

> It's washing day,
> It's washing day,
> My Py-jams are all soap.
> They'll shrink and shrink
> And shrink and shrink,
> Oh dear there is no hope.
>
> It's washing day,
> It's washing day,
> The things are on the line.
> There's me ma's things,
> And me da's things,
> And next to them are mine.

She couldn't have made it rhyme if she had stuck their Michael's name in, and she hadn't thought of turning "me ma's" to "my mother's", or "me da's" to "my father's", and this seemingly had detracted still further from the poem's merit; yet, in spite of this, Mother St. Bede had praised her, and apparently for the very thing that she had condemned which she called misconstruing.

She hadn't pointed out to Mother St. Bede that "Flag Day" was how her da referred to the washing in the back lanes; Mother St. Bede, she felt sure, wouldn't have understood if she had.

And now to write a poem, a beautiful poem, that would win not only the house prize but be the top of the four houses and be set to music, as the winning poem always was. Just that morning they had all sung last year's winning song, which had been won by a girl not in the Upper House, but in the Middle one.

She hummed it to herself:

> Come fly out of doors and see the rain,
> Rain that won't come for a year again;

99

> *Golden rain, brittle and brown*
> *Singing as it floats waverly down.*
> *Come, let joy sing in your veins,*
> *For only once a year it rains*
>
> *Leaves of Autumn*
> *Yet promise of Spring.*
> *Come fly out of doors and let your heart*
> *   sing."*

It was a lovely tune an' all. Oh, if only she could write a song like that. So filled did she become with her desire to write a song that the day was but a prelude to the recreation hour, and she waived all thought of letter-writing so that she could get down to it. Having begged her favourite seat near the window she was down to it when Marian made her appearance.

Marian, Mary Ann was finding, could be a bit of a nuisance. If she wasn't crying about her da she was talking about him. This side of her Mary Ann understood perfectly, and she always allowed her to go on for some time before butting in herself to continue the same theme, but, of course, with a very different da. When she spoke of Mike to her friend she continued to use the forbidden term, and through repetition Marian had come to think of Mary Ann's father as her da.

"What are you doing?" she asked now flatly.

"Writing some poetry, a poem." Mary Ann didn't look up.

"It's a waste of time, you won't get anything. Beatrice'll win it."

Mary Ann's head came up now, and quickly she retorted, "She won't! Mother St. Bede didn't take no —any notice of hers."

"Shush!" Marian looked slyly up and around. "She's over there. . . . You know what?" She sat down and brought her head near to Mary Ann's and, in a voice scarcely audible above the buzz in the room, she said, "She was going at Lolo about you."

Mary Ann's attention was successfully brought away from her task. "She was?"

"Yes." Marian nodded and nuzzled nearer. "She said you were common, and this place would never alter you, and—and you were the biggest sow's ear she had ever known here. A sow's ear, that's what she called you."

Mary Ann had heard the first time. Sow's ear, she knew all about sows' ears. Mrs. Flannagan had said she was one, and Sarah Flannagan had shouted it after her, adding that you couldn't make a silk purse out of it. But Father Owen had told her that you could, for he had been a sow's ear himself once. But in this moment Mary Ann found no consolation in Father Owen's ancestry, which was apparently akin to her own. That Beatrice was a cheeky thing. She cast her eyes to the far corner of the room, where Beatrice was writing, surrounded by three of her cronies. For two pins she'd go over to her and say, "Who do you think you're calling a sow's ear! You're a brass-faced monkey. Take that!" She had a beautiful mental picture of delivering a ringing slap that would knock Beatrice clean off her feet.

"Don't look over there," begged Marian now in some fear, "she'll come over and then she'll give you more marks. Let me see what you've done."

"No." Mary Ann put her hand over the paper.

"Oh, well, all right, if you want to be huffy." Marian moved away a little and idly opened a book, and Mary Ann returned to her composing. But she had scarcely begun to think when Marian's voice came again, insinuatingly, "Aren't you going to write to your—da, tonight?"

"No."

"Oh."

Mary Ann's mouth went into a tight line. Why couldn't Marian do something? She was always "just asking". She wasn't going to take no notice of her, she was going to do her poetry. What went with . . . lawns of green? Bean . . . lean . . . sheen? Yes . . . sheen, lawns of green sheen . . . No. Glossy sheen. Yes, that was it: lawns of green and glossy sheen.

"I wish it was the holidays." There was a sigh from Marian, which elicited no response whatever from Mary Ann.

Falling like—like what? Mary Ann pictured the lawns outside below the terrace. What fell? . . . Waterfalls . . . oh yes, falling like waterfalls. But that wasn't long enough . . . and then there was something about de-da-de-da's that Mother St. Bede said you had to count to get the lines right. Oh, she couldn't bother about that, she would forget what she was making up. Lawns of green and glossy sheen, falling like waterfalls —to—to valleys . . .

"Do you know that all the nuns—Sisters, too—were called to Mother Superior today? I wonder what for. Do you know?"

Mary Ann did not raise her eyes, but let out a long-drawn breath that sounded like the leak of a bicycle tyre. Bust Marian. And nuns and Sisters. . . . Oh, bums and blisters, she had lost it now. But her disappointment was suddenly turned to excitement by this last thought, which rhymed, nuns and Sisters, bums and blisters. Eeh! but you couldn't say bums, not here! A little laugh wriggled inside of her and found its way up to her lips and eyes. Eeh! but it could be funny. She liked doing funny ones, she was good at funny ones. Her pencil was now away ahead of her thoughts.

"Let's play needles and pins, Mary Ann." It was a whisper from Marian.

"No, not now, I'm working. Can't you see?" She would want to play needles and pins now. . . . Needles and pins, needles and pins, sit on them pronto for your sins. You see, she could write funny ones.

> *Needles and pins,*
> *Needles and pins,*
> *Sit on them pronto for your sins;*
> *If you don't eat your cabbage there'll be some fun*
> *And a whack on your bum by a Sister or a Nun.*

Eeh! it was funny. She could make a really funny one up out of that. But she'd have to take that "bum" out.

"What on earth are you writing?"

As the hated voice fell down on her a hand came over her shoulder, but before it could reach the paper Mary Ann's hands, aided by sheer terror and panic, had grabbed it up, and she had sprung from the table. And now both of these emotions were directing her self-preservation, for her hands, as she backed from her tormentor, endeavoured to tear up the paper.

"Give it to me!"

"No, I'll not!"

"Do as you're told."

"I'll not for you, so there!"

The whole attention of the recreation room was now turned on Mary Ann. And Beatrice, seeing that in a few more seconds there would be no evidence left of the self-convicting of this, to her, common individual, made a lunge towards her. But Mary Ann's riposte, owing to her slightness of form, was as quick as any foil in the hands of a master, and as she leapt to the side Beatrice, losing her balance, sprawled forward and aided by the glib surface of the floor, skidded some distance on her stomach being brought to a stop by a chair and Sister Alvis's thick Irish voice, crying, "Beatrice! get up out of that. Mother of God! what do you think you are playing at! Keep your hockey demonstrations for the fields, child."

Sister Alvis can be forgiven for lacking sympathy, for half the room had dared to burst into laughter at the result of Beatrice's attack; moreover, Sister Alvis had very little liking for Beatrice—a hoity-toity piece, and full of pride. Jesus forgive her for passing judgment—and so now, if she were under the impression that anything was amiss, she passed it over by crying loudly again, "Come on now! Come on now, all of yous, all of yous. And pick up those pieces, Mary Ann; you're spraying the floor with them. . . . Are you hurt, Beatrice? You're a big girl to go throwing yourself about like that. Away you go upstairs and tidy yourself; there's five minutes before supper. Now go on. Go on." She shook her head. "I can't listen to any chatter now."

Mary Ann could have flown to Sister Alvis and flung her arms about her. She was lovely, she was wonderful, she was holy, a saint—everything—the lot. A minute ago she had thought that the Devil didn't appear only in men who wanted you to go for rides in cars. She had seen him plainly advancing on her, dressed up as Beatrice. But Sister Alvis had come and saved her. Her faith in human nature, as supplied by

103

convents, and justice, about which she had always had her doubts, were both revived and strengthened.

She picked up the pieces of paper with lightning speed, ran from the recreation room straight to the lavatory and pulled the chain on them. There! what could Beatrice do now.

Later, in chapel, she looked across at the Holy Family. Wooden as they were, and without colour or feeling, tonight they seemed to be a little alive, warmer somehow, and for the first time since her coming here she addressed them as she would have the group back in Jarrow. "Thank you, dear Holy Family." Eeh! if she'd got hold of that paper I'd have been in for it. Oh, she's awful. . . . "Thank you for making Sister Alvis come in. She's lovely, like Mrs. McBride. I like her best next to Mother Mary Divine and Sister Agnes Mary, although she did clout me, Sister Agnes Mary, I mean. God bless me ma and da and our Michael, and make him write to me. And will you help me with me poetry, cos I want to get some marks. In the name of the Father and of the Son and the Holy Ghost. Amen." Eeh! where was she, they were giving the responses. She hadn't her mind on her prayers, on the real prayers. . . . "Spare us, O Lord—" she spoke up loud and clear. Then not yet being in her stride and over-excited by the preference God had so openly shown her to-night, she forgot that she should read the next line to herself and leave the verbal oration to the priest, and so to her own horror she heard her voice, saying, still loud and clear and joined now solely with that of the priest: "AGNUS DEI QUI TOLLIS PECCATA MUNDI." Her Latin pronunciation was something akin to her English and "Paa—car—ta—Moon—day" trailed horribly away in the silence, and her head drooped to pew level, forced there by the quick glances of those about her. Eeh! Eeh! she had no words terrible enough to pour on her own head over this sacrilege, yet away behind a boarded-off section of her mind, the boards being constructed of convent veneer, the real Mary Ann was crying out in her own defence: What could you expect from a wooden Holy Family—they should have stopped her. It would never have happened in Jarrow.

Strange as it seemed to Mary Ann, she never even got ticked off about the chapel incident, but it had its repercussions, one nice . . . lovely, and one horrible . . . beastly.

The first occurred the following morning. When bumping into Mother Mary Divine in a temporarily deserted corridor, the nun had bent above her and touched her cheek softly and whispered, "Agnus Dei, qui tollis peccata mundi . . . bless you. Indeed, bless you," and then had glided away. And Mary Ann had stopped for a moment to gaze after her, speechless but filled with a . . . lovely feeling . . . a holy feeling, and this feeling persisted right through the morning in spite of Mother St. Bede going at her again for the way she spoke. You never knew how you had Mother St. Bede. One minute she was praising you for your poetry, and the next she was going at you just cos you said "cassel" instead of "carsal"; and then the blooming word was spelt castle—it wasn't fair. But the unfairness was not strong enough to force its way beyond her holy feeling. What completely shattered her celestial affinity, however, and brought her to mundane earth with a bump was when she ran into a group of four girls in a carefully prepared circle round by the side of the gymhouse and all wearing mournfully long faces, behind which laughter was bubbling to escape. With eyes raised to heaven and with hands joined as if in prayer, they were groaning quietly, one after the other, in voices fitting their expressions:

"Agnes Dei qui tollis peccata mundi,
Spare Mary Ann Shaughnessy, O Lord."

"Agnus Dei qui tollis peccata mundi,
Spare her da, O Lord."

"Agnes Dei qui tollis peccata mundi—and their Michael."

Now it was Beatrice's voice, groaning with emotion and strangled laughter:

"Agnus Dei qui tollis peccata mundi,
And her ma . . . and the farm and Mr. Lord—and —and the whole of Jarrow."

The last word was drowned in a concerted splutter, and their heads fell together. Then their arms flung round each other, their laughter burst high, crackling, almost hysterical.

Mary Ann stood as if glued to the spot, the whole of her body twitching, but especially her face. Her eyebrows jerked, her eyes blinked, her compressed lips rotated in a circle, and then she burst out, "You—you rotten cheeky beasts! I'll tell me——" She shut down on the word in time. But Beatrice supplied it for her. Stopping in her laughter, she cried, "Me da! You'll tell me da, won't you?"

Mary Ann stared up at her. The words on Beatrice's tongue sounded strange to her—she would not give them the stigma of "common" and she told herself that wasn't how she said them at all.

"I hate you!"

"Do you? Thank you very much, it is reciprocated." Beatrice was beginning to enjoy herself. She had at last got this foreign being on the raw.

"Mary Ann, there ees a letter for you."

Lola had come hurrying round the corner and she delivered her message while looking at the group facing Mary Ann. Now she pushed her hand out to Mary Ann and continued: "Go on, Mother St. Francis is waiting, go on." It was an order and for Mary Ann it carried more authority than if it had come from a prefect, for Lola had said it. And so she turned, still raging with her anger, and went away, leaving someone much more capable of dealing with Beatrice than she was.

The letter was from Michael—she recognised that by the writing on the envelope—and the relief it brought soothed away her anger and humiliation, and hugging it to her, she went into the recreation room—empty on this blazing hot noon—to read it.

Swiftly she opened it, and when she saw three whole pages with writing on both sides, she said "Coo!" and wriggled with excited anticipation further on to the window sill. But after reading the first paragraph her body became still and her expression fixed. What was the matter with their Michael? What was the matter with their da and ma? What did Michael mean? What's he getting at? she thought.

She was up to page five before light began to dawn on her, and by the time she had reached page six she was thinking: Mrs. Polinski! and her old fears were back, swamping her in great waves. They were the fears that had filled her when her da thought her ma was going off with Mr. Quinton, and although Michael hadn't put the thing in actual writing, she was seeing it happening again, but with her da this time, and Mrs. Polinski.

Michael ended his letter again by saying, "I wish you were here."

As with the last trouble between her ma and da, Michael, in spite of his four extra years, was in no way fitted to deal with it—he could only be hurt by it. Mary Ann knew this, as she also knew that something was up, there was trouble. . . . That's why he hadn't written last week. And now, although this letter from his point of view, was actually giving nothing away, he had told her everything as plainly as if he had stood before her and said it—that her mother was unhappy —that her da and her had had a row, and all over Mrs. Polinski, who, he said, was causing trouble on the farm an' all, for her da, as well as Mr. Lord, had gone for Tony for wasting time, and it wasn't his fault. Mrs. Polinski, when she couldn't talk to their da, would talk to Tony, and Mr. Lord didn't like Tony at all.

Back was the weight of the family on her shoulders. It brought a pinched look to her face and a wildness to her eyes. Folding the letter up, she went slowly out of the room and up the stairs and put it in the bottom drawer of the chest by her bed, forgetting that the dormitory was out of bounds except for ten minutes following prayers. Sister Catherine, finding her there and adding another black mark to her list, did not throw her into the depths of despair, for black marks had suddenly lost their potency. What did black marks matter anyway—there was something wrong at home, something drastically wrong. What could she do? If she wrote to their Michael and asked him, Mother St. Francis would have to see the letter, and then she'd want to see the letter she had received.

When she reached the hall again she was waylaid by Marian.

"What's the matter? I've been looking for you."

"Nothing."

Marian accepted this without comment; then after staring hard at her friend for a moment, she said, "Come on out and play and tell me about that hickaty-pickaty."

"Oh, I don't want to." Mary Ann shrugged her off.

Marian's face fell, and Mary Ann, seeing the suggestion of tears, tossed her head impatiently and went out and into the larger of the playing fields. And in a corner, with only a small portion of her mind applied to it, she began to instruct Marian further into the mysteries of North Country games.

Pointing first at herself and then at Marian, she began to chant half-heartedly,

> *"Hickaty-pickaty, I-sill lickaty,*
> *Bumberrara jig;*
> *Every man that has no hair*
> *Generally wears a wig.*
> *One—two—three—*
> *Out goes she!"*

Of course, as previously arranged, it meant that out went Marian, leaving Mary Ann the first to have a go with the ball. This she did in a most desultory fashion; and she was on the point of giving up altogether when she saw Lola. Although there were many girls playing she knew that Lola was running towards her. So sure was she of this that she stopped her play and went to meet her. Lola was out of breath from her running and could not for the moment speak. She stood over Mary Ann, gazing at her, her eyes wide. And Mary Ann, drawn out of her apathy, muttered, "What's up?"

"You leetle fool."

"What!"

"Why do you write such things?"

"Me?" Mary Ann's mouth fell open. "What have I writed—written?"

"What have you wrote? You know that. But do you know that Beatrice found eet and gave eet to Sister Catherine?"

"Give what? She couldn't—I tore it up." Mary Ann's now clear conscience was pointing to her particular effort of last night.

"You might have thought you tore eet up, but eet is now in the hands of Sister Catherine, and she wants you. Go on—go on." She pushed Mary Ann away with an angry gesture.

Mary Ann, no fear in her, for the same conscience told her she had done nothing, went towards the main door, up the steps, across the hall and to the office.

She had no need to knock on the door for it was open, and inside she saw standing round the table, and all looking at a piece of paper, Sister Catherine, Mother St. Bede and Sister Alvis.

Her presence made known by the diligent wiping of her feet, although perfectly dry, Mary Ann was not bidden to enter in the usual way; instead, Mother St. Bede, pointing a long finger at the floor, indicated what she should do, and Mary Ann, in spite of her clear conscience and feeling that here an' all something was up, walked slowly into the room.

The three nuns looked at her, but it was Sister Catherine who spoke first. "You are a wicked child," she said, "and you will go to Hell. There is no doubt about that."

"Wait a minute." Sister Alvis's thick voice interrupted her, and promised something of a reprieve from so final a destination as she said, "Let us go into this. . . . Mary Ann, you've been writing poetry lately?"

"Yes, Sister."

"Funny poetry?" These words of Sister Alvis's brought the heads of Sister Catherine and Mother St. Bede quickly upwards. But Sister Alvis went on, "When did you write your last funny poem?"

"Last night, Sister."

"Where is it?"

Mary Ann's eyes darted from one to the other. It was no use telling lies. Although all those pieces were now floating down some main sewer she felt that the three dark-robed figures would know all about them. "I tore it up."

"Not all of it—definitely." Sister Catherine's hand swept to the table, and taking up the piece of paper she thrust it before Mary Ann's eyes, so close that Mary Ann could see nothing but squiggles. "You recognize this piece of paper?"

Mary Ann's nose jerked up above the paper as she said, "No, Sister."

"You don't remember putting this in the back of your prep book?" It was now Mother St. Bede speaking.

"I never put any paper in the back of me homework book, Mother."

"I never put a paper—a—singular! Oh, what's the use!" Mother St. Bede's head drooped with her exasperation.

"You don't remember putting a paper in the back of your book? You don't remember, I suppose, writing these words? Look at them. Read them."

Mary Ann's eyes now went to the paper and she read:

"You must not kiss, you must not wink,
You must not smoke and you must not drink,
You must not gamble and you must not swear,
Or wear high heels or curl your hair.
Should you not follow this advice,
You'll be taken to Hell by Sister Alvise."

Signed by Catty Kath
and Old Ma Bede.

Mary Ann's lower jaw now hanging, her nose straining upwards and her eyes bulging, she again looked from one to the other. But she found she was unable to speak. They thought she had written this. Eeh! She had never written things like that . . . ever. Eeh! What made them think it was her?

"Well?"

Mary Ann swallowed. "It's not mine, Sister. I never did it."

Mother St. Bede snatched the piece of paper from Mary Ann's hand and looked at it. "You say this is not yours? I couldn't mistake your writing, child, if I could overlook the context which points to your naughtiness. Your usual way of thinking . . . your—your——"

The latter part of Mother St. Bede's words were unintelligible to Mary Ann, she only knew she was being blamed for writing this poetry when she had never done it, and so she defended herself and strongly, although her lips were trembling. " 'Tisn't my writing, I never done it, I didn't. I don't know nothing about it, so there."

Grammar, delivery, attitude were passed over by Mother St. Bede, or did these things stun her, for with joined hands she turned away.

And now Sister Catherine took over. "You'll be punished for this, severely punished. Reverend Mother will be told about this. You forget where you are—we don't allow this kind of thing. . . ."

"Ssh! ssh!" Sister Alvis interrupted her and looked down on Mary Ann. "Now, my child, if you tell the truth you won't get into trouble. Why did you write this? It was a silly thing to do, wasn't it? Have you written any more like this?"

Mary Ann looked up at the Sister, so like Mrs. McBride in her manner, and her voice shook as she said, "I didn't write it, Sister, honest. I don't know nothing about it. Somebody's done it for spite, not me."

"Huh!" Sister Catherine was coming again to the fore, and her attack was just stopped by the sound of the bell, so that all she said was, "Get away! Get away to your class this minute."

Mary Ann got away. She went along the corridor and into the hall; and once round the corner she stood with her four fingers in her mouth, biting at one after the other. But it was Sister Catherine she was biting, and it was to her that she silently spoke. "You! I didn't, I didn't do it. Somebody's done it, it wasn't my writing! You're always at me. I hate you, I do! You're mean, you are. You! . . . I don't like you."

"What's the matter?" It was Marian again, excited and eager to know what the trouble was. "What did they want you for? I saw Sister Catherine. Oh, she looked wild."

Mary Ann, tears now welling into her eyes stammered, "They said I'd—I'd written some bad poetry, and I never did."

"Who?"

"Sister Catherine and Mother St. Bede and Sister Alvis. That Sister Catherine—she thinks she's Mrs. God!"

As this blasphemy was uttered the earth seemed to

111

open, but not far enough to swallow Mary Ann, for there, not a few feet away at the entrance to the corridor, stood the three nuns in question.

Her eyes darting from one to the other of her contemporaries as if in confirmation of her opinion of this child, Sister Catherine, with foreboding quietness, said, "Go to the dormitory this minute, and don't move until I come."

Trembling as if with ague, Mary Ann squeezed past the three pairs of eyes and like someone drunk went up the broad, picture-laden stairs towards the dormitory.

Twenty-four hours had lapsed since Mary Ann had committed the heinous crime, not of writing cheeky poetry, but of insulting Sister Catherine. Each individual in the dormitory, with the exception of Lola, had given her own version of the affair as she had heard it—the different versions ranging from simply swearing at Sister Catherine to hitting, biting, and, lastly, spitting in her face. But Mary Ann heard none of these versions, for she was being ostracised. Marian, after her many accounts of the incident, had not the nerve to be seen openly talking to her; only the steadfast Lola still spoke to the culprit.

Mary Ann had spent all yesterday afternoon in the punishment room—a form of solitary confinement; no books, no paper or pencil, not even an underground comic to look at—and last evening, two full hours on her knees in the chapel, during which time the Holy Family had been less than useless; and this morning she had appeared before the Reverend Mother.

Had the Reverend Mother put her thoughts on this matter into words, it is probable that the whole of Mary Ann's life would have been changed, for the Reverend Mother did not believe that this child had written the words on the paper presented to her although the writing seemed to prove that she had. No, the Reverend Mother believed Mary Ann when she persisted in her denial of any knowledge of the paper but admitted frankly to having written cheeky poetry the previous night; and when with bowed head the child had repeated what she could remember of the rhyme, even

112

to the mention of blisters on unmentionable anatomy, the wise woman realised that this child was confessing to something decidedly more vulgar than the words which were written on the paper. So she believed the child, but she didn't tell her so—that would never have done—she only dismissed her, with a caution to write nothing that she wouldn't want the whole world to see.

Following this, the Reverend Mother went on to tell Sister Catherine her real opinion of this matter, which, from the many things reported to her, she linked with Beatrice. Her final word was that the child was to be punished no more, and if she misbehaved in future she was to be brought straight to her.

It was with some surprise then that Mary Ann received the order to get ready for the afternoon walk. Once again she found herself out in the sunshine, in the crocodile, walking with Marian. But now she was paying Marian back in her own coin, for she would have nothing to say to her—in her own words "she wasn't kind to her".

The same two nuns were in charge of the walk, Sister Agnes Mary and Sister Alvis. Sister Alvis appeared to Mary Ann slightly aloof, and whenever Mary Ann's eyes caught hers she was made to feel her past sins by a gentle, hurt look on the Sister's face. But not so Sister Agnes Mary—it would appear she had found favour in the eyes of Sister Agnes Mary. Forgotten was the beach episode. It could have been that this particular Sister had never lathered her behind, and when the hearty Sister took hold of her hand her love and gratitude rushed out to her.

On these walks each child was allowed sixpence to spend, and today when they touched on the town they were told off in threes to go into a sweetshop and spend their money. Mary Ann was one of the last three, and she was standing at the counter after giving her order for three-pennyworth of "Dolly Mixture" when a voice from behind her said, "Why, hallo, Mary Ann."

Mary Ann's eyes, as they stared at Mrs. Wilson, lighted up as if she was seeing her mother, and she turned from the counter and flung herself at the old woman. "Oh! hallo, Mrs. Wilson. Oh! hallo."

Mrs. Wilson, holding both of Mary Ann's hands, said

feelingly, "I'm glad I've seen you, hinny, we're going back the night."

"Home?"

"Yes, my dear. Mr. Wilson can't stand it no longer here." She laughed. "He's lived too long in the North."

"The night?" There was hungry longing in Mary Ann's voice and eyes.

"Yes, the night. Oh, I'm glad I saw you, hinny. I'll tell him—he often talks of you. Did you get wrong the other day?"

"No—well, yes, a little. Oh!" Mary Ann gripped the hands in hers. "Oh! I wish I was comin' with you and Mr. Wilson."

"The holidays will soon be here, hinny, and I promise you we'll come and see you when you come home."

"Thank you, Mrs. Wilson. Look," she reached up eagerly and whispered, "will you go and see me da and ma when you get back, afore I come home?"

"Yes, we will, hinny, I promise you. And now I'll have to be going, I just slipped in to get a few sweets for the train. We're gettin' the four o'clock, we just live near here. Oh, Mr. Wilson will be glad I've seen you. Good-bye, hinny, and God bless you." Mrs. Wilson stooped and gently patted Mary Ann's face.

"Good-bye, Mrs. Wilson."

Then she was gone.

"Come on, the woman's got your sweets." One of the girls pushed Mary Ann, and she turned towards the counter, and took the bag and handed over her money. And when she got into the street she looked quickly up and down, but Mrs. Wilson had gone, and with her all comfort, all hope. Never before had she felt so alone in the world. She wanted just to stand and cry, but she was hustled into line and the march back to the convent started.

It was unfortunate that within five minutes of her entry into the convent two things should happen to breathe life into the thought that at the moment was but a germ in her mind. The first was a letter from her mother, very short, telling her nothing, only as usual to be a good girl, to do her lessons, and that the holidays would soon come. But at the bottom Mary Ann noticed something that hadn't been on her previous let-

114

ters—the cheap paper was raised in a blob where a drop of water had hit it.

Mary Ann recognized that blob. When she first came to the convent it had dotted her own letters—that blob was a dried tear. Her mother had been crying, and a longing to see her that would brook no cautionary advice such as "Eeh! but you know you can't, not till the holidays" assailed her. And then, as she folded the letter and went to move out of the recreation room, there was Beatrice standing in her way, laughter filling her eyes.

There was no retaliation left in Mary Ann at this moment with which to meet her enemy; she had not the power even to thrust out her chin. She knew that she could not fight Beatrice—she was not on her own ground, this was Beatrice's ground.

She could not realise that in a year or two this would be her own ground, too, and she could meet Beatrice as an equal; she only knew that Beatrice was the one who had written that bit of poetry and stuck it in her book, Beatrice was the one who had caused her all this trouble, and there was no way of showing her up.

Like a small, fascinated rabbit, and very unlike herself, she watched Beatrice go out. Then she shivered, as if from a chilling wind, and waited, so as to give her enemy sufficient time to get well ahead before she followed her but not to the playing fields to join up with the rest of her form. There was a milling of girls in the corridor as the lessons changed, and she mixed with them; then made her way to the cloakroom. There she took up her gaberdine hat and mackintosh, stood for a moment swallowing hard, then, with the hat in her hand and the coat over her arm, she walked out of the cloakroom, across the great hall, down the steps and, unbelievingly, down the drive and out of the convent gate without a soul stopping to question her. Perhaps she had the appearance of a child who had come in from a walk and been sent quickly on some errand down to the lodge.

Only at the main gate did she pause, and that was when she had to make her way round a lorry that was unloading sand on to the side of the drive. She did not see the caretaker. If she had, some lie would have leapt to her lips that would have convinced him of her right to be there. And when once outside she did not pause in fright, nor start to run, but walked, with her heart pumping so hard that it made a knocking sound in her head, towards the main road where the buses ran.

She had still threepence left out of her sixpence and two pounds in her locket. She kept one hand over the locket as she waited for the bus, and when it came and she was firmly seated in it, she asked the conductor with a stammer that sounded natural, "How much is it to the station?" And when he said, "Threepence half," she tendered the coppers with a feeling that God had started to direct the proceedings, for if the conductor had asked for more she would have had to get off and she didn't know where the station was.

As she alighted from the bus a clock confronted her and it said ten to four. She felt sick now and terrified, but it did not enter her head that she should return to the convent. She walked into the booking office, her eyes searching for the familiar faces of the Wilsons. And now the feeling that this whole business was out of her hands was confirmed, for there, among the numerous people standing in the hall, was Mr. Wilson, and he was alone. He was counting his change and looking at his tickets. When she pulled at his coat he looked at her as startled as if she had been an apparition.

"God in Heaven! hinny, where have you sprung from? Have you come to say us good-bye?"

"Mr. Wilson," the tears were now in her eyes and she choked on his name; then started again, "Mr. Wilson, I wanta go home."

Mr. Wilson straightened his back and pressed his hand backwards as he said, "But, hinny, you canna do that!"

"I want to, Mr. Wilson. Take me—oh, please!"

"Take you, hinny—home? Look, what's up with you? Is any thing the matter? Have they been goin' for you?"

Now she nodded dumbly, and then added, "It's not only that, it's me ma—there's something wrong at home."

"What makes you think that, hinny?"

116

"I know by the letters me brother's sent—that's our Michael—he's always goin' on about me da and another. . . ."

When she stopped Mr. Wilson said angrily, "I knew from the beginning they should never have sent you this far. I've said all along to the missis. All this way for a bairn like you, I've said. You're North Country, you belong there like meself. This is no place for God nor man. I've found that out." He bent nearer to her as he delivered this last statement. "I'll be glad to see the Tyne again, hinny. Aye, by God! between you and me I will. But about taking you home." He straightened. "Aye, that's another kettle o' fish."

"Oh, Mr. Wilson, please." She lifted her face up. "Please. I've got the money, it's in me locket where you put it."

" 'Tisn't the money, hinny, it's what's going to happen. And Mrs. Wilson, she'd never stand for it. No, hinny, it's out of the question."

Mary Ann's whole face crumpled, and then she whimpered, "I can't go back now, I'll get wrong and be put in the punishment room."

It was the two last words that did it.

"Punishment room!"

They altered Mr. Wilson's whole expression, for before his eyes he saw a cell, a convent cell, with high, grated windows, cold stone floor, and dry bread and water for sustenance.

His face was hard and flushed as he said, "Have you been in the punishment room, hinny, here?"

"Yes, yesterday. They said I wrote some bad poetry, and I didn't. And——"

The sound of a train passing through the station cut off her words, and Mr. Wilson looked round him, his thoughts written plainly on his face. He knew that if Mrs. Wilson caught sight of the child the game would be up, there would be no chance of getting her on the train, and now he was determined to get her on the train.

Mr. Wilson saw himself bringing his battle into the open—he was fighting a convent, all convents, because a convent had taken one of his grandchildren from him. "Look, hinny," he said in a strangely controlled

117

voice, "stand aside, I'll get your ticket; we'll settle up later. Do as I tell you now," he said quickly, "the missis is in the main hall. When you come through the barrier after me make yerself scarce, for it'll be all up if she sees you." He nodded at her. "Keep out of the way —you understand?"

Mary Ann nodded quickly back at him, and stood to one side, her eyes riveted on the old man. Mr. Wilson had now taken on the form of God—everything was in his hands and she trusted him implicitly. Father Owen's warning of the Devil and his many disguises was forgotten. Had she thought of it she would not have made it applicable to Mr. Wilson. Anyway, if Mr. Wilson had sprouted horns at this moment he would have had her vote of confidence. When, having bought the ticket, he turned from the booking office and did not look at her, but walked to Mrs. Wilson and pushed her ahead through the barrier, her heart began to race at an even faster pace. Close on his heels she followed him. But when the tickets were punched and they were through she kept her head down, and when she saw his legs going one way she turned and walked in the opposite direction, until in the distance she saw the very end of the platform. The emptiness this indicated brought yet another kind of fear to her; and so she stopped and glanced cautiously over her shoulder along the platform. But from where she stood there was no sign of the Wilsons, and in panic she scampered back between the groups of people. And just as she caught sight of them standing at the far end there came the train.

The panic in her head yelled, "Eeh! eeh! ee . . . eh!" and the sound was much louder than the noise of the train. As the doors were flung open, Mr. Wilson marshalled his wife into a carriage, then furtively turned and thumbed Mary Ann towards another compartment. This action seemed to bring her out of her state of petrification, and she dashed towards the open door, scrambled up the high step and threw herself on to a seat opposite to two women, and there she endeavoured to compose herself to wait for Mr. Wilson.

She had no book, nothing to look at, so she looked at her hands, and the women from time to time looked at her and smiled. But she didn't smile back; instead

118

she turned and fixed her gaze on the window, in case they should ask questions.

Ten minutes later, when the train stopped and Mr. Wilson had not yet been along to her, she had a sudden desire to scream and jump out. But she put her fingers into her mouth and pressed her face closer to the window. The train moved again and she began to feel sick. And just when the sickness was about to get the better of her and she knew she would soon do something on the floor Mr. Wilson appeared in the corridor.

The old man's eyes moved swiftly between her and the two women, and then he smiled and said, airily, "Oh, there you are! Come on, hinny." Under the staring eyes of the women he held out his hand, and Mary Ann, grabbing it eagerly, left the compartment.

In the corridor, Mr. Wilson's smile vanished and he bent above her, saying, "Now, look. The missis is up in the air—she's not for having it, she wants to send you back. It's up to you, come on."

Mrs. Wilson looked a different person altogether from the one Mary Ann had seen only a short while ago in the sweetshop. Her face was white and strained and she didn't look at Mary Ann in a nice way, and on first sight she didn't even speak, her lips were pressed tight together. Then she sprang them apart, and began to talk as Mary Ann had never heard her talk. Much quicker than Mr. Wilson she talked . . . on and on.

"Look . . . you're a naughty girl . . . you shouldn't have gone and done it. You know you're a naughty girl, don't you?" Mary Ann just stared. "What d'you think's goin' to happen? We'll get into trouble, it's like kidnapping. Just think of the state they're in at the convent. They'll get the police, and then it'll be on the wireless and then you'll be found. You've got to go back . . . d'ye hear? As for you"—Mrs. Wilson now turned on her husband—"it's you who started all this, you and your talk about convents. You won't give credit that Teresa is the best off of all our grandbairns. Oh, no! it's because she's in a convent. And then you're the one to talk about bigotry—you started all this—you! But now I'm goin' to finish it—she's goin' back."

Mary Ann looked at Mr. Wilson. He wasn't the Mr.

Wilson that she knew either, it was as if Mr. Wilson had become Mrs. Wilson, and Mrs. Wilson had become Mr. Wilson. He sat with his head bowed, his back stooped, and his hands dangling between his knees, and to her astonishment he didn't open his mouth. And she realised, as he had said, that it was now up to her. But what could she do against this force? Nothing.

Her heart was so heavy its weight was unbearable. She began to cry, silently, the tears in great blobs rolling down her cheeks. Mrs. Wilson watched her with her lips falling again into a hard line, and she seemed to draw them right into her mouth before emitting almost in a shout, "You're a bad lass! That's what you are, a bad lass. Why did you do it?"

"Me da . . . me—me ma. She—she must have been crying—it was on her letter—there's something up at home, it's Mrs. Polinski, she's after me da. Oh! Mrs. Wilson, I want to see me—me ma." In desperation she flung herself against the old woman's knee, and, throwing her arms around her waist, gave vent to a paroxysm of sobbing.

Mrs. Wilson hesitated only a second before gathering her up and saying, "There! there! All right, but something must be done." Then turning her eyes in the direction of her husband she spoke one word. "You!" she said.

The exclamation spoke of surrender, but Mr. Wilson's head did not lift but drooped lower. His hands came together in a tight clasp and he let out a long-drawn sigh.

7

With a rhythmic beat Lizzie hit the rough stone wall of the scullery with her clenched fist, while the mutterings from her lips sounded unintelligible even to herself; then turning with a swift movement she went and stood over the sink and retched. She retched as if she wanted to throw up her heart. Mary Ann! Mary Ann! Mary Ann! Even her pores seemed to ooze the name; every blood vessel in her body was beating out the name: Mary Ann! Mary Ann! Mary Ann! Since six o'clock this evening she had started. Was it the miss of her that had brought it about? the mirror she could not believe she was not looking at a very old woman. . . . Her child was lost, her child had been taken away by a man. And on the thought she cried, "Oh, my God . . . Oh, my God!"

All her life she had known worry, nothing but worry, worry; but during these last few months she had thought she was being repaid for all her tribulations, especially those of her married life. Hadn't Mike landed this grand job. After setbacks and trials he was now settled, and the child was away at a grand school receiving first-class education. And then the other trouble had started. Was it the miss of her that had brought it about? When had Mike first begun to notice Mrs. Polinski? She retched again and exclaimed, "Damn Mrs. Polinski! Damn everyone—everything! Mary Ann! Mary Ann! Mary Ann!" Where was she at this moment? Would nothing ever be heard of her again? It had happened to other bairns. Oh, my God! would she never hear anything? She raised her head and looked round the lighted scullery. Nearly midnight. Where was Mike? Where was Michael? Would they never come and tell her.

She stumbled into the kitchen trying to shut down on the terrifying thoughts racing into her mind. But there was no power in her strong enough to keep them at bay, and she stopped dead to look at the picture presenting itself before her eyes. . . . Dead by now. Raped . . . raped!

"No! no! no!" She cried this denial aloud, then clapped her hands to her mouth. She would go mad, stark, staring, raving mad. And it was all her own fault. Why had she let her go? The child hadn't wanted to go. She had pushed her, pushed her to save Mike, pushed her to satisfy an old man's whim. She could have been educated at a school near here, just as well as all those miles away. It was as Mike had said, the old fellow had wanted to separate her from them. Damn him! Damn money and farms. Damn youth! Young girls, empty-headed with big breasts, flaunting them under a man's nose. Mike had laughed at her and said she was crazy. "I'm old enough to be her father!" he had said. "What! me take notice of that empty-headed piece when you are around? Don't be so damn silly, Liz! Be your age."

She had been her age and looked at Mrs. Polinski, a young sex-starved girl. Mike was missing Mary Ann. He wanted her laughter, her young hand in his, and so he talked to Mrs. Polinski. He just talked to Mrs. Polinski, that was all, but how she hated Mrs. Polinski. And then he had said, "You're jealous, Liz!" He enjoyed her being jealous. "Now you know what I felt like over Quinton. Now you know what it feels like, that feeling that somebody's stepped into your shoes. But you're mad, Liz, you're quite mad." She could hear his voice interrupting her thoughts that cried, Mary Ann! Mary Ann! Mary Ann! He had held her close in his arms one night and said, "We're missing her, that's what's the matter with us, that's what's the matter with all of us. The house isn't the same, nothing's the same. There's only one person happy out of all this, and that's the old boy. Damn and blast him—him and his money, him and his power." Oh, my God! She gazed about her wildly. What was she thinking? With a wave of her arm she swept everything from her mind but her child, and again she was crying aloud: "Please, please, Jesus, save my bairn. Oh, Holy Mother of God, do this for me. It doesn't matter if he loses his job, it doesn't matter if we go back to Mulhattans' Hall, nothing matters, security or nothing, only bring my child safely back to me. Don't let her come to any harm. Do you hear?" She raised her eyes to the ceiling: "Don't let her come to any harm!" She was shouting now. Then dropping into a chair, she buried her face in her hands and tore at her thick hair. She was going mad, stark, staring mad—she couldn't bear it.

The latch of the door clicked, and she flung up her head, her eyes clutching at Mike's face. But when his eyes moved quickly away from hers she turned round and joined her hands together and pressed them into her chest.

Mike moved slowly across the stone floor, his steps ringing with the weight of his body, the weight that seemed to have increased in the past few hours. He was heavy all over, his head, his limbs, his mind. He was old; he, like Lizzie, knew he was old. Never again, he felt, would he find an urge towards life. The latest news was that she had been noticed leaving a Hastings train on Charing Cross Station. She had been in the company of an old man, he had had her by the hand. Her being with an old man had been confirmed earlier by the two women in the train who had rung up after the nine o'clock news.

He stood looking in the fire, his thumbs in his belt. He could see himself standing that way. He seemed to be outside of himself, and he saw himself possessed by an odd quietness, part of a terrifying quietness, a quietness full of calculated premeditation, and this part was talking to Mr. Lord. It was saying, "You're to blame for this, you and you only. You wanted to take her away from me, didn't you? Well, now you're going to pay for it." And as he watched this side of himself he knew that if she was not found by the morning he would make the old man pay, and pay thoroughly.

Then there was the other side. He both saw and felt this side—a tearing, raging, cursing side—wanting to run, to fly hither and thither; to search and kill; to turn men round in the street and stare in their faces and demand, "Have you seen her? Have you seen her? Have you seen her?" He saw himself taking a man by the throat and bearing him to the ground and stamping on his face until there was nothing left. . . .

The latch moved again, and now both swung round towards the door as Mr. Lord entered, accompanied by Michael. With a pitiable frailty the old man came into the room. Gone was his brusqueness and supercilious manner; he looked like any old man who had lost all he possessed, and when he spoke, even his voice sounded frail. He addressed himself to Mike, as he said haltingly, "I've just heard—there may be a chance she's on the North-bound train."

"What? Who? How did you hear?" Lizzie stood before him, standing close and peering into his face.

He put out his hand and patted her arm. "They phoned. I'm going to Newcastle now." He turned towards Mike, who said nothing but picked up his cap from the table and went out.

Mr. Lord now spoke to Michael, but without looking at him, as he made for the door. "Don't you come, you stay with your mother."

Michael stood watching him until he went out, and when the door was closed he turned, and looked at his mother. Then throwing himself into a chair, he flung his arms across the table and, dropping his head on them, began to sob.

Lizzie, going swiftly to him, put her arms about him, and drew his head to her breast, saying, "There! there! She'll be all right. Very likely she'll be on the train. Yes, that's it. She wanted to come home." For a moment she tried to make herself believe this, until Michael, raising his head from her chest, muttered between gulps, "How—how could she?" Then again, "How could she? She couldn't come by herself." His head dropped, and Lizzie, her hands still on his hair and hope gone, murmured, "No, she couldn't come by herself."

It must have been three-quarters of an hour later when Lizzie, with her arms still around Michael but now sitting beside the fire in a form of stupor, heard the car come back. The sound seemed to inject them both with life again, and they sprang up and reached the door together, then stopped dead, peering into the night. The farm looked as if lit up for a gala. There were lights on outside the byres, there were lights in Mr. Lord's new house on the hill, which meant that Ben was also keeping vigil; the Jones's light was on too, but not the Polinskis'. The voice of Mr. Jones came to them from the farmyard. It was loud as if he was crying across a distance, and it asked, "You got her?"

When there was no answering voice, no scampering of feet, Lizzie's hand tightened on Michael's shoulder and they both turned slowly back into the house, leaving the door open.

Within a few minutes Mike came in. He looked wild, half mad, his hair was matted with sweat and falling into corkscrews, like a piccaninny's, about his brow. His eyes were sunk deep in his head, and he seemed to have lost his height. Lizzie looked at him across the table, and Michael looked at him, and he returned their glances with a wild stare.

Lizzie's voice sounded like a whimper when she said, "You heard nothing?"

"No." He beat his clenched fist on the corner of the table; then striding to the fireplace he leant his head against the mantelpiece.

Lizzie stared at his back. She could give him no relief—for a moment she was barren of everything but fear—it was left to Michael to offer a crumb of comfort.

"Tony's been in, Da. He's got the idea she'll make her way home somehow. He's gone back to Pelaw Station to the phone. He says——"

Mike swung round from the fire. "Make her way home! With an old man?" He was speaking to Michael now as one man to another, and Michael's eyes dropped before the knowledge his father was imparting to him.

"Oh, God in Heaven!" Now Mike's voice was high and rough, and he was shouting as Lizzie had been shouting, and using almost the same words. "She should never have left this house. But who's to blame for her going? Him! him!" He was still addressing Michael, but he was really speaking to Lizzie. "The old boy—the old boy who must be placated. Well, this is the end, I've had enough. I'm finished, but before I'm done I'll put paid to him. He wanted her away from me—I know, oh! I know, I wasn't blind—and now she's away—away! away! And he'll go away an' all. My God! he will."

Into Lizzie's misery came a terrible fear. The look on Mike's face was not sane, and his jealousy of the old man because of his love for Mary Ann was turning into something grim and gigantic. It was like a madness developing before her eyes, and what it would lead to she could see as plainly as if it was happening. By this time tomorrow tragedy could have been heaped upon tragedy.

125

She attempted to swing his thoughts away from his mad intent by saying angrily, "Yes, go on! Blame someone else, put the blame on anybody but yourself. Mr. Lord, what's he got to do with her going away? It was for you, you, she went away!"

"Me?" The demand filled the room.

"Yes, you—you who were never capable of doing anything on your own—you who had to be sustained by her. Why did she go away? Why? I'll tell you." In her effort to turn his mind from Mr. Lord she knew she was going too far, she was going to tell him things that in a saner moment she would have cut out her tongue rather than voice, she was going to make him plain to himself. "She was giving you security, she was buying you a job. Yes!" She screamed at him now, "Raise your eyebrows, open your mouth—she was buying you a job. She sold herself, if you like, to get you this job. Did the old man send her to school? Yes, but she only went because she knew that you owed him a debt and she was paying it. She was paying for your job, do you hear?"

Before her eyes Mike seemed to swell, and then up from the depths of his being, he dragged his voice, deep and terrible. "You're a bloody liar! Tell me you're a bloody liar!" He went a step nearer to her, just one, and he looked like a mountain shifting itself heavily. "Tell me!"

"I've told you the truth." Now Lizzie's voice was screaming, and her hands were pressed against each cheek, holding her face as if to give herself support for she had gone too far, she knew she had gone too far, but she could not stop herself and she went on yelling, "She's always borne your burdens, she's always directed your cause—you, the big fellow. And as soon as she was out of your sight what did you have to do? Laugh and lark on with a lazy, dirty, young——"

It was Michael's voice now, high-pitched, yelling, "Stop it! Stop it, Ma!" that checked hers. So hysterical was it that immediately it had a calming effect on them both, and when they turned from each other and looked at him he jumped with both feet from the ground, he jumped and stamped on the stone floor and yelled again, "Stop it! Stop it! Both of you." Then before they could react in any way he made a wild dash for the open door, and Lizzie, remembering another occasion when their fighting and the hopelessness of their lives had got the upper hand of him, rushed after him and caught him just on the threshold. But what words she would have said to him were checked, for there, coming up the path, was Mr. Lord.

Stepping back into the room and pulling the struggling boy with her, she made way for the old man to enter. When he had done so, he stood looking from one to the other. Nothing escaped him. Unasked and uninvited, he walked towards the table and slowly turning a chair round he sat down and, addressing Mike without looking at him, he said, "Sit down."

Mike did not move, and Mr. Lord, in a voice utterly unlike his own because of the touch of humility in it, said, "All right, I know how you feel, and I'm going to tell you now that I'm taking all responsibility. It was my fault the child went away." He raised his eyes to Mike's red-rimmed, staring gaze. "I wanted her to be different, I wanted to give her a chance that you hadn't it in your power to give her. I know I was wrong."

When Mike spoke, his own voice sounded calm, even normal: "Did you give me this job on condition that she went away to school?"

There was a long pause during which Lizzie's eyes were on Mr. Lord and Michael's were fixed on his father. Then Mr. Lord, his eyes dropping to his hands, said slowly, "Yes. . . . It was her idea in the first place. She came to me and told me you could manage this farm. I hadn't thought about it, it was the last thing that would have entered my mind, but I grant you that once it had entered I saw the possibility of it—of it being a good thing. And you've proved that, there is no doubt about it."

"Huh!" There was a smile on Mike's face, but a terrible smile, a smile devoid of pride, devoid of all the things that gave a man self-respect, and of all the qualities that any man needed Mike needed self-respect.

Lizzie had wanted to lift the blame from Mr. Lord's shoulders and put it on Mike's, and she had succeeded, but with an agony filling her she saw that the weight

127

was too heavy for him. She need not now fear for what he might do to Mr. Lord, but she need fear, and fear terribly, what he might do to himself.

She moved towards him, until she was standing at his side, and she looked up into his face, all her love and tenderness returning, and just as she was about to put her hand on his sleeve it was arrested. Not only was her hand, but her whole body was stiffened into a state of immobility. And not only hers, but Mr. Lord's and Michael's. Only Mike moved. His head jerked upwards on the sound of running steps, light, tripping, running steps. They all heard the gate bang; and the flying steps came up the path, accompanied now by short, sharp gasps of breath, and before their unbelieving gaze there stood the child, hat in hand, in the doorway, and it was evident in this moment that in spite of her audible breathing not one of them thought her to be real.

She stood, as it were, transfixed in the frame of the door, held there by their eyes. All the way from the cross-roads her mind had gabbled what she would say. "Oh! Ma," she'd say, "I'm sorry, but I had to come. Oh! Da," she'd say, "I missed you, I had to come. Oh! I did miss you. Oh! Ma," she'd say, "it was awful. . . . And Beatrice and Sister Catherine . . . and I can't go back. I don't care, I can't go back; I want to stay home." But now all that was pressed down by their eyes, and what she said was, "Hello." Just a small whisper, "Hello." The one word went to each of them, saying, "Hello." It made them all tremble in their combined relief at the memory of their fears of the past hours. It was Lizzie who spoke first.

"Child!" she said, "Child!" She flew towards the doorway, and Mary Ann, with a bound now, sprang towards her and flung her arms about her waist. And Lizzie, gazing stupidly down at her head, her hand smoothing her hair, repeated, "Child, child!" She did not ask, "How have you come? Where have you come from? Who have you been with?" but just kept saying, "Child! Child! Child!"

Mr. Lord was standing now by the table. He looked even older than he had done a moment ago, if that were possible. His wrinkled skin was moving in little tremors all over his face and his eyes were blinking as if he had just woken from sleep. Quite suddenly he sat down again. Nor did Michael rush to greet her, but groping behind him he felt for a chair, and he too sat down. This left only Mike.

Across the room Mike looked at Mary Ann, pressed hard against her mother, and a terrible feeling overcame him, a sort of hatred for this flesh of his flesh, this power embodied in the smallness of her, this power, without which, even his wife had said, he was lost. A wife was there to bolster a man, but when she told him the truth it was the truth, as he only too well knew now. He was nothing without his daughter. She had got him a job, a job as manager of a farm, a job beyond his wildest hopes and imaginings. He had imagined he had achieved this all by himself—him, the big, red-headed, burly, one-handed Mike Shaughnessy had secured a grand job with his own ability. But no, he had been given the job because of his child's power. She held the power to take hold of a heart—an old man's heart. And now, because of her, his whole life had been rent; he had been stripped naked, split open and presented to himself; it was as if he was gazing at his bowels and he could not bear the sight of them . . . and all because of her, because she had run away from school. He could see it now. She may have been with a man, but she had come to no harm, she had come in through the door just as if she had returned from school in Jarrow. Just as easy as that. But during the time she had left the convent and arrived in this room, his whole life had altered and he had become old. The first thing the news of her flight had done to him was to press the weight of years on to him. Never again, he felt, would he know what it was to feel young and virile; never would he be able to laugh, to bellow from his belly great sounds of mirth. And then the knowledge that she had bought him the job had stripped him even of his remaining manhood—he was nothing, only something that a child could buy. Inwardly, he had always resented the fact that it was because of her that Mr. Lord had first employed him, but his work on the farm, he felt, had proved his capabilities and carved his own niche. Now he knew that that was only a wishful thought in his mind—he had carved nothing. The old man had said, "Make your da a manager! Well, all right, I'll do it if you go away to school." He had carved nothing.

Mary Ann raised her wet face from her mother's body and looked through blurred vision across the room. There was her da, big as she remembered him. She could only see the outline of him, but now she rushed towards him, muttering, "Da! Oh, Da!" Her hands were outstretched and her body seemed to leap over the distance, but when she clutched at the remembered flesh something happened—she was thrust roughly back. She stood blinking up at him. Her vision cleared and she saw his face, and her mind told her that he was mad, flaming mad. He was vexed with her for running away, that was understandable, but nothing told her that she couldn't get round this. She thrust out her hand to grab his sleeve, and when the blow hit her, her thinking stopped and she became frozen inside. Her stunned mind did not even say, "Me da's hit me!" This was too big for even thought.

As Mike had raised his hand and struck at the fingers clutching at him, Lizzie had gasped and sprung forward. Michael too had gasped, only Mr. Lord remained still. And when Mary Ann, the tears flooding silently down her face, turned for an explanation and looked from one to the other, she saw that all eyes were not on her, but on her da. But no one spoke, no one said, "You shouldn't have done that."

Mr. Lord raised himself slowly from the chair. Not now did he say, "There's no need for that;" not now, as he once had done, did he check Mike from threatening to smack her bottom; instead he appeared indifferent to what might happen to her. His eyes looked at her but did not seem to see her; they rested on her as if he was making a conscious effort to blot her out of his mind, and when he turned from her, she found that for a moment the feeling of horror at the blow her father had given her was lost in a new feeling that made her want to rush to the old man and cry, "Oh! I'm sorry, I didn't mean to do it, but I wanted to come home. I'll tell you all about it and then you'll see." But she said none of these things. She knew Mr. Lord only too well, and her mind told her that he was finished

130

with her, and this thought brought a pain into her body, surprising in its effect, because it was equal to that pain which her da had caused.

As Mr. Lord disappeared through the door Lizzie sank on to a chair. She, too, had felt something of what the old man was experiencing. She did not pay any attention for the moment to her daughter. Only Michael now turned his attention to her, and after staring at her for a moment his face screwed up, trying as it were to associate this small sister with the trouble and agony that had come upon the house, and finding it an impossibility. He turned from her and rushed upstairs, and when his door banged overhead, Mary Ann, shaking with sobs, walked slowly to her mother and put her hand tentatively on her knee, as if to question her welcome in this quarter, too. Lizzie's arms came out, slowly, but steadily, and pulled the child once again into her embrace. And across her head she looked at Mike.

For the first time in his life Mike found he had nothing to say, good or bad, to his daughter. He had threatened to bray her often enough because of her escapades, because of her constant fighting with Sarah Flannagan; now, he hadn't brayed her as a child, but hit her a blow that he would have dealt to a grown-up.

He was standing staring into space, as if he were riveted to the spot on the hearth-rug, and the silence in the kitchen, apart from Mary Ann's sobs, was terrible. As always Lizzie's mind went out like that of a mother to him, and she asked herself over and over again, "What has she done to him? What has she done?" But not only the child was to blame, oh no, she must be fair, she herself had done a lot of damage tonight. Never in a thousand years would she have told him the truth, at least she had thought not, but the events of the night had rent tact and diplomacy from her, and deprived her of all wisdom, and although the relief of having her child back safely was now relieving the tension of her body, once again, as always, she was worrying, worrying about Mike and what would happen next.

Mary Ann's spluttering through her sobs, "I—I—I'm sorry, Ma, I'm sorry," told Lizzie that what she should do now was go for the child, spank her and send her to bed, but she knew that Mary Ann's entire world had dropped apart. Mike had thrust her off; Mr. Lord would have none of her; they weren't even interested in how she had got here—even she herself had forgotten to demand how she had come home, for from the first sight of her she knew that however she had come she was unharmed. She said gently to her, "How did you get here?"

Gulping and sobbing, Mary Ann said, "With Mr. Wilson."

"Mr. Wilson?" Lizzie's face screwed up.

"Yes. You know, the man me da met in the train and told to look after me." She cast her eyes hesitantly towards Mike's averted face. "They were coming back home, and I got into trouble at school and I got your letter, and——" Again her eyes flicked towards Mike, and she said, "I thought—I thought something was wrong. There were marks on it—I thought you were sick."

Puzzled, Lizzie muttered, "Marks on it?" Then rising angrily and almost upsetting Mary Ann off her feet, she exclaimed, "It's him that's at fault! He should be locked up for bringing you. He'd no right."

"He didn't want to, Ma, and Mrs. Wilson neither. She was frightened of the police."

Lizzie, her face set now, demanded, "How did you get here then?"

"He got my ticket, and we got off at Durham. Mrs. Wilson wouldn't come through in the train, and we got the workmen's night bus from Durham. They put me off at the corner."

Just as simple as that. Mr. Wilson got her ticket; they got off at Durham; took the night bus and put her off at the corner, and in a few minutes here she was; and the agonies, the passions, the crucifixions of each of them were explained away in those few words. . . . But Mike?

Over Lizzie flooded an overwhelming sense of helplessness. Now she had another situation to cope with —Mike. Before, the situations concerning him had been mostly one-sided. She'd known their substance; Mary Ann had known their substance; and they both, as it were, had worked together for his good, leaving Mike happy in his male fantasy. But now the covers had been ripped off—Mike would be gulled no more, always he would be on his guard. His rejection of the child showed her the depth to which his hurt had gone. She didn't lay it all down to false pride, she knew that he himself had thought the worst had happened to her this night, and his relief in part had taken this form of rejection. And so, thinking that if he were left alone with the child it might help, she turned to Mary Ann and said, "Go on to the fire, I'll go up and get your bed ready."

When her mother had left the room, Mary Ann stood, her fingers in her mouth, looking towards the door through which Lizzie had disappeared. She did not turn to Mike; he still seemed frozen and unable to move, only the movement of his eyes showed his brain was working rapidly.

Mary Ann, never being able to bear silences at any time, was finding this one almost excruciating in its loudness. Her fingers still in her mouth, she turned slowly round and looked at her da's profile. Her da had hit her—and hard. Her hand hurt, her arm hurt. Some part of her told her that she deserved all she had got, and more, but she still could not get over the surprise that he had lifted his hand to her, for she had expected wide-open arms ready to greet her, she had imagined herself flinging herself against him, hanging on to his hair, kissing his face and watching his eyes moving over her features in the way she loved. Now, in spite of herself and the fear of another repulse, she moved towards him, and when she was at his side, with her first finger and thumb tentatively extended, she gently nipped the sleeve of his coat, and in a very, very, small voice, she muttered, "Da, I'm sorry." And then, as with her old apologies, she added, "I won't do it again."

The implied probability of a recurrence of this particular incident seemed to rouse Mike, and he moved his feet in a grating gesture. Her downcast eyes became fixed on them. She dare not look up into his face, but she waited for his hand to come on her head. And after a while, when it didn't, she slowly raised her eyes upwards. He was still mad, very mad, but it was a different kind from any she had ever witnessed before. He didn't look the same as she'd remembered him and, a trembling, terror-riddled feeling told her, he wasn't the same. This feeling urged her to cry out, and now she flung herself against his legs, with her arms round his thighs, crying, "Da! Oh, Da!"

He did not push her away, but he did not fondle her. What he might have done within the next minute cannot be known, for at that moment Tony entered the room. On the sound of footsteps, Mike turned his head, and across the room his eyes met the young man's.

Tony's entry seemed now an excuse that he turn from her, and without a word he left the kitchen and went out into the night.

Tony stood looking across the table at the bowed head of Mary Ann. In the short time that he had been on the farm he had learned of this child's influence. He had only known her for a few hours, and thought her a taking—a fetching little mite. He liked these people—especially did he like Mike—and over the last few weeks it had hurt him to see the tenseness between him and his wife. Furthermore, since six o'clock last night their suffering had torn at his own heart, for, although he hadn't shown it, he, too, had thought only the worst could happen. And now apparently, from Mike's attitude, nothing of a very serious nature had happened, at least to her.

He had learned that she was a little devil for her escapades; he had taken it that she was an individualist of the first order; and now he had no doubt whatever about it, for after all the upset, here she was unscathed. Yet something about her touched him, she looked so forlorn, so very small, and however she had gone about the business of coming home, she had got here and that was an achievement for anyone of her size and age. So he went to her, and putting his hand on her head, he said, "There now, don't cry."

Snuffling she looked up at him, "Me da's mad at me."

He smiled a little smile. "Well, do you expect him to be anything else? You've had everybody very, very

134

worried. . . . Do you know they were broadcasting on the wireless about you?"

Did a little bit of excitement flicker across her sorrow-laden face? Something very like it came over in her voice as she exclaimed quickly, "The wireless? Me?"

"Yes, the whole country's been looking for you."

Again she exclaimed, "Me?"

He nodded solemnly. "They thought you might have come to some harm." Not wishing to explain what he meant by harm he added, "It's a long way."

Blinking, sniffing and gulping, she looked away from him towards the fireplace, and said flatly, "I wouldn't come to no harm, I had a St. Christopher medal in me pocket."

This simple statement of faith caused his eyebrows to rise. . . . She would come to no harm because she was carrying on her person a piece of tin, depicting the saint who was supposedly a protector of travellers! The simplicity, the profundity of this small child's faith amazed him and caused the feeling of bitterness which he was rarely without, to rise and swamp him again in something like envy now, for never could he remember even as a child having faith.

When a fresh spasm of sobbing began to shake her and her head drooped once more, and she slipped her small hands between her knees and pressed them together, he bent swiftly down and lifted her up and placed her on his knee, saying, "Ssh! be quiet. There now. There now."

Desperately, she turned her face into his chest, as she had hoped to do in Mike's, but without any of the feeling of comfort she would have experienced from contact with her da. It was all so different from what she had expected; her da would have nothing to do with her; nor their Michael; and Mr. Lord was finished with her; even her ma, knowing she was feeling bad, had left her to go upstairs. . . . The fact that of all the people in the house only this boy had stayed with her added to her bottomless sadness, for, as she thought of it, he didn't belong to them. She liked him all right, she had liked him on that first day, but he wasn't her da, her ma, their Michael, or Mr. Lord.

Her crying mounting, she pressed her mouth hard against his shirt, and with his arms about her he sat stroking her head, until Lizzie, like someone sleep-walking, returned to the kitchen and, showing no surprise at finding Mike gone, carried her upstairs.

8

Twenty hours precisely had elapsed since Mary Ann's dramatic return, and they had been filled with everything contrary to what she had expected. She had talked to more policemen than ever she thought had existed. And not policemen as she knew them, but just in their ordinary clothes. And even men from newspapers. These men wouldn't believe that she didn't know Mr. Wilson's address. Had she known it and was trying to protect him she would surely have failed under their battery of questions. Mr. Wilson was going to get wrong, and she didn't want Mr. Wilson to get wrong. Mr. Wilson was nice, so was Mrs. Wilson, but it was Mr. Wilson, and he alone, who had brought her home. The day had been filled with talk, but no one had spoken to her personally, no one had spoken to her as if she was Mary Ann Shaughnessy. Her mother had said, "Eat your dinner," "Eat your tea"; their Michael had avoided her eyes; her da had not spoken at all; and she hadn't seen Mr. Lord. Only Tony had talked to her, or let her remain with him, but as yet in her mind he wasn't in the circle of the family, he was just "the hand".

And now she was lying in bed, wide awake, her eyes staring and blinking at the sloping ceiling, listening to her ma and da fighting, fighting quietly in the kitchen.

Like the wind at night, their voices rose and fell at intervals. From time to time she had strained to hear what they were saying, but couldn't; now, when her da's voice rose high for an instant and she heard him crying plainly, "I'll do what I bloody well like," she found herself out of bed and on the landing at the top of the stairs, listening, as was her old habit, feeling that she must know the torments of her parents and seeing their every move in her mind's eye.

Down in the kitchen, Lizzie sat by the table, automatically pushing her plate an inch first one way and then another, her eyes following its course as if it were something of deep interest. When Mike had yelled at her she hadn't answered, and now he was standing, his foot on the fender, his arm on the mantelpiece, his fingers beating a tattoo that seemed to fill the room with their angry, rebellious thumping.

Addressing her plate, she said quietly, "Whether you believe it or not, you've always done what you like."

"Aye, you've let me think I was doing what I like. You were very clever, Liz, but now all that's finished. I thought I was a man with a mind of me own and knew where I was going, but all the time you've been leading me—leading me through her. Well, that's over, I'm giving up. There are other jobs besides this, thank God, and I'll get one, but I'll get it on me own. Do you hear?" He turned round to her, his voice rising again, "I'll get it on me own, under me own steam. Under me own steam, d'you hear? Propelled by no woman or bairn." He paused, glaring at her downcast head. Then he flung out his hand at her, "Don't you realise —don't you see I've got to do things on me own?"

He watched her head sink lower towards the plate and his voice sank, too, as he said, "You used to understand—you knew me at one time better than I did meself. Perhaps that's what you did this for, manoeuvred her to manoeuvre me. You might have done it for the best, but. . . ."

Lizzie lifted her head. "I've never manoeuvred her. Whether you like to believe it or not the manoeuvring's been between the two of you. I couldn't come between you, not even if I'd wanted to. And now you're thrusting her off, not because of what she's done, but because of your own vanity. You always want to be the big fellow, don't you? Well, when you're thrusting her off you're thrusting yourself off because you're afraid to see yourself, because she's you, every bit of her. All her fighting, all her unthinking actions, the idea that she's only got to make her case plain and everything will be all right—that's you, you all over. And I'm telling you this, if you don't relent you'll be sorry. You always say you are like the elephant, well, so is she—she doesn't forget. She's likely to get over this if you drop it now, but if you keep it up, this silence, this putting her away, you'll live to regret it. I'm telling you, you'll live to regret it, for there are others, and I don't need to mention any names, who will be only too willing, even after what she's done, to step into your shoes."

Mike was in the act of turning away, and now he flung himself round at her and the words "Nobody can take her from me, the old boy nor nobody else" spurted into his mouth, but he didn't say them, he simply stared his anger at her. Since he had seen the child enter the door last night he had pulled down an iron shutter on his feelings for her and was refusing, even at this distance of hours, to recognize that they were beating for release against the barricade. But now the insinuation of the old man into the battle again brought his love bashing and crashing out of himself. He knew the agony of last night would leave an indelible stain on his mind, in fact it would alter the course of his life from now on; because of what had come to light through it he would be suspicious of every action of both Lizzie's and the child's for his welfare; he would fight to go his own road, fight for his right to support them all on his own merits, fight for the right to feel himself a man, his kind of man, his idea of a man, be what it may.

Instead of the words that were filling his mouth, he said, "And you think the old fellow will still have an interest in her after this, after all his high-falutin plans for her are brought low? Old Ma Flannagan said that you couldn't make a silk purse out of a sow's ear, and she's right. And you think the old fellow would be interested in the sow's ear? No, not if I know him. He had a prodigy in her, someone he thought he could mould, but he picked the wrong clay, she'll never be

138

moulded by him or anybody else. . . . All right—if you like, she's like me. She'll remain herself, and to hell with the old man and his power, and his money, and his dictating, and that's what I'll tell him when I see him the morrow."

Lizzie's head jerked up and her eyes became startled, and seeing her fear he now became cruel and said, "Oh, don't worry; you won't starve, I'll get a job that will support you. I suppose you know Polinski's going? He's going as far as Dorset. Foreman he's going as. Told me only the day. And they're wanting a manager on that farm an' all." His eyes narrowed. "How would it be if I put in for it? I wouldn't be separated from her then, would I?" He paused. "That's another thing we've got to get straight, isn't it?"

Lizzie's eyes were stretched, very like Mary Ann's when surprised by pain, but she made no retort at all, she merely rose and with her hand pressed to her mouth went towards the door. She didn't reach it, however, for in a couple of strides Mike had her by the shoulders and had swung her round, and his arm pinning her to him, he was talking into her hair, crying, "Liz! Oh Liz! My God! what's come over us? Listen, Liz. Listen. Forget about the child. I'll deal with that. I'll deal with the old boy an' all—nothing can alter what I'm going to do. But about the Polinskis. My God! Liz, believe me on this; I would much sooner have thought of starting something with old Ma Jones than I would with that young, dirty piece. And I mean what I say, dirty in all ways . . . lazy, a lazy good-for-nowt. But Liz, she was the wife of one of the men, and I liked Polinski and was sorry for him. And, aye God! I was sorry for her. I knew what was the matter with her, Polinski didn't suit her. She wanted a man, any man who hadn't his whole mind as Polinski had on the farm and getting on. I laughed with her, cos I knew her game, and I laughed at her, that's all, Liz. Liz, where's your conceit—her against you. Oh no!" His arm tightened still further around her, and helplessly now she began to sob, and the sobs filled the house.

Mary Ann was leaning against the banister, all her fingers in her mouth. The tears slipping softly from her lashes were missing the wells of her eyes to drop on to

139

her cheek-bones and roll heavily to her chin. They were kind, they were kind to each other again. That's all that mattered, nothing else mattered, not the policemen, or the men from the newspapers, or which school she was going to, or her da leaving the farm and getting another job. They were kind, nothing mattered. She stumbled into the bedroom and into bed, and lying down she stuck the corner of the sheet into her mouth, and in a short while fell asleep.

The following morning Michael couldn't go to school, he had a fever. His body was hot, his hands were hot, and he wanted nothing to eat. Lizzie sat on the side of his bed and pushed his wet hair back from his brow. She knew that something was worrying him—she knew her son better than she did her daughter—and she said, "What is it? Tell me, what is it?"

She had asked this a number of times during the past few hours, but he had just tossed his head. And now he did it again. Then, when she did not persist in her enquiries, he swung himself round and burying his face in the pillow muttered something brokenly, and she bent her head to hear, and said, "Yes? Go on, tell me what's happened."

Slowly he turned his face so that he was looking into her eyes, and muttered, "I was to blame for her coming back like that."

"You?" Lizzie pressed her head away from him to see him better, and again repeated, "You?" as though she thought the fever was causing a slight delirium.

Snuffling, he nodded. "I wrote and told her." His eyes dropped. "I wrote and told her that I thought ——" He paused again; then suddenly sitting up in bed and holding his knees tight and dropping his head on to them he ended, "I told her about Mrs. Polinski."

"Oh, Michael!" Lizzie was aghast. "Oh, you shouldn't have done that. Oh, Michael."

She was about to add, "But how did you know?" when she checked herself. How could he not know? How could anyone not know what went on in the house, they were all so closely knit together? She bent towards him and put her arm around him, saying, "You only did what you thought was right. You missed her, like all of us. And if she had been here there would never have been any mention of Mrs. Polinski. And I must tell you now, Michael"—she raised his head and looked into his eyes, demanding by her look that he believed her—"that was my fault, not your da's. It was my imagining things. I was lonely for her an' all. Look"—she now put her hand under his chin and raised his face—"do something for me, will you? Go and tell your da what you've told me."

She felt him shrink from her, and she pleaded, "It'll be all right. You see, things have been said. I've said things I shouldn't have. It was all through the worry of this business—and I've upset him terribly. Do this for me, Michael. Tell him it was your fault . . . you wrote and told her about things that you shouldn't have. He won't blame her so much then."

She saw that he was making a great effort to conquer the fear of confessing to his father his share in the trouble.

"But will he wallop me?" he asked softly.

"Oh, no!" said Lizzie hastily. "Of course he won't wallop you. Anyway, I'll see he doesn't. He'll be only too pleased to know that all the blame isn't hers. Come on now, get up and go down to the farm."

Lizzie left him, and as he dressed he asked himself as he had done dozens of times since last night if he had really told her anything in his letters. Sometimes he thought he had and sometimes he defended himself flatly by saying, "I never said a thing about me da going with Mrs. Polinski."

Michael's bewilderment was caused by his failing to realize that he had the kind of sister who never read what was on the lines but the substance that lay between them. . . .

Mary Ann had wandered aimlessly about for hours. She was home, she was on the farm. There were the cows, the bull, the young calves, the hens, the ducks, the geese, everything that she had longed to see again, yet now they held no interest for her. She had looked into the cowshed and met the cold stare of Mr. Jones. Mr. Jones had looked at her as if he could have walloped her, and Mrs. Jones, from the backyard, had not waved to her. Len had grinned at her and exclaimed, in awe-filled tones, "Eeh! by, you're not half a star!" Mrs. Polinski had looked at her coldly. Mrs. Polinski looked different, older than when she had last seen her, and she realized that she not only disliked Mrs. Polinski, she hated her. Another time she would have felt the strong desire to stick her tongue out at Mrs. Polinski, but today she just turned her head away and made for the barn.

Then she saw her da was in the barn—she saw his back bending over the bales—but she did not go to him. There was something high and unscalable between her and her da and she knew that she could do nothing herself to surmount it, so slowly and sadly she turned away and walked up the hill towards Mr. Lord's house. But only because she knew that Mr. Lord wasn't in it. She had seen him depart for Newcastle in the car earlier on. Although Mr. Lord was now living in the house and the men had been and put up fine curtains at the windows, the house itself looked raw and unfinished. All around lay mounds of bricks and mortar and builders' refuse. Slowly, as if picking her way over new territory, she walked round to the back entrance, impressed, in spite of herself, by the grandeur she glimpsed through the long, low windows. She would have loved to go inside but she felt, in fact she knew at this moment, that she would never, never be asked inside Mr. Lord's house.

As she reached what was to be a walled courtyard with a pool in the middle, the place as yet merely roughly dug out, she saw Ben come out of the glass kitchen-door. Ben stopped when he saw her, and his grave and forbidding countenance, which had once frightened her to death, did not soften, nor even did it take on a sign of recognition. Ben was a reflection of his master, he was not seeing Mary Ann. Within a minute he had returned through the glass door, and Mary Ann hurried out of the yard and made her way down the hill again, her fingers now, one after the other in turn, being pressed into her mouth, and her mind crying at all these people in her own defence, "I wasn't to blame all the time . . . I wasn't. It was Mrs.

Polinski and our Michael and that Beatrice, and Sister Catherine . . . I wasn't to blame, I wasn't. I don't care if nobody ever speaks to me, I don't care. Me ma's all right. Me ma's not like them. I don't care—I don't."

As she reached the gate near the farm, she saw across the yard a car draw up at the main gates, and she thought, "Them men again." This description covered policemen and newspaper reporters, but when she saw stepping from the car not only one of "them men" but also Mr. and Mrs. Wilson, she clapped both hands over her mouth. An urge bid her fly to her old friends but reason prevailed and she turned and dived behind the big barn, across an open space to the little barn, and dashed into its cool dimness and stood with her back to the wall, her whole body trembling. There would be a row, there was bound to be another row, and Mr. Wilson would get wrong. Eeh!

"And now what's the matter?"

She swung round, startled to see Tony. He was standing near a number of old, battered and belabelled trunks, and she went to him swiftly and said, "It's Mr. and Mrs. Wilson, they've just come." She stared at him for a moment then added, "There'll be a row."

"No there won't. It'll be all right. Stop trembling now." He took her hand and bent his face to hers and smiled, an unusually wide smile that momentarily took all the brooding sombreness from it. "What'll you bet that this time next week everybody's forgotten about the whole affair?"

She stared up at him. "They won't forget, cos nobody's speaking to me. But I don't care. . . . If only me——"

She didn't go on to say that she didn't care if nobody spoke to her again if only her da would, but Tony seemed to be able already to read her mind, and to understand Mike, and he said, "Don't worry, this time tomorrow you and your da'll be like—that." He crossed his long, lean fingers and held them up for her inspection and comfort. And she stared at them trying to see herself and her da joined again like them, but she couldn't and her head drooped and once again she started to cry.

"Come along, don't cry. Dry your eyes. You'll be back at your old school next week. You'll like that, won't you?"

Her tears stopped quite suddenly, cut off as it were by this small shock, and she jerked her head up towards him and repeated, "Old school?"

"Yes, don't you want to go back to your old school?"

She looked away from him around the barn, stocked with things that she had not noticed in it before. Old rubbish, she thought, from Mr. Lord's other house—trunks and cases and boxes. School . . . her old school . . . Going back to her school in Jarrow, she found, did not bring her any comfort at all—it could be said she abhorred the thought. Sarah Flannagan and all them, jeering at her. For the first time she asked herself what she had done, and answered quite truthfully, "Eeh! I must have been daft," and the convent, from which up to a moment ago she was glad she had escaped, now appeared to her as something personal and valuable she had lost. And all through Mrs. Polinski and their Michael, and that Beatrice and Sister Catherine. But what school would she go to if she didn't go to Jarrow? She knew that Mr. Lord would send her to no other school. Mr. Lord was finished with her good and proper, there would be no forgiveness forthcoming from Mr. Lord. If he had been mad and stormed at her she would have had some hope, but no, Mr. Lord's silence was as final as death.

She was startled by Tony's next question. It was as if he had a looking-glass on her mind, for he said, musingly, "Do you like Mr. Lord?"

Her voice was very small and low, "I used to."

"He's been very good to you, hasn't he?"

Her conscience was heavy, and it weighed her head down as she murmured, "Yes."

"He's not good to many people, is he?"

She raised her eyes slantwise to him. "No, I don't think so; he's bad-tempered."

"And cold and hard as iron inside."

Now her eyes were wide and staring. Tony's face had taken on not only his solemn expression, but a hard, bitter look that made him suddenly appear old, and not a little frightening to her. She saw that his eyes were blazing, and she watched him lift his foot and savagely kick at one of the trunks. Then her eyes widened as she heard him swear under his breath, using bad words, as bad as any she had heard her da use, like, "Damn him to blazes!" "Who the hell!" and "Blast him!" The only difference was he said them swanky.

Eeh! it was Mr. Lord he was at. He didn't like Mr. Lord. Mr. Lord had been at him, but to kick the boxes like that and to swear!

As if remembering her presence, he turned to her, his face still dark but his voice normal, saying, "I'm sorry, Mary Ann. Don't take any notice. I'm like you, I take the needle."

She slid off the box and, looking up at him, she asked as one sufferer to another, "Has he been getting at you?"

A smile that had no movement in it came into his eyes, and she thought, "He looks nice—sad-like, but I like him." And when he nodded, she said, as if in comfort, "Never mind, he's always getting at somebody." Yet as she said this she felt somehow that she was betraying a trust.

"Yes, he's always getting at somebody."

He turned away towards the door, and she fancied she heard him mutter, "He always has." And she thought, That's funny. What's he carrying on for? He hasn't been here very long. She felt that she had known Mr. Lord for ever, not just one year, while Tony, although he was "nice", was really a newcomer on the scene. She watched him walk away, then stop abruptly, grope in his pocket, then turn and come back to her.

"There's only three left. You like Buttered Brazils?"

"Yes. Oh, ta. Oh, Buttered Brazils!"

Buttered Brazils were far and away above her finances, and she said again, "Oh, ta." Then it struck her that she shouldn't say "Ta" to him, because he didn't talk like she did, he talked like them back at the convent. She looked at him now with new interest in her eyes. And he was like them back at the convent. She had noticed something different about him at dinner time when she sat opposite him at the table. The way he sat, the way he ate, the way he talked to her ma. Yes, he was like them at the convent. She said now, "Thanks," in her politest tone, and he smiled down at her for a moment, before moving away. She thought again, He's nice, and not because he had given her some sweets. Mrs. Polinski gave her sweets, but she didn't think Mrs. Polinski was nice—but he was. She became very firm in her mind about this. She liked him—he was nice.

Thinking it policy to do so, she stayed in the barn for what seemed to her hours, not making a move to go outside until she heard from the distance the sound of the car starting up. And then, in spite of her relief, she felt a tinge of disappointment that nobody had come in search of her and a touch of curiosity as to why they hadn't.

When the fading *brr!* on the road told her the car was safely speeding away she walked into the yard again, around the big barn, and towards the house. There was no sign of her da or her ma, the whole place looked deserted, as if everyone had gone away in the car. But as she neared the back door she heard her mother's voice, and the words that came to her told her she wasn't speaking to her da, and for a moment Mary Ann was riveted to the spot. Not her grannie, not to-day, she couldn't bear it if her grannie was here today.

"It wasn't really her fault," Lizzie was saying; "she should never have been sent in the first place."

Mary Ann, with her hand pressed tight to her chest, waited, and when the thick North-Country twang came bouncing out to her, "Yer right there, Liz. Aa've said it all along, it was a mad thing to do, separating her from him," a feeling akin to a great laugh swept over her, and she raced through the scullery and into the kitchen, crying, "Mrs. McBride! Oh, Mrs. McBride!"

Mrs. McBride's ox-like arms opened, and Mary Ann flung herself against her billowing bust, and the old woman cried, "Ah! hinny, it's good to see ye. Aw! it is, it is. Here, let me hev a look at ya. Stand away." She pushed Mary Ann to arm's length; then nodding her head and without a word of reprimand on her tongue,

146

she said, "You're grown. You're grown up in the last few months."

"Have I, Mrs. McBride?"

"Ya have that, hasn't she, Liz?" The old woman looked up at Lizzie, and Lizzie, smiling for the first time in days, said, "Yes, I think she has, a little bit."

"When did you come, Mrs. McBride?"

"Just a minute ago, hinny."

"How?" Mary Ann was eager for details.

"By the bus, of course—me car isn't ready yet. But it will be soon, it's being made to measure!" She punched Mary Ann playfully and Mary Ann laughed and grabbed at her hand and said, "Oh, Mrs. McBride!"

There was so much feeling in Mary Ann's tone as she spoke her old friend's name that Lizzie turned away and went into the scullery to fill the kettle, and Mrs. McBride said, with a tremor in her voice, "So you're back, me bairn?"

Mary Ann's face sobered, and she nodded solemnly.

The old woman touched her cheek and, shaking her head and with a smile spreading over her fat wrinkled face, she said, "Eeh! ye know what? it's a good job there are not two in the world like you, or else we would be in a state, wouldn't we?"

At this, Mary Ann moved into the comfort of the old woman's knees, and tracing her finger around Mrs. McBride's frayed and rusty coat sleeve, and with one eye cocked upwards that held just a trace of amusement in it, she said, "There was a nun like you in the convent, Mrs. McBride."

The shout that filled the kitchen brought Lizzie to the door, and Mrs. McBride, her hands in the air, bellowed to her, "Have you heard this 'un?"

Lizzie, smiling, shook her head.

"There's a nun like me! Can you see that, Liz?"

Again Lizzie shook her head and her smile broadened, and Mary Ann, looking from one to the other of the women, for the first time in days, laughed freely. "But there was, Ma. It was Sister Alvis; she talked like Mrs. McBride, and she looked like her."

The roar filled the kitchen again, and Fanny cried,

"Well, I've been likened to many things, and everything on the farm from a heifer to a cow in——" She rubbed her finger across her nose and did not finish her description, but cried, "And many more things I've been likened to. But a nun! Begod, I'm going up in the world. What do you say, Liz, eh? A nun. Eeh! Oh, hinny!" She touched Mary Ann's cheek tenderly. "That's imagination for you. God help her, poor woman, if she was like me."

"She was, Mrs. McBride, and I liked her."

"Bless you, bairn."

"Mrs. McBride——" Mary Ann started playing with the buttons on the old woman's blouse as she said, "You know something? I can speak French and German."

"No! French and German?"

"Yes, I learnt it at the convent."

"Go on, let's hear you."

Mary Ann considered a moment, then said very slowly, as if each word was being dragged from as far away as the convent, "Nous avons—une grande maison —et—un beau jardin. . . . Je vive—avec ma mère et mon père. That's me ma and da, that last bit."

"Your ma and da in French? God in Heaven! D'ye hear that, Liz? That's what education does for you. Makes you into a foreigner." She laughed. "Go on, tell us some more."

"German?"

"Aye, German. Oh my, you can speak German an' all?"

Mary Ann, all woes forgotten for the moment, and in an accent that was more Geordie than German, was telling her friend that this was her brother Hans, and Mrs. McBride's eyes were stretching to a complimentary width when an alarmed exclamation of, "Oh, no!" from Lizzie made them both look towards the window.

Lizzie was carrying a tray full of tea things which she now held stiffly suspended, and her gaze was fixed on something outside. Again she exclaimed, "Oh, no!" then quickly turning she looked across the room and said, "Your grannie!"

"Me grannie?" Mary Ann had pulled herself from Mrs. McBride, and Mrs. McBride exclaimed, "Oh, God

148

in Heaven, not her! How did she get here, she wasn't on the bus?"

Lizzie wearily putting down the tray on the table said, "She sported a taxi seemingly."

Mary Ann could say nothing. She looked from her mother to Mrs. McBride, then towards the door, but she did not attempt to make her usual escape. She was experiencing very much the same feeling as she had done when she had been confronted by Beatrice at the door of the recreation room. She felt tied to the room, to the spot. She turned towards a chair and sat down. She had no fight in her with which to combat what was surely coming from her grannie, and all for her, exclusively for her.

Within a minute, there came a sharp rat-tat on the front door, and walking heavily Lizzie went to open it, while Mrs. McBride arranged herself as if ready for battle. She opened her coat, smoothed down her skirt, hitched up her enormous bust, then folded her arms under it, while Mary Ann, from her chair, kept her eyes on the door.

As Mrs. McMullen's strident voice was heard from the hall, Fanny hissed across to Mary Ann, "Don't look like that, that's not you. Give her as good as she sends. Go on, up with that chin of yours."

With an effort Mary Ann lifted up her head, and as soon as her grannie entered the room she made herself look straight into her face. The look seemed to hold Mrs. McMullen, and she stopped and stared back at her grandchild. Then, with her eyes slowly drawing to slits, she gave a pregnant exclamation.

"Ah!" she said. Then looking towards Mrs. McBride, she added, "Huh!" and Fanny, her face and voice amiable, replied, "Aye, huh! We're all out the day, eh, like Flannagan's Fleas."

Mrs. McMullen, wearing a stately dignity, moved to the big chair near the fire. "You must speak for yourself, Mrs. McBride, I am visiting my daughter."

Now it was Fanny's turn to say, "Huh!"

"Will you have a cup of tea, Mother?" Lizzie stood near the tray, and Mrs. McMullen with raised eyebrows, said, "Well, I should think that goes without saying after this journey."

149

"Was your journey really necessary?" Fanny, trying to imitate a refined twang, muttered this under her breath, and it brought into Mary Ann's worried being a little gurgle of laughter. Oh, Mrs. McBride was funny. Oh, she was glad she was here. Her grannie wouldn't start on her surely, not in front of Mrs. McBride . . . she'd hold her tongue for a while.

But Mary Ann had misjudged her grannie's powers of self-control, for no sooner had she received a cup of tea from Lizzie's slightly shaking hand than she turned her eyes on her grand-daughter and again gave her pregnant exclamation, then added, "So you're back!"

Mary Ann said nothing, she only looked at her grannie, and her grannie began to stir her tea while she peered down into the cup. Then without raising her eyes she said, "I suppose now that you've had the whole country on the alert for you you're feeling fine. Trust you to draw attention to yourself."

Mary Ann's eyes slid to her mother and Mrs. McBride and then back to her grannie. She had found no help in the sight of her ma's shoulders stooped over the tray, nor from Mrs. McBride's face which seemed to be expressionless—she had no one to rely on but herself. But the forced proximity to her grannie was restoring her fighting feeling. Her grannie's words were now stinging her all over, like hailstones.

"I suppose, as usual, you were greeted with open arms and patted on the head, and told what a clever girl you were, eh?"

There was a clatter of cups as Lizzie moved the tray, and there was a wriggle of Mrs. McBride's hips as Mrs. McMullen went on, "And I suppose the big fellow said 'Well done'? Like father like daughter!"

"Mother, I'm having none of this. It's finished, it's all over. If you want to stay, please forget it."

Mrs. McMullen reared her head so high that it looked as if her hat was going to topple off the top of her abundant hair as she said, "Am I getting the door again?"

"There's no need to talk about the door, Mother. Only leave her be, she's been through enough."

"Huh! huh!" Mrs. McMullen sipped her tea then

150

exclaimed bitterly, "You were always soft with her—like clarts."

There came a deep sigh from Fanny and she exclaimed quietly, "Well, in this case, it isn't like mother like daughter, is it? Eh?"

Mrs. McMullen turned her haughty gaze on Fanny, and replied icily, "I didn't think I was addressing you, Mrs. McBride."

"No," said Fanny, "neither did I. But tell me"—she leaned towards Mrs. McMullen—"tell me, what do you think of this fine job your son-in-law's landed? Isn't this one great, big, grand farm?"

"I am not in the habit of discussing my family's business with outsiders." Mrs. McMullen put down her cup and folded her hands.

"No. Only when you want to kick them in the backside, Mike in particular, with old Ma Flannagan." Fanny's voice was hard.

"Look," said Lizzie, her eyes darting between her mother and Mrs. McBride, "I want no more of this, one way or the other."

There was silence in the kitchen for a moment, during which Mrs. McMullen stood up and deliberately took off her coat and hat. Then sitting down again and unable to restrain her tongue or curiosity, she asked of Lizzie, "Well, and what's going to happen to her now? You can't tell me that the old boy will have any more interest in her after this. She's made him the laughing stock of the country." There was another tense pause, and Mrs. McMullen slowly turned around to meet Mary Ann's eyes. "Jarrow school, I suppose again, and serve you right. I hope you have a nice time when you meet Sarah Flannagan and the rest of them. I wouldn't like to be in your shoes when you go back there!"

"I'm not going back!" The words seemed squeezed out of Mary Ann's throat.

"Oh!" Mrs. McMullen's head bounced slowly. "And where are you going, pray?"

"I'm going to another school—a better one." Mary Ann's nose was twitching, a sure sign of her inner agitation. "Bigger—nicer."

The wishful thinking was only all too plain to her

grannie, and she laughed as she said, "You've got some hopes. If I heard aright, the old boy's washed his hands of you, and not you alone by all accounts. No, not you alone!"

Mary Ann knew instinctively who the "not you alone" meant. That meant her da. She was saying that Mr. Lord had washed his hands of her da. Her grannie was a liar. Her grannie was bad, wicked—the Devil. Yes, that's who her grannie was, the Devil dressed up! She wished she would have a fit and die in it.

And her grannie's next words caused Mary Ann to make an effort to bring her wishful thinking into operation. For just as Mrs. McMullen was placing her empty cup on the table she made a statement. "It's the case of the sow's ear all over again," she said.

No one was more startled than Mrs. McMullen as a sample of concentrated fury flung itself at her, and before her flabby hand could prevent it happening, her cheek was scratched in several places.

What followed was a good five minutes of sheer pandemonium, during which Mrs. McMullen poured her vitriolic venom into the air of the kitchen and Lizzie held the struggling and screaming child, while Mrs. McBride, yelling her loudest at Mrs. McMullen, and that was saying something, told her what she had thought of her, not only for the last year or so either, but from the time they had been girls together in the neighbourhood of Jarrow.

When at last Lizize managed to quieten Mary Ann's screams, she picked her up in her arms and made for the stairs, and just as she reached them Mike came hurrying into the kitchen. He stood for a second on the threshold, taking in the whole situation, then growled, "What's going on here? You can hear you all over the farm!" His eyes moved swiftly from Mary Ann in her mother's arms to his mother-in-law's bleeding face, and he spoke directly to her, cutting off her own tirade just as she was about to flood him with it. "We always get what we ask for. For my part I can say it's a pity it wasn't the other side an' all." Then moving across the room, he addressed Fanny briefly by saying, "Hello, there, Fan."

"Hello, Mike," said Fanny, just as briefly.

Then when he reached the door he gathered up Mary
Ann from Lizzie's arms and went up the stairs.

9

Father Owen was very weary. He sat in the confessional box, his hand shading his eyes and only half
listening, it must be confessed, to Jimmy Hathaway's
confession. Jimmy had made the same confession for as
many years as Father Owen cared to remember. It began, "Drunk, three times last week, Father . . . very
sorry." Only the number of times he had erred ever
varied. It could be as many as six or as few as one, but
whatever the number his reactions to his lapse were
always the same, and his way of confessing it never
varied. "Knocked her about a bit, Father."

It was as well, Father Owen sometimes thought, that
Peggy Hathaway could not become any dafter. Jimmy
Hathaway was beyond hope, and, years before, the
priest had given up any idea of earthly redemption for
him, but this had not stopped him from trying to save
his soul. But tonight he dismissed him without even the
usual advice, with only a curt, "One Our Father and
ten Hail Mary's," wondering as he did so, if they would
ever be said.

Father Owen sighed as he heard Jimmy stumbling
out of the box, and when next a thin whine came to him
he repeated his sigh. It was a bad night, all the hopeless
cases of the parish seemed to have got together at once.
This penitent, he knew, was Mrs. Leggatt. Although he
did not know what would be forthcoming in Mrs. Leggatt's confession, he knew her well enough to expect
nothing but a tirade of petty spite and pilfering, and
his mind said, "Oh dear, dear!" Altogether, it had been
a trying day.

Father Beaney had been at his most pompous, his most patronising, his most overbearing. Of course he knew that his superior's attitude had been invoked by the young curate. The newcomer had tested his own nerves, for what was more putting off to a man in his sixties than a warm-blooded enthusiast out to outdo even God Himself . . . out to reform all human nature in his own way . . . which was the best way, of course, being the latest way. Oh, yes, between Father Beaney and God's latest lieutenant, he'd been sorely tried this day. And not only today, but all the week. And this had brought about his own lapse. Only in extreme emergencies did he allow himself a double dose of his "cough mixture" before retiring. His weak will had tempted him to tell himself that the events of the week could be constituted an emergency. His patron saint, Miss Honeysett, his housekeeper, and the good God, together allowed him one glass, but at times he was apt to ignore all three and take a second helping of his comforter . . . his conscience didn't trouble him so much at night, for the flesh was warmed and weak then. But in the morning it was a different kettle of fish, for then it loomed at the side of his bed, looking at him, nodding its head and saying, "The LINO penance for you, me boy—the LINO penance for you." To an outsider the lino penance might seem so light as to be no penance at all, but when one of the things you have been unable to stand during the whole course of your life is your bare feet on cold linoleum, what more harsh treatment could a conscience extract from you but bid you get out of a warm bed and put your feet on to slabs of ice and to keep them there while you dressed—and the blood in your veins already like water. Oh, it had been a trying day. What was that? He pricked his ears up as Mrs. Leggatt's voice whimpered, "And it wasn't gold at all, Father, so I didn't feel so bad about it. Six shillings I got on it; that was all."

"Have you taken it back?"

"No, Father."

"And you come here expecting absolution?"

There was no answer from Mrs. Leggatt.

"Now away with you, and go and get that brooch out

of pawn, and when you have returned it to its owner you can come back and we'll discuss the matter further. Away you go now."

Father Owen sounded angry. He was angry. Would they never learn?

He heard Mrs. Leggatt's heavy breathing and noticed, not without some satisfaction, that she tripped heavily on leaving the box. God had His ways.

His hand was again covering his eyes when the door opened and the usual shuffle to the kneeler was made, and he became slightly impatient when no voice started on the act of confession. He said, somewhat sharply, "Yes? Go on."

"Pray, Father, give me thy blessing, for I have sinned. It's been a week since my last confession . . . but not here."

Some feeling, not incomparable with the warmth of a good glass of whisky on a cold night, shot through Father Owen. It was Mary Ann. Well, he had been expecting her—it would be good to see the child again. Oh, my, yes, but he must not let her see this, he must give her a sound ticking off. She had really gone beyond all bounds this time. Stirred up the whole country for a few hours, and what was more had thrown over the chance of a lifetime. Wilful, wilful. And that chance, if he knew anything, would not be repeated. Old Lord was not a man to give second chances, even to bewitchers like Mary Ann. He checked the eagerness in his voice and said flatly, "Go on."

Mary Ann's voice came to him clear and soft through the grill. "I've never missed Mass, Father, or Communion, and I've said me morning and night prayers every day, but I've been bad, Father." There was a pause. "I run away from school." There came another pause which he did not break, and her voice when she went on was much more definite. "There was a girl there. She was really the Devil, like you said, so it wasn't my fault."

There was a gulp from the box and the priest muttered, "We won't go into whose fault it was. Get on with your confession."

The voice had a little tremor in it now as it came to

him, saying, "I'm sorry, Father, I didn't mean to do it, but I was worried. Me ma was worried. It was all over me da."

Oh, that da! That child and her da! What had the man done now that had caused her to run away from school and throw up the chance of a lifetime? "What was the matter with your da?"

"Nothing, Father. Only there was a girl on our farm and our Michael told me about her. She was always running after me da, and me ma was worried, and I got a letter and she had been crying, and I wanted to come home."

Dear God! Drink, and now women. Would he never do anything right, that man? And having landed a job out of the blue like he had. And to jeopardise it by women now!

"Father?"

"Yes, my child?"

"Do you know it's me, Father? Mary Ann Shaughnessy?"

"Yes, I know it's you, Mary Ann."

Mary Ann sighed. The priest undoubtedly was blind but he wasn't deaf. She said again, "I'm sorry, Father, I didn't mean to do it. I'm very sorry."

The sincerity in her voice made Father Owen say, "Yes, I believe you are, child. But you committed a grave wrong, and now what's going to happen to you?"

"I don't know, Father."

"Mr. Lord won't give you a second chance."

"No, Father."

It was only a whisper, and Father Owen said, "No. At least I think we're agreed about that. . . . Well, it'll be back to school for you."

There was a long silence, and into the silence Father Owen read Mary Ann's reluctance to return to her old school. No matter what had made her run away some part of her had undoubtedly liked the taste of the convent, and now there'd be no more convents for her. Ah, it was a pity, a great pity. He'd had high hopes of her. Well, that was that. Perhaps God didn't want it that way. His ways were strange, and he himself mustn't be too harsh on her. No, no, he couldn't be too harsh with the child. Who could be harsh with someone that loved so much . . . she loved that great, big, red-headed lump of trouble with a heart that was as big as her body, if not bigger.

When he heard a slight snuffle his voice dropped to a tender tone, and he said, "Well, now, my child, don't worry any more. The thing is done, we can only look forward. Trust in God and pray. In the meantime, say a decade of the Rosary each night for a week. . . . On your knees mind, not in bed!"

"Yes, Father. . . . Father."

"Yes, what is it?"

"I've done something else bad, Father."

"And what was that?"

"I hit me grannie yesterday."

"You what?"

After a heavy silence, Mary Ann repeated, in a voice that was scarcely audible, "I hit me grannie, Father."

"Oh, that was very wicked of you, very wicked—an old woman. How could you, Mary Ann? That's the worst yet. I trust you're heartily sorry."

He waited, but no words of remorse came through the grid, and he repeated, "Did you hear what I said? I trust you are heartily sorry. Are you?"

After an extended pause the priest received the truth. "No, Father."

This answer seemed to floor Father Owen and he made fluttering noises, and then demanded sternly but softly, "Did I hear aright? You're not sorry you struck your grannie?"

"I've tried to be, Father. I prayed to Our Lady last night that I would be, but I woke up this morning and I wasn't cos she said I'd always be a sow's ear. You remember, Father, you said you'd been made out of one, an' all, didn't you?"

Father Owen did not confirm this kinship, and in the heavy silence Mary Ann proceeded. "But it was what she said about me da that made me do it. She said——"

"I don't want to hear what she said. Say your act of contrition."

"O my God, I am very sorry that I have sinned against Thee, because Thou art so good, and by the help of Thy Holy Grace I will never sin again. Amen . . . . Good night, Father."

157

"Good night, my child, and—and God bless you. I'll be seeing you." The voice held no reprimand now, and Mary Ann said, "Yes, Father. Good night, Father."

The priest sighed heavily. God help her, for only He could now. No earthly persuasion that he could see would make old Lord fork out any more money on her behalf, and if he knew anything of the old man, Mike Shaughnessy would likely suffer because his plans for the child had gone awry. He must trip over there some day soon and see how things were shaping. . . . And she had hit old Mrs. McMullen! He rubbed his hand over his face. The day wasn't so far gone when he'd had the strong desire to do the self-same thing. But now he must pray for her—pray for them all. . . .

As Mary Ann said her penance at the side altar and gazed with moist eyes up at the Holy Family, she experienced the first semblance of peace since her arrival home. She did not go over the business of the journey with them—they knew all about it—nor did she mention her attack on her grannie—like Father Owen, she remembered, they did not always see eye to eye with her over her grannie, but she did cover the gamut of her errors over the past few days by saying, softly and contritely, "I'm sorry." This they accepted and looked at her kindly, but no word on the incense-laden air came to her, and she knew they would have little to say until she had proved her contrition. They were, she knew, biding their time—but they weren't vexed, and the sight of their beloved faces was a salve on her heart and had a steadying effect on the shivering anticipation that was filling every pore of her body, the anticipation of even a more serious nature than her being bundled back to Jarrow school, the anticipation of her da leaving the farm.

What happened after she had hit her grannie was hazy in her mind. She could remember very little until she found herself in bed and alone with her da. When her ma had left the room he had lifted her from the bed and on to his knee, and pressed her face into his neck, and without him saying a word she knew that everything between them was all right again. At least, that was how she had felt as she went to sleep, her hand in his. But this morning she wasn't sure, not really sure. He had smiled at her at breakfast time and put his hand on her head. But there was something still wrong, and as the endless morning had worn on she came to know what it was. It was the farm—her da's job, it was hanging in the balance. She saw it in the way he walked with his shoulders pushed back; she saw it in the way he talked, his voice over-loud and cocksure. In all, she knew he didn't care any more whom he vexed or pleased.

Before leaving the Holy Family she stared hard up at them for a moment, and without her usual preliminary preamble she stated simply, "Please look after me da, will you? An' don't let him get vexed."

In this short plea she had said everything, for she felt that if her da kept his temper he'd keep his job.

She genuflected deeply to the altar, turned about and walked slowly up the church, past the grown-up penitents dotting the pews and out into the porch.

She had especially picked Saturday night to come to confession, for it wasn't usual for any children to be there, having all been marshalled from school on the Thursday in an unrepentant horde, and so it wouldn't have been a matter of surprise to her to encounter Mrs. Flannagan, but to see Sarah startled her. There they both were on the edge of the pavement, right opposite the church door and, although Mrs. Flannagan had her back towards her and Sarah her profile, instinctively she knew they were waiting for her. A concealed tug by Sarah of her mother's sleeve told Mary Ann's sinking heart that this was a prepared attack.

"Oh!" Mrs. Flannagan turned casually round, and with well-simulated surprise confronted Mary Ann squarely. "Well!"

Only two words, but they halted Mary Ann as firmly as a weighty hand on her shoulder, and she looked, with almost a plea for leniency in her eyes, up at the tall woman. She was trapped in front of her enemy, Sarah, and her mother's enemy, Mrs. Flannagan, and even if she had wanted to fight she would have been unable to do so, for she dare not cheek a grown-up, even such an awful grown-up as Mrs. Flannagan.

"So you're back. Well! well! It's a short career you've

had, isn't it? Not sufficiently long enough to turn you into a lady, I would say. You were going to be a lady, weren't you, Mary Ann?"

Mary Ann said not a word, humiliation was sweeping over her. The loud snigger from Sarah did for a moment stiffen her spine; but only for a moment, for Mrs. Flannagan took up the attack again.

"Well, have you lost your tongue? Aren't we going to hear your refined accents . . . or wasn't that wonderful convent used to dealing with sows' ears?"

No part of Mary Ann moved—except her eyes. For a second they fell away from the gimlet stare, but were brought back again to her tormentor as Mrs. Flannagan continued, "But, of course, they hadn't time to curb your craving for sensation. Rome wasn't built in a day, was it? But I doubt if that will ever be curbed. You went to town this time, didn't you . . . got on the wireless . . . nation-wide search. My! my!"

Another snigger from Sarah.

"Well, you must always remember, Mary Ann, the higher you climb the farther you fall. But I don't suppose there'll be another opportunity for you like that, will there?" Another pause, during which Sarah changed her balance from one foot to the other, then hung affectionately on to her mother's arm and looked up at her as she continued, "I saw your grandmother last night. She had a nasty mark on her face—it would take more than a convent to change YOU, wouldn't it?" In her last words Mrs. Flannagan had dropped her bantering tone, and her bitter feeling of enmity was stark as she went on, "She was telling me she had a long talk with Mrs. Jones on the bus back. You've shot all their bolts, haven't you? Your Fairy Godfather's got fed up, washed his hands of you, so if your da can't hold a farm job down by favour he certainly won't hold it down by experience, for he's had as much experience of a farm as I've had of ballet dancing. And unless you're well in favour with them that matter nobody's going to be fool enough to give a handicapped man such a responsible job. It stands to reason, doesn't it?"

The tears that Mary Ann would not allow to run from her eyes were blocking her throat and seemed to be forcing their way out through her pores, for she had broken into a heavy sweat and she stood helpless as Sarah, her voice filled with laughter, spoke for the first time. "She was going to learn French and German an' all, Ma."

"Yes, so I understood," said Mrs. Flannagan, bestowing a tight smile on her daughter. "You can learn French and German in Jarrow, but, of course, it wouldn't be the same French and German that you would learn in a posh convent, would it?"

Sarah giggled, and Mrs. Flannagan, hitching her coat up on to her shoulders preparatory to moving away, fired her last shot. "The attics in Mulhattans' Hall are empty again, tell your ma."

Even after they had moved off, Sarah joyfully skipping along by her mother, Mary Ann still stood where they had left her, and not until they had disappeared round the corner did she stir, and then it was only to shudder. She stood for some long time staring down into the gutter, while she chewed on her fingers in an effort to suppress a tearing spasm of weeping.

Finally she moved away and to the bus stop, and when the bus came she mounted head down and made for the top end, where, there not being a seat, she stood, supposedly taking an interest in the driver through the glass partition. Not until she had alighted at the crossroads and was almost to the farm did she raise her head and her eyes from the contemplation of the ground and look about her and release some of the pain in her heart, by saying, "It's my fault. It's all my fault." She did not think now, "Oh, that Mrs. Flannagan! Oh, that Sarah!" but, "Eeh! what have I done?"

For a moment, she had a wild idea of contacting, in some way, the Mother Superior, or Sister Alvis, and telling them she was sorry and wanted to come back. She saw herself leaving here as secretly as she had left the convent and arriving back in the south, and her presence there automatically wiping out the whole disastrous episode. But the picture quickly faded. Even if she could, she wouldn't want to go back—not all that way. She wanted to go to a nice school again, oh, yes, she wanted that, and with a desire the strength of which surprised her. But she wanted to be home, if not every day, at the week-ends. Above all, far, far above all that, she wanted things back as they had been on the farm—her da settled and everything lovely. And now it would never be that way again. She felt this to be true, for as Mrs. Flannagan had said, she who had made everything lovely for her da and ma had "shot their bolts".

How true this was was proved as she neared the farm gates. The sound of a car coming out made her move off the road, and on to the grass verge, and when Mr. Lord, sitting at the wheel of his car, went by she glued her eyes on him, and in a flurry of prayers willed that he would look at her, just look—it wouldn't matter if he glared. But Mr. Lord never took his eyes from the road. It was impossible for him not to see her, but he didn't see her, he was blind to her.

Depressed beyond measure she went on and into the house, but here no comfort awaited her. Lizzie, with hard pats and thuds was busy cooking, but she was not drugged, as she usually was, into a cheerful calm placidity by the warmth and mixture of smells; instead she was immediately short with Mary Ann, telling her she had a half-hour before bed and no more. Michael was doing his homework on the table near the window, and he did look up at her for a moment, but he didn't smile as he had done this morning. His face had a familiar, funny look, and it brought fresh anxiety to her . . . something had happened. Had her da and Mr. Lord been at it? Oh no! no!

She left the kitchen, trying not to run, and when she reached the farmyard there was no sight of her da, or anyone else. The look on Michael's face had told her she must find her da, but he wasn't in the cowshed, nor yet in the big barn, nor in the loft. She shouted up, "Da! Da!" and when no answering call came to her, she ran towards the hill on which Mr. Lord's house stood. Halfway up was a stark gate-post, and if you climbed it and sat on the top you could see a number of fields around. But when she was perilously balancing on its foot square top, she still could not see her da.

On the ground once more, she stood, her forefinger between her teeth, again seeing the look on Michael's face. There had been a row . . . her da had gone out to—to Jarrow? No! No! She bit harder on her finger . . . . That was why her ma had been tossing about like that, thumping everything. Eeh! no, he wouldn't do it. After all this long time, he wouldn't go and get drunk again—anything but that. Suddenly her arms were round the post, and she was holding it tight. Her stomach gave a nervous heave, and she felt sick. Eeh! where was her da? He had gone out, but where? Perhaps he'd gone to the market about the cows. On a Saturday night? How long had he been out? Was he even now in The Long Bar or The Ben Lomond? She gazed about her in panic. She couldn't go back to Jarrow and look for him, her ma wouldn't let her, she'd only have to wait—wait and wait.

Then she saw Tony. He was crossing the yard. She saw him go round the big barn and make for the small one. He might know where her da was. Her da liked Tony, he liked him a lot—he might have told him.

On the thought, her legs carried her at a tearing pace down the hill. It was just when she left the grass and reached a section of the cinder track that she fell. She was used to falling, and she usually recovered herself with a "Dash! hang! bust!" but this time she lay for quite some time, sprawled out, the tears flooding from her eyes into the dirt, before she raised herself. The palms of her hands and her knees were scraped and bleeding and covered with black ash, and at the sight of them her crying became very audible. But there was no one in sight to console her, so between sobs she picked off the largest pieces of the ash, and, spitting on her handkerchief, she dabbed at the blood, first one knee, then the other; then at her hands, exclaiming all the time, "Eeh! oh, it's bleeding all over. Eeh! Oh, oh, Ma."

She was telling herself that she would go home to her ma when she again thought of the reason for her running, and so, making a gallant effort, when she reached the yard she turned off and limped in the direction of the little barn. As she neared the corner of the big barn, the blood from one knee began to trickle down her leg and produced a feeling of panic, and the inward cry of, "Eeh! I'm bleeding."

She would bleed to death. To prevent this catastrophe she bent down and pressed her hanky to the spot, and as she did so her eye was caught again by

163

the sight of Tony. He had come to the door of the little barn and was looking out, but from where she was he couldn't see her, and before she could call to him he had disappeared again.

Holding her hanky to her knee, she hobbled slowly towards the barn door, and just as she neared it and came in sight of his back she was stopped from calling out to him by the sight of what he was doing. She even forgot for the moment about her wounds, for Tony was opening one of Mr. Lord's trunks.

There were six trunks in the barn. Four big ones, ends up, which stood higher than herself, with lots of labels on them, and two old black ones with rounded lids and brass bands. It was one of these that Tony had opened, and his hands were now groping amongst the things inside. She watched him lift up and open a little box, and then slowly close it again. The next thing he lifted up was a blouse. She saw it was a bonny one, all lace and stuff, and cream coloured. He looked at it a long time before laying it down. Then she watched him bend farther down, his arm thrusting towards the bottom of the trunk, and when he straightened himself he was holding three small-framed pictures. She saw him spread them out like her da did cards, then select one, and with his eyes still on it, lay the other two down.

It was at this point that she sniffed. It was a very loud sniff, for her nose was full of tears and she seemed to have been holding her breath for a very long time. The sound brought Tony round as if it had been the report of a gun. His hand was thrust behind him, the picture in it; his thin face was pinched tight and no longer looked nice, but dark and frightening. And as her eyes met his, she shivered and would have turned and run, but his voice came to her, belying his looks as he said in relief, "Oh, it's you, Mary Ann."

"Yes." She didn't move.

"What's the matter?"

"I fell."

"Let me have a look."

It was as if he had not been rummaging through Mr. Lord's boxes. She watched him turn and put the photograph back on top of the other two, and with his back to her, he said, "Come here, and let me have a look."

164

Slowly she entered the barn, and he turned and came to meet her, then lifted her up on to the top of the other black trunk.

"My! you have had a toss. How did you do this?"

"Running down the hill." She kept her eyes on him while he wiped the dirt from her knees with his handkerchief. As he dabbed the blood with a clean corner of the handkerchief, he said, "You'd better go home, they need washing."

There followed a pause, during which he kept dabbing, even when there was no more blood to dab. Then quietly, without raising his eyes, he said, "I wasn't stealing anything, I was only looking for something."

Mary Ann said nothing, and now he brought his eyes up to hers. They were nice eyes again, not like they had been a moment ago. "Do you believe me?"

She did not say yes or no, and he said, "There's nothing to steal in these old trunks, there's only clothes and things."

Mary Ann's gaze slowly dropped sideways to the photographs, and quietly she murmured, "They're silver frames." She knew silver when she saw it because Mr. Lord had a lot.

She was surprised when Tony started to laugh, for it wasn't often he laughed, and more surprised when he sat on the box beside her and dropped his face on to his hand and his shoulders began to shake—she could see nothing to laugh at.

"Oh, Mary Ann!" He looked down on her and his eyes were wet. "I'm glad you're back; don't go away again."

She did not answer his laughter with her own, for her hands and knees were stinging—something awful. She really felt like crying again, and found it impossible to give to this situation all the attention it deserved, for she sensed something funny was going on. There was something funny about Tony, yet not nasty funny, she told herself, although she had been frightened of the way he looked a few minutes ago. Then him talking like that, jumping from one thing to another, like what she herself did, which made her ma pull her up and say, "Stick to the point," and her da would laugh and say—

At this point her mind was wrenched from thoughts of her da's sayings by the actual sound of his voice, which chilled her to the heart, for he was singing. Not loud and yelling as he did sometimes in the house in the morning, but just quietly. It was this quietness, this softness of his voice that made her close her eyes and want to die.

On the first sound of Mike, Tony had risen sharply. Going towards the trunk he hastily smoothed out the things and pulled down the lid. The lace of the blouse caught up on the iron clasp as he did so and he had to raise the lid again in an attempt to extricate it.

With her eyes Mary Ann watched, but her mind did not take in anything he was doing. She did not make any attempt to move off her seat, it was as if the sickness in her heart had taken the life out of her body. Not even when Mike stood in the doorway, his hand on the stanchion, did she move. In boundless pity she gazed at him. He wasn't right drunk, just a little bit. He's only a bit sick, she told herself. But it was poor comfort; in fact, no comfort at all. He had promised Mr. Lord . . . he had stood in the cottage kitchen and said, "I'll try my best, Sir." And he had tried his best, she knew that; but now he was back where he had started, and all through her. No it wasn't—she refused to take the sole responsibility for this terrible catastrophe—it was Mrs. Polinski, it was their Michael writing, it was Sister Catherine.

"Hello! hello! hello! what have we here, eh? Look at them knees." Mike pointed at her, laughing lightly. "By! wait until your ma sees you. . . . What have you been up to, eh?"

He moved towards her saying as he came, in an aside to Tony, "Hello, lad."

Tony didn't answer. His brows were drawn to a deep furrow between his eyes and his gaze was hard on Mike.

Mary Ann looked up at her father and said in a small voice, "I fell, Da."

"You fell?" He sat down heavily on the lid beside her; then continued ponderously, "You'll always fall, Mary Ann. Me and you, we're of the same kidney, we'll fall and fall. But we'll get up again, won't we?"

"Yes, Da."

"And start afresh, eh?" He bent over her.

"Yes, Da."

"In places where our fame hasn't gone on afore us, eh?"

"Yes, Da."

"Aye, we will." He nodded at her, then looked towards Tony where he stood before the trunk, and again said, "Hello there, lad."

"Hello, Sir."

Even in her misery Mary Ann could not help but be impressed by Tony's deference—she had never known anybody else call her da Sir. And to keep on calling him Sir even now, that was something—Tony liked her da, she liked Tony.

"You think us a funny crowd, lad, don't you? A lot of things puzzle you, eh? I puzzle you, don't I?" Mike did not wait for a reply but went on with a wave of his hand, "Oh, yes, I do. You've wondered how I could be running a farm when I know damn all; you with your book learning could buy and sell me. An' you've taught me a lot, lad. You've helped me to surprise me Lord and Master by glibly repeating some of the things you've said. Oh aye, I've played the learned boy. Johne's Disease, I've talked about. 'That pond in bottom field wants filling in,' I said. 'Better be safe than sorry.' And Bloat—I even remembered you called it Tympanites—not that I didn't know about Bloat and have got rid of it with a twist of the knife in their hunkers afore now. But did I tell the old boy that? No. I spouted it from your book, word for word. 'The best method,' I said, 'is to insert a trocar and a canula into the rumen. The old methods are dead,' I said. He was impressed—an' you know something? So was I. I was impressed by all the things you knew out of books . . . not that they'll be any good to you without the experience." Mike paused and looked at Tony with his head on one side, then said slowly, "There's summat, lad, I've wanted to ask you, but in me sober senses wouldn't dream of doing it. But now I'm"—he paused and glanced derisively down on Mary Ann—"a bit sick . . . I'm a bit sick, aren't I, hinny? . . . Well, now I'm

167

a bit sick I've the cheek of the devil. Your da always has courage when he's like this, hasn't he?"

Mary Ann had slid to the ground and was standing by his knee, and for answer she swallowed, and he turned to Tony again, his hand to his head now, "What was I saying, anyway?" He gripped the skin of his forehead tightly between his finger and thumb in an effort to clear his thinking. "Oh aye. You were wondering how I came by this job, how I could kid the old fellow. Well, I didn't kid him. He won me in a raffle sort of. S'fact. I was the penny that was tossed up between two gamblers and the old man won me. It's a fact. But you know, it's also a fact that gamblers always lose in the end, for what good does their winnings do them. The old boy won me and see how I've turned out. . . . And here's the loser." He put his hand on Mary Ann's head without looking at her. "She had to pay—pay the old boy—a child, he made her pay. What'd you think of that, eh? I'm talking rot, you say, I can see it in your eyes, but I'm not. . . . Or you didn't say anything. No, you wouldn't, you're a tight one all right. I know that much about you, lad, and I know you have as much love for the old boy as I have. Yet what has he done to you, except growl? He hasn't stolen your bairn, he's done nowt to you—yet you hate his guts. That's why you and me get on together, isn't it? And that's what I was going to ask you. Aye, I knew it was something different to what I've been on about. Why did you pick this farm, you can learn nowt here that you don't already know? What you here for? That's what I've been wanting to ask you. . . . What's that?"

Tony had been supporting the lid of the trunk with the back of his leg—he had not been able to close it before Mike's entry—but on Mike's last words his body had seemed to jerk and the lid slipped into place with a click. Now showing up, almost white against the black leather work, was a piece of the blouse, just a couple of inches of lace, and it caught Mike's eye, and although his mind was fuddled it did not prevent him from associating the piece of lace with the click of the catch.

"Ah, ha! what's going on?" He rose as heavily as he had sat down and walked towards Tony, and when opposite to him he looked down at the age-seered lace, then up into the boy's face, and again repeated, "What's going on?" His voice was now no longer friendly. "I'm having none of that here, lad. I'm still manager, don't forget, and I've never pilfered in me life. I've done many things but I've never been for 'what's yours is mine'. That's the old boy's property. What've you taken?"

"Nothing, Mike, nothing. Honest. You don't understand."

Tony had called her da Mike, not Sir. Mary Ann stared at his white, strained face.

"Don't I! I understand you've opened this trunk, an' I want to know why. . . . Out of the way!" With a thrust of his arm, Mike pushed Tony violently towards the wall of the barn, almost knocking him off his feet. Then he lifted the lid and looked down on the jumbled contents of the trunk, and the first things that met his eye were the photographs. But his mind and his hand passed over these as not worthy of stealing. He was stirring up the contents as if he had his hand in a bran tub when Mary Ann let out a squeal. It was only a small squeal for it was strangled in her throat by the sight of Mr. Lord standing in the barn doorway. Only the Devil himself could have appeared so silently, and her turbulent, panic-stricken thoughts suggested that it was that very gentleman who was standing there, for never had she seen Mr. Lord look as he was doing now. He looked terrible, like, like——Her mind boggled for a description, and when the voice thundered, "Yes! and what may I ask, are you doing, Shaughnessy?" the whole barn seemed to become full of devils. She watched her da swing about with his eyes blazing and his jaw thrust out, and she saw on Tony's face, from where he stood in the shadow of the barn wall, the same look that had frightened her earlier. They all looked like devils.

"Well!"

The word seemed to splash into Mike's face, spurring him to retaliation. His head jerked upwards and he blinked once before saying, thickly, "It was knocked over, the catch broke. I was . . . putting things straight."

If his pursed lips and slowly blinking eyes had not

betrayed him, his voice would have done, and Mary Ann, in a sweat of fear, saw Mr. Lord's mouth become a thin grim line, and his eyes draw out into steely slits. Then whatever he might have said to her da was checked by Tony's voice crying, "I opened it." Her eyes sprang towards him as he moved quickly from the wall to the side of the trunk, one hand held behind him.

Mr. Lord's eyes swivelled slowly, as if reluctant to move away from Mike, and came to rest on the young man.

"It was me who opened it, do you hear—me!"

Mary Ann's blood and ash-smeared hand went to her mouth as she saw Tony take a step towards Mr. Lord, and a voice, loud within her, cried out to him, "Eeh! don't—don't you be cheeky or you'll get the sack an' all." Then the expression on Tony's face froze even her thinking. He looked as if he loathed Mr. Lord, as if he would hit him. She saw her da reach out and catch his arm. It was the arm that Tony was holding behind him, and when his hand was dragged forward he had in it one of the silver-framed photographs.

It was the sight of the picture that seemed to change Mr. Lord. From being like a dark, furious devil, ageless in his wrath, his entire body appeared to shrink; he became old, very old. For a moment his face moved into wrinkles of perplexity, then flushed into impotent rage, and he spluttered as he cried, "Wh-what are you doing with that! Stealing? . . . stealing? Who—who are you, anyway?"

Although Tony was still held in Mike's grip he leaned forward and strained his face towards Mr. Lord's, and with his eyes on the twitching mouth, and his words coming slow and bitter, he said, "Who am I? I've news for you, I'll tell you . . . I'm your grandson."

There was silence in the barn; the whole farm was silent, no mooing of cows, no cackling of birds, no barking from the dogs; no footsteps, no voices, not even the soft scrambling of one of the many barn cats disturbed the dreadful silence. Then Mr. Lord, in a voice high, almost like a scream, cried, "You're a liar! A liar! I had no son. Never had a son . . . never had a child . . . never . . . never." His voice stopped abruptly.

He had the look of someone just awakening from sleep. His eyes became wide, his mouth stretched and his jaw hung slack, as if it wanted to fall off.

Distressed beyond measure, Mary Ann watched it, and her own mouth widened and dropped into a gape, for she was seeing what Mr. Lord was seeing, in fact what she had unconsciously noticed the first day this man and the boy had met, they were alike. She watched Mr. Lord's hands go first to his head and then to his throat, and he made a gurgling sound like the cows did when the grass went down the wrong way. Then she heard herself screaming as he fell. He went sideways, and although her da lumbered quickly forward, he couldn't save him.

The screaming was filling her head as on the day her da got his hand in the machine. Then it was silenced by a blow. Her da had hit her again, boxed her ears.

"Stop it! Stop it, d'you hear!" It was her da yelling at her and his voice was no longer fuddled. "Go and get your ma—tell her to go up to the house."

"Oh, Da! Da! Oh!—oh! he's. . . ."

"Go on—do as I tell you. Go and get your ma."

She dragged her eyes from the crumpled form up to Tony, then muttering, "Yes. Yes, Da, yes," she ran out of the barn, carrying with her not so much the impression of the prostrate figure of the old man but of Tony standing stiff and white and frightened.

"Ma! Ma!" She went screaming across the yard, "Ma! Ma!" out into the road and to the gate, through it and up the path. "Ma! Ma! Oh, Ma!"

Before she reached the door Lizzie was there, fear on her face. "What is it?" She stopped Mary Ann's madlong rush.

"Oh, Ma, it's, it's——"

"Calm yourself. Is it your da?"

Mary Ann could have said yes to this, but she shook her head and gasped, "Mr. Lord. He fell—he's bad—in the barn. Come on. Me da says come on."

Lizzie was now running down the path, Mary Ann beside her, and when they entered the farmyard it was to see Mike crossing it, carrying Mr. Lord in his arms. And supporting the old man's head to stop it from dangling was Tony.

As Lizzie came up Mike said briefly, "Go and warn Ben. Phone a doctor."

Without comment Lizzie ran on ahead, but Mary Ann did not run with her, she stayed where she was. She did not even attempt to follow the trio up to the house. She was feeling sick, Mr. Lord was dying. She was experiencing a great depthless sense of loss; if only they had been kind. If he died and they weren't kind what would she do? Love for the old man blotted out everything at this moment, it even smothered the worry over her da and the latest trouble—his lapse.

She stood tearless, her head bowed on her chest thinking. She had a theory that you could never ask God for two important things at the same time. Five minutes ago she had wanted only one thing in the world—the well-being of her da—and, as on other occasions she had bargained with God to bring this about, now she was willing that if only one request could be asked of Him, it should be for Mr. Lord's life, and if it could only be paid for by neglect of her da, and such neglect she imagined would mean his complete fall, then let it be so.

She turned slowly and went towards the little barn again, and kneeling down by the open trunk, for somehow she felt close to him here, she began to entreat the Holy Family for Mr. Lord's life, offering them, in exchange, her own blameless and lieless life in the future.

10

Mary Ann lay on the kitchen couch with her face turned to the wall. Her hands were smarting, her knees were smarting, and her heart was sad. Moreover, the place was alive with excitement, and she was shut out of it—or, to be more correct, shut in from it.

After she had said her prayers in the barn she had intended going to the house, for then Mr. Lord would be in bed and looking, if her prayers had been answered, all right again, but she had hardly finished blessing herself when their Michael had come running in to say their ma said she hadn't to go near the house but was to go indoors and stay there. She had protested, as was only natural, even going so far as to emphasise her protests with a number of pushes, but Michael was adamant and she found herself hauled to the kitchen where he none too gently washed the grazes on her hands and knees, then applied Dettol—raw. When she bawled loudly at this torture, he liberally applied more, whereupon he received just payment by a good hard kick on the shins.

Following on this, her plans to slip out, when he was gone, did not materialise, for he didn't go out but settled himself down to his homework. His lack of feeling and refusal to be drawn into a discussion as to what was happening nearly drove her frantic, until at last she flung herself on to the couch and suffered agonies of frustration when she heard, at intervals, the sound of cars coming into the yard. By this time she wasn't speaking to their Michael, and as Michael had the only view of the yard from the window and she wouldn't demean herself to go near him, she had to remain in ignorance as to the identity of the visitors.

It seemed years later when the kitchen door opened and her da appeared and brought her from the point of sleep. She swung her legs dazedly off the couch, but had to sit for a moment to collect herself, and in that moment she saw that her da was in no talking mood, for his face was tense, his expression closed, and he was now quite sober.

"Your mother wants you. Go on up to the house." He was looking and speaking to Michael, and Mary Ann thought, "It isn't fair, it should be me, and I want to know how he is." She looked up at Mike, but couldn't say, "Is he better?" in case he wasn't. She felt sick, her head was aching, her hands and knees hurting,

173

but it was the pain in her chest which centred around Mr. Lord that felt the worst.

Michael, after one hard look at his father, went out, and Mary Ann rose from the couch and went towards Mike.

"Da."

"Yes?"

"Da—is he——?"

"He's all right." Mike turned his back on her and stared down into the fire. "Go on up to bed."

"I don't want to go to bed, Da."

"Then go on the couch."

Mary Ann looked up the broad expanse of Mike's back, then turned slowly about and went back to the couch. Her da wanted to be quiet, she knew the signs, he would only get mad if she kept on. She lay down, her eyes on him for a time until the sound of his knuckles beating on the mantelpiece made her throw herself round and face the wall again.

Her da was worried—upset . . . perhaps Mr. Lord was dying. Eeh! no, he mustn't die. If he died Tony would be to blame. What had Tony said? Eeh! yes, that Mr. Lord was his granda. Eeh! . . . Well, she had said the same thing herself. But she had only been making on; Tony hadn't been making on, he had meant it. And she had a feeling that he didn't like it . . . didn't like Mr. Lord being his granda.

Her mind puzzled itself about this new problem, and when some time later she woke to the sound of Tony's voice she couldn't believe she had been asleep and wondered how he had come in without her hearing him. He was talking softly to her da, and she couldn't make out what he was saying, for she was lying on one ear. When she did move her head her da was speaking.

"Why didn't you come openly and tell him? This was no way to do the thing, sneaking about."

It was some time before Tony's voice came to her, and then she could only just hear it. "I had no intention of telling him at all. I was paying him out because of my grandmother's life. . . ."

"She did her own paying, I would think, to go off like that and not let on she was having his child. I don't hold much to her."

"You didn't know her."

"I know the old fellow, and I know this much, if he'd had a child, son or daughter, he'd have been a different man. He's the loneliest creature on God's earth, that's why he tried to take her."

Mary Ann felt their eyes on her back, but she didn't move, for if her da knew she was awake they would stop talking.

"You don't know what a life my grandmother had."

"By the accounts I've heard of it, it was a pretty gay one. It nearly broke him, anyway."

"A woman will spend money if she can't get anything else. He had no more feeling than an iceberg, and he was old enough to be her father."

"She knew that in the first place. What happened to the fellow she went off with?"

"He left her when my mother was six."

There was silence now in the kitchen, and Mary Ann waited, trying not to turn round to see what they were doing, and just when her curiosity was about to get the better of her, Mike's voice said, "Well, she's not the first woman that's had to work to bring up a child, and she won't be the last."

"But it was different for her, she had never worked in her life, she was made for pleasant things." Tony's voice held sorrow.

"Aren't we all!" Mike's tone was mocking.

"You don't understand."

"I understand all right. I understand you've been brought up by a woman who had the knack of making you see things and people exactly as she wanted you to see them. It's my idea that your grandmother knew that she had wronged the old man and that made her keep talking about him—her conscience was at work. Were you brought up with her all the time?"

"Yes, my mother and father had to travel about, they were in Rep. I was only ten when they died. They both went together . . . they were trapped in a fire in an old theatre."

Again there was silence, and now Mary Ann was saying to herself, "Eeh! poor things."

"If your grandmother was hard up why didn't she write to him?"

"Write to him? You say that when you know him! Wouldn't it have given him a kick to know that she was begging!"

"I wonder . . . I wonder. Anyway, I think she did him a great wrong. If he'd known he had a child. . . . My God! When you come to think of it, it was wicked, damn well wicked. I could say evil. . . . It's no use your rearing up like that, Tony. You're a young lad, you've got all your life afore you. Just imagine someone withholding the fact that you had a child. But you've never been married, you don't know how it'd feel . . . you don't understand."

Mary Ann heard her da pacing the mat, and then his steps stopped and his voice demanded, "If she had such a struggle to bring you up how did you manage the money to go to college?"

"I didn't have to have much money, I passed for the Grammar School. Left when I was sixteen and got a grant to the agricultural college. The little money that I did need had to be borrowed. I've still got to pay that back." His voice was bitter.

"What's happened to your grandmother?"

Mary Ann waited for quite a while before she heard Tony mutter, "She died, a year ago."

"Damn good job, I should say."

Mike's words had been quick, and Tony's response was even quicker. "Shut up! Don't you dare say that. I'll have none of it. As I've said, you didn't know her."

Mary Ann held her breath in the silence that followed. Her body was nerve-stiff, they were nearly fighting.

"I'm sorry, it's none of my business." It was Mike speaking.

Then after a moment Tony said, as if struggling with his emotion, "You didn't know my grandmother, I repeat that, she was a wonderful person, but you know him, and yet you're taking his part."

"Aye, I am in this. I know he's a hard man, and I know if he sets his heart on anything he doesn't care who he tramples on while getting it. But there's another side to him, and I've had to admit this, as much as it's irked me. Up to a point he's just, and sometimes beyond the point. And you must remember this,

176

lad, a man isn't born hard—something makes him hard. Anyway, what I'd like to know is, why, if you hated him so much, did you seek him out?"

"I didn't seek him out. I came this way looking for a job. Oh, I know it looks like it. Perhaps I really did come this way to see him, I can't tell exactly what my feelings were, but at the time I was looking for a job and was given three farms to go to. I didn't know he had a farm. It was the name, Lord, that first suggested that this one might be his. Even the day I walked along the road I still didn't know if I was on the right track, but as soon as I saw him in the yard, then I knew."

"If he dies, what about it then? Will you claim?"

Mary Ann stiffened—they thought he was going to die.

"I don't know."

"You'll have some job proving your case. Your grandmother gone, your parents gone. Anyway, if he survives what's to stop the old boy saying that you're a fraud? How can you prove your mother was his daughter, couldn't she have been the other fellow's?"

"What do you think?"

Mary Ann could feel them looking at each other.

"I think you're his grandson all right. Something puzzled me about you from the first. I couldn't quite place it. It was your temper, your manner when vexed —it's just like his." Mike gave a soft, consoling sort of laugh, and then he said, "Well, whichever way things go there's going to be an upheaval."

"Do you think I had better go?"

"Go? What in the hell are you talking about! How can you go now?" Mike's voice was harsh. "Don't you realise that it's the fact that the old boy recognised you as his that brought the attack on? What's going to happen if he comes round and you're not here? You wait a minute—" Mary Ann could see her da in her mind's eye, holding up his hand—"let me have me say. You've got to face him. And what's more, and I say this, you've got to hear his side of the affair. You needn't go black in the face. Anyway, you knew there'd got to be a showdown some day. I feel that's what you came here for."

"I didn't!" The protest was vehement.

"Well, why the hell were you messing about with that trunk?"

"Because my grandmother used to talk about when she was first married, and how, in her lonely hours, she would wander about that great house waiting for him coming home, and likely as not, end up in the attics. She happened to mention the old black trunks with the quaint brass bands, and it was because I thought I might find something of hers that I looked in them."

"I'm sorry to keep harping on about this—" Mike's voice was plainly sarcastic—"but from what I've heard she wasn't the kind of girl that would spend her time sitting in an attic waiting."

"Do you know how old she was when she married him? Seventeen. After the honeymoon she sat at home like a good wife for nearly a year, and then she realised that she could go on sitting like that for the rest of her life. There were times she didn't see him for days—he would sleep at the office—but when he came home he'd expect to find her there."

"Couldn't she understand what he was going through? He was trying to save his business."

"Get a beautiful woman in her twenties to understand that when a man won't go near her for days on end. You say I have no experience—I know this much of human nature. Five years is a long time when you're young. She had nothing to do but spend money."

"And not caring a damn that she was taking it out of a swiftly sinking ship." Such was the tone of Mike's voice that Mary Ann's muscles jerked and she would have turned round and spoken in order to break up their conversation, but at that moment she heard the door burst open and Michael's voice say quickly, "Da! me ma wants you to go into Newcastle with the doctor."

There were no more words between Tony and Mike, and a moment later she heard the door close again and she knew that Michael had gone back with her da. She had the desire to turn round and look at Tony, but something kept her with her face to the wall, and then she heard an odd sound, mixed with the scraping of the chair on the stone floor. Then came the very faint but recognisable sound of crying, the smothered difficult crying like their Michael did. . . . Tony was crying! He was a grown up, like her da, and he was crying! Her ma could cry; their Michael could cry; but not her da, not men; and Tony was a man. The situation had become such that she felt she was unable to deal with it, so she lay stiffly staring at the wall while the quietly muffled sound went on.

11

The school holidays had started, as was evident in the back streets of Jarrow. Tumbling, gambolling, squatting groups covered the pavements, and the roads, and as Mary Ann threaded her way amongst them, often being pushed or jabbed and returning the thrusts with interest, she thought: I wish I was home. She had been sent on errands to the butcher's, the chemist's, and the Home and Colonial, and in all three she'd had to wait. Waiting always irked her, and now she gladly saw the bus stop ahead. In another minute or so she'd be on the bus and back home—and be experiencing once again the waiting feeling. She was thinking about this waiting feeling that was permeating the farm, when her mind was swept clear of the sombre issues by being brought swiftly to a personal one, and one that set her mouth agape. There, coming towards her, was none other than Sarah Flannagan, but not accompanied by her mother or her cronies, but by—two lads.

Mary Ann's eyes widened; her mouth contracted again and slowly formed an "O" and her eyebrows went up even farther. In this moment she did not know what to expect. Would Sarah Flannagan stop and attack her, aided by her male escort? If so, she was lost. Reluctantly she kept walking, every step bringing her nearer to the trio, until they were almost abreast. And not till then did she realize that something was wrong with Sarah Flannagan. She knew Sarah wasn't blind—she had second sight where she herself was concerned—but she wasn't seeing her! She was looking straight ahead. One of the boys was talking to her while the other moved silently along, his head down and his hands in his pockets, yet seemingly, and this was evident to Mary Ann, seemingly pleased to be where he was.

How anyone could want to be with Sarah Flannagan was quite beyond the powers of Mary Ann to understand. These two lads must be daft.

The three were abreast of her now, and she stared pop-eyed at them. Could it be that Sarah Flannagan was sick, ill, or had she really been struck blind, for she was going past without a word, without even a look? The only sign that could be taken for recognition, Mary Ann's hypnotised stare told her, was the slight lift of Sarah's chin. They were past, and Mary Ann was brought to a stop and forced round to stare at the three receding backs, walking all very decorously along the street. And then it dawned on her. . . . Eeh! Sarah Flannagan had a lad. Eeh! Sarah Flannagan was going with a lad. Eeh! two lads.

This astounding knowledge seemed to press heavily on her, and her steps, as she approached the bus stop, were weighed down. She couldn't get over it. For the first time in their lives she and Sarah had passed each other without a blow or a word, and all because Sarah Flannagan had a lad. There was something here that needed strong concentration and, of course, some condemnation. You shouldn't have lads, not when you were only nine or ten. But then Sarah was eleven. Perhaps when you were eleven you could have a lad. Suddenly she remembered Sammy Walker. Sammy Walker had been in her class last year in Jarrow, and he would sometimes give her a sweet. But there were times when he didn't and pinched her bottom. She didn't like Sammy Walker. Yet she did like Bobby Denver. But Bobby Denver never looked the side she was on.

The bus came, and it was a very puzzled Mary Ann who took a seat, as was her wont, near the front, so she could think by herself. If Sarah Flannagan had a lad, why shouldn't she have a lad? If she went back to Jarrow School next term and Bobby Denver was in the same class. . . . Her thoughts came to an abrupt stop. She didn't want to go back to Jarrow School next term, even if she did want to see Bobby Denver and he should take it into his head to slip her sweets. Perhaps she could get another lad. If Sarah Flannagan could have two, then why not her? Why not! She'd ask her ma when she got home. She would say to her, "Ma, how old have I to be afore I can have a lad?"

For the rest of the journey her mind was taken up, apart from Bobby Denver, in selecting a lad. Fat ones, thin ones, dirty ones, and clean ones, she went over all the boys she knew, but somehow she didn't fancy any one of them, and by the time she approached the farm, even Bobby Denver no longer appeared desirable.

She was coming under the influence of the waiting feeling again.

She had just reached the cottages when she saw her mother. She was some way down the road from their gate and was waving frantically to her. On the sight of her Mary Ann sprinted forward, her mind saying, "Eeh! what's up now?" As she neared her, Lizzie's hand came out and grabbed at the basket. This she put down straightaway on the road, then automatically began to straighten Mary Ann up as she talked, her words low and rapid. "Now listen: you're to go to the house, he wants to see you. And mind——"

"Me? Mr. Lord . . . he wants to see me?"

"Yes . . . what am I telling you! By! you've been some time. Where have you been? It's over an hour since he asked for you."

"I had to wait in the chemist and the Home and Colonial, Ma."

"Let me have a look at your hands. . . . Here!" Lizzie wetted her apron and rubbed at a mark on Mary Ann's palm. "Now there you are, you're all right. Now mind, listen to what I'm saying. Mind your p's and q's and be careful what you say."

Mary Ann made no reply to this, she only stared wide-eyed at her mother, but she did ask, "Is he all right?"

181

"As right as he'll be for some time. Don't be cheeky, don't fidget, just speak when you're spoken to, you understand?"

"Yes, Ma."

Mary Ann made to move hastily off when Lizzie grabbed at her, and stooping down and pulling her foot up, she quickly dusted her shoes, one after the other, gave another tug to her coat, another touch to her hat, another push, and said, "Go on. And mind, be civil to Ben."

Mary Ann had no time to think, no time to wonder what she was going to say. As if she had been dropped from the wind she found herself at the back door of the house, and it would seem that Ben had been standing behind the door waiting for her knock, for immediately he opened it and looked down on her. His face was the same as ever, grim as the grave, yet now, it seemed to Mary Ann as if it was older. How that had come about she didn't know, for to her mind Ben could get no older, he was as old as old. Without a word she stepped into the kitchen. She hadn't been in the house since the furniture came in, and now she scarcely recognised it. It was like one of them kitchens in a magazine, all colour and light, and the woman in her said that such a kitchen as this would be lost on such a man as old Ben. Now if her ma had it. . . .

Ben, too, like her mother, was looking at her clothes. He pushed her hat to one side, in the opposite direction to that which Lizzie had placed it; he pulled her coat straight; and he, like Lizzie, looked at her hands. Then he spoke. "Come along," he said.

Mary Ann came along through the hall, splendid with its antique furniture. There were no big bits from the other house, only little bits, she noticed, tables with curved legs, chests against the walls, with brass standing on them. Then up the stairs, deep and soft to her feet, the colour startling to her eyes, cherry red, and this against startling white walls, with bits of gold here and there.

Such was the change in the house that the furniture and decorations had made that for a moment or two her mind forgot why she was here. Then they were on the landing, big, too, as big as the kitchen and again all white and yellow and cherry. Then a pause before a door, and Ben's wrinkled face coming close to hers, his breath hot on her cheek as he muttered, "Mind you be careful. Don't upset him."

She did not answer but gave the slightest shake of her head. Then Ben tapped on the door and they were in the room.

The first thing Mary Ann saw was not Mr. Lord but a nurse, a great big nurse, nearly as big as her da, and when she smiled, her smile was big, too, cheerily big, and when she spoke her voice matched everything about her.

"Ah! there you are," she said. "Now you mustn't stay long, ten minutes, that's a good girl. Go on."

Before Mary Ann moved towards the bed, over the foot of which she had not yet raised her eyes, she looked back at Ben. But Ben was looking at the nurse and it was evident to Mary Ann that he disliked her as much as he had, at one time, disliked herself. It wasn't until the door closed on them both that she looked over the bottom of the high bed to the propped-up figure, and such was her relief that she nearly blurted out her thoughts: Eeh! he didn't look much different, only thinner, perhaps, and whiter. But that, likely was his nightshirt that was buttoned up to his chin. The look in his eyes was as she remembered it, penetrating and hard. But she didn't mind this for he was seeing her; he was not pretending that she wasn't there. Slowly she walked round the bed and to the head, and there they were, close together again, his hand only a few inches from hers.

His eyes had never left her face, and although she remembered that she hadn't to talk, the silence between them was really unbearable and she said, very softly, "Hello."

Mr. Lord did not speak, but lifting his hand slowly from the coverlet, he pointed to a chair, and Mary Ann, realizing that if she sat in it she would be unable to see him, gently and with some effort, lifted it round. Then, getting on to it, she sat up straight. But even so he seemed miles away.

"Sit here."

Mary Ann stared in surprise. "On the bed?"

He did not reply, but pointed to the chair, indicating that she could stand on it to reach the bed. This she did and when she let herself down very gently, near his legs and with her face now almost on a level with his, only with an effort did she stop herself from laughing and saying, "Eeh! what if Ben comes in."

"How are you?" His voice was very low and thin, not a bit like she remembered it.

To this polite enquiry she blinked her eyes. That's what she should have asked him.

"I'm all right, thank you. How are you?"

"I'm all right, too."

He didn't look it, not now, for though he didn't look as bad as she had expected him to look, close to, like this, he looked awful. The silence fell heavily between them again, and she became a little embarrassed under his stare and sought in her mind for a topic of conversation which they both could share. Then a brainwave, as she put it, made her remember the nurse, and she asked, but very quietly, "Is she nice?"

"Nice? Who?" His brow puckered.

"The nurse."

It was evident immediately that she had said the wrong thing—the nurse mustn't be nice—for she felt his legs jerk to one side and his head moved impatiently on the pillow. Then he said, "I didn't send for you to talk about the nurse."

"No? Oh."

"No. I want an explanation."

"An explanation?"

"You heard what I said." He took a few short breaths. "Are you sorry for your escapade?"

Mary Ann's head drooped and she started to pluck at the bed cover with her fingers, pulling at the threads of a handwoven design. "Yes, I'm very sorry—very."

"You didn't like the school?"

Her head was still lowered as she answered, "It wasn't that, I did like the school except Sister Catherine and a girl there, but——" She stopped. She'd better not tell him about her da and Mrs. Polinski, that would make him mad, so she finished, "I missed everybody. I wanted to be home."

184

"That wasn't the only reason, was it?"

She raised her eyes to his and was forced to say, "No."

He did not press her any further, but moved again with some impatience, then said, "They'll push you out in a few minutes. I want to ask you something. And mind——" he stopped again and took some breaths——"I want a truthful answer."

She looked up and watched him strain his neck out of his nightshirt, then her eyes dropped to his hands, for very much as her own had done, his were plucking at the bed cover. "That boy——" There was a pause, and he started again, his voice rasping, "That boy on the farm, do you like him?"

Her face must have shown her surprise, for he demanded, in a voice that was much stronger, "Well?"

"You mean Tony?" She waited; then went on, "Yes, I like Tony very much."

"Why?"

"Cos he's nice."

"Do you like Mr. Jones?"

"No."

"Why?"

"Cos I think he's silly, he tries to make rows. He tells me da about this one and that one."

"And Len?"

"Len's all right."

"Just all right?"

"Well." Mary Ann being unable to explain Len's dimness shook her head. "He's all right, he's nice enough, but he's not nice like Tony. Tony's different somehow. Me da likes Tony." Immediately after saying this she bit on her lip. Had she said the wrong thing again? His eyes were fixed hard on her now, but he showed no reaction whatever to her words.

"What do you know about him?"

She blinked at him. "Eeh? I mean, what? Tony?"

"I said, what do you know about him?"

"Nothing." She wasn't going to give Tony away.

He seemed to sink down into his pillows now. His disappointment was evident, and his voice sounded tired as he said, "That's very unusual for you. As I remember you, you made it your business to know something about everybody."

"Well, I said he was nice, and he is nice—in spite of having a nasty gran——"

She closed her eyes tight against herself as Mr. Lord's body came slowly up in the bed. She dared not look at him. Eeh! now she had done it. What had she said? She was unable immediately to form the connection between Tony's grannie and Mr. Lord, but there was a connection, a strong connection, and something that she should not, under any circumstances, have referred to.

"Open your eyes."

Slowly she opened her eyes. Their faces were close now. "What do you know about his——" There was a considerable pause and a number of laboured breaths before Mr. Lord added the word "grannie?"

"Only that she wasn't nice, she was a bit of a tartar."

"Who said she wasn't nice?"

"Me da."

Now Mr. Lord's bewilderment was evident in his face, for it was screwed up as he repeated, "Your da?"

"Yes. Me da went for Tony when he was talking about his grannie and saying how nice she was, and me da said she wasn't."

"Why did he say that . . . your father?"

Mary Ann's eyes seemed to do a revolving stunt before she added, softly, "Cos she ran away from you."

Mr. Lord swallowed, the blue veins on his temples stood out, his chin dropped down to his chest, and he swallowed again before raising his head. But now his eyes were not on Mary Ann, they had moved beyond her to the end of the room, and beyond that, down into the past. And when he spoke his voice seemed far away. "How did you come to know all this?"

"I was lying on the couch and I heard me da and him talking. They thought I was asleep. It was the night you were took bad. Me ma wouldn't let me come up here, nor our Michael, and I woke up and me da and Tony were nearly fighting. And then when me da went out, Tony began to——" She stopped. She wouldn't say what Tony had begun to do.

Mr. Lord's gaze came back to the room, and to her, and he questioned softly, "Yes? What did he do?"

The jerking of her head increased and the thread between her fingers puckered up the material. "Nothing."

"Look at me."

Reluctantly she raised her eyes, and when he said again, softly, almost in a pleading tone, "Tell me," she muttered, "He was crying, with his head on the table."

After giving Tony away, her own head dropped again, and she felt the old man sink slowly back on to his pillows.

His silence once more weighed hard upon her, and she could find no word of her own to break it, so steathily she began to take in her surroundings. She found them very pleasing to the eye, and a section of her mind which was always open to appreciation said, "Eeh! isn't it a lovely room."

"Mary Ann."

"Yes?" She brought her attention quickly back to him.

"I want you to come here every day until I'm up again, even if they only let you stay a short time. I want you to keep your eyes and ears open, and tell me all you see and hear."

"But what about?"

"Everything, everybody."

Something about this request, or was it a demand, hurt her. She felt that she could jabber about people but not tell tales, and what she was being asked to do was a form of tale-telling, and she imagined that if her da knew he would raise the roof. Well, her good sense told her, her da mustn't know. She wasn't going to carry tales about Tony, but she'd tell Mr. Lord little things, just to keep him quiet.

Once again she was coming into her own, her mind was working along the old lines. The fact that they were friends was smoothing away all her fears. Now, without reasoning, she could see a way out. She did not give way to the old bargaining thought, "If I do this for him, he'll do something for me da," but it was there in her mind, making her alert once more. But the feeling was separate from the protective one that was fill-

ing her now. She smiled at the old man and very gently put out her hand, and with the tips of her fingers
touched the raised blue veins on his.

The hand had scarcely touched the old man's before it was buried within his palms, and he had once
more edged himself up from the pillow. And now there
was a deep note of urgency in his voice as he whispered, "Listen, Mary Ann, I want you to——"

The door opened and the big, smiling nurse stalked
in.

"Ah, there you are. You've had your nice little talk.
And on the bed! Well, well. But come along now."

Eeh! Mary Ann's attention was drawn from the
nurse back to Mr. Lord. Eeh! he had sworn worse
than her da. It was the first time she had ever heard
Mr. Lord swear. His face looked black again, as if he
was in one of his old tempers, but strangely enough
he didn't go for the nurse as she had expected him to,
he just lay back on his pillows and when she said,
"Ta-ra," and did not even amend it quickly by saying,
"Goodbye," he made no effort to check her by word
or look.

She was escorted out of the room as if her visit had
just been an ordinary one, and she knew, oh, she knew
very positively that her visit had been no ordinary one.

Her legs had wings, and they took her out of the
house and down the hill, into the road and up the
farm path in a jiffy, and as she hurled herself into the
farm kitchen crying, "Ma! Ma!" she was brought to a
dead stop, for there, and as if they were all waiting
for her, was not only her ma, but her da, their Michael—and Tony. Never had she seen them altogether
in the house except at meal-times and at night. It was
her ma who stepped towards her and, quickly voicing
her anxiety, asked, "How did you get on?"

Mary Ann's eyes left her mother and touched over
the other three. They did not rest on her da particularly, although of them all she felt most his keenness to
know what had happened. And the look on his face
told her that this was the time for real diplomacy, or
as she put it, keeping her mouth shut. If she wasn't to
make any slips she had to be careful, so looking at her

mother again she answered, "All right," then walked past them all to the table.

Lizzie turned and followed her, and sitting down opposite to her pressed her face forward and said, "But what did he say, child? Tell us."

Once again she looked at the faces about her, and after stretching her nose, and searching assiduously for her hankie, remarked, "Oh, nothing."

Lizzie sat back tight against the chair back and repeated, "Nothing?"

Mary Ann now moved her finger around a little bundle of crumbs on the table, then exclaimed, "Well, just about the farm and things."

Into the hush that followed this evident lie burst Mike's laugh. It was deep and loud, but not his nice laugh, and it startled them all. Mary Ann looked sharply up at him, then back to her mother, who was looking at him, too. Then, much to Mary Ann's surprise, she heard her ma's laugh join her da's, but it was an uneasy laugh, and even their Michael's face was showing signs of a laugh. Only Tony's countenance remained the same.

Then her da, taking no notice of anybody, not even herself, and with his laugh still ringing, buttoned up his coat and marched out of the kitchen. It was as if he had gone daft, as if they had all gone daft—except Tony.

Mary Ann had made seven visits to the sick-room. At eleven o'clock every morning she had been ushered in and exactly ten minutes later she was ushered out. She always returned straight home, and after her third visit Lizzie ceased to question her but would say something like, "Do you want a drink?" or "Have you had anything?" to which the answer was invariably, "Yes, please," or "No, I've had nothing."

Her da, after his queer, laughing bout, had started to look at her funnily, and after her second visit he had stood at the farthest point of the kitchen and, staring at her while making small movements with his head, had said, softly, and did she detect with bitterness, "So it's starting again. After all this, it's starting again." Her ma had said sharply, "Mike!" and he had gone into the scullery saying, "No, by God! It won't, not if I know it. No more bargaining for this bloke."

She had not been able to understand fully the gist of his remarks, but she knew that it had to do with herself and Mr. Lord. And now, preparing herself for her morning visit, she wished from the bottom of her heart that she wasn't going. Not that she didn't like visiting Mr. Lord—she admitted to herself, she loved it—but her da didn't like her going. She knew that, yet she also knew that it was for his good that she was going . . . for all their goods.

As she crossed the yard she saw her da and Tony up in the loft. She did not hail them, but walked sedately up the hill to the house. As usual Ben let her in, and as usual took her up to the door, where, as on every occasion, he cautioned her with the same words, "Mind, you be careful." The nurse, too, nearly always greeted her in the same way and informed her as to the length of her visit. But following on these the visit did not follow its usual pattern, for hardly had the door closed on her this morning, and even before she had time to say, "Hello," Mr. Lord, sitting up much straighter today, said, "Go and get your father."

Her brows shot up as she exclaimed, "Eh?"

Mr. Lord's eyes closed, and he muttered, "If you use that term again. . . . We went into that yesterday, remember?"

"I'm sorry."

"You heard what I said, go and get him."

Mary Ann did not linger. She passed the astonished nurse at the bottom of the stairs and Ben in the kitchen, and was out of the door before he could check her flight. And such was her haste that the poor old man was positively sure in his mind that she had at last achieved the death of his master, which, owing to her capers, he had from time to time foretold to himself.

Yelling at the top of her voice she raced across the yard: "Da! Da!" Then coming to a halt at the ladder leading to the loft, she stared up into Mike's questioning face and answered his abrupt "What is it?" with "You're wanted."

"Who wants me?"

"Mr. Lord."

She saw him turn his face away, and she knew he was looking at Tony. Then through the aperture she saw Tony's legs. They had turned away from her da. The next minute Mike was standing by her side, and he looked down at her and said abruptly, "What did he say?"

"That's all. I just got into the room and he said, 'Go and get your da.' That's all."

Mike turned from her, saying sharply, "You stay where you are." He dusted down his trousers, lifted his coat from a nail, gave it a brief shake and put it on while crossing the yard. His mouth was grim and his body tight, as he showed himself to Ben and briefly explained his presence there.

Without any questioning, for he had a respect for this big, one-handed fellow, Ben led the way upstairs. But before they reached the landing their glances met sharply as Mr. Lord's voice came to them, crying, "Get out woman and leave me alone! I'll see who I like, and when I like. Get out!"

The door opened before they reached it and the nurse flounced out, no longer smiling. She paused for a moment to say something to Mike, then, changing her mind, passed him with only a jerk of her head.

Mike entered the room and slowly closed the door, his eye on the knob as he did so. Then he turned, and across the room looked straight at Mr. Lord.

Mr. Lord said nothing, but with a gesture indicated that he take a seat. Heavily, Mike covered the distance to the bed, then swivelling a chair round he sat down and faced the old man and waited for him to speak.

"Well, Shaughnessy?"

"Well, Sir?" Mike's voice was not harsh, for in spite of himself he was touched by the frailty of the old man. He saw that he was much changed, better of course than when he had last beheld him, but he could not see him ever again being as he was once, a virile, steely, strong old man. He had a sapped look that touched Mike and forced him to say, "I hope you are feeling better, Sir."

"I'm well enough." Mr. Lord examined his hands now as they lay palms down on the cover, as if he was looking at them for confirmation of his own remark. Then he surprised Mike utterly with his next words. "Loneliness is a dreadful thing, Shaughnessy. I don't suppose you've ever experienced loneliness?"

After a moment of staring at the white, downcast head, Mike moved his hand hard down one side of his face, then said, "I've had me share, Sir. I was brought up in a workhouse. Perhaps you didn't know that."

Mr. Lord raised his eyes without moving his head. "No, I didn't know. I'm sorry. And yet because of that I feel you'll understand me a little now. You may not have done so before. You thought I would like to take the child, didn't you, to estrange her from you? Well" —his eyes dropped again, and now both his hands began to move in a sliding movement back and forward over the cover—"perhaps you were right, perhaps I was doing just that, but she was the only person I ever met who wasn't afraid of me. She talked to me." He made a little sound in his throat that could have been the shadow of a laugh, as he added, "At times I found her more than my equal, even my superior. But I am beating about the bush, I'm misleading you. I didn't bring you here to talk about her. She's yours, and she'll always remain yours—money and possessions cannot buy her. I've always envied you, I suppose I always will, but that's finished. I want your advice about another matter."

Into Mike's heart had come a great feeling of easement. He did not speak, but waited for the old man to go on. He watched him lie back, join his hands together, the fingers linked tightly; he watched his thin, blue lips move in and out with the mobility of the aged; but when his eyes came up there was no weakness in their penetrating stare, and his voice, too, was strong as he asked, "Do you believe he is my grandson?"

Without hesitation Mike replied, "Yes, Sir, I do."

"Give me a reason."

Mike now gave a little quirk of a smile, as he replied, "Well, his temper for one thing."

Mr. Lord's eyelids drooped and he asked, "Is that the only thing?"

"No, Sir; he's got the look of you. I knew there was

something about him from the first, and I couldn't place it. It puzzled me. I suppose I would have noticed it if you both hadn't——" He stopped.

Mr. Lord's eyes were on him again, tight, and he demanded, "Yes, if we both hadn't what?"

Mike moved restlessly on the chair before saying, "Well, you know how things were, Sir, you both went for each other, from the start."

"Yes, we did." It was a softly-spoken admission. "What's your opinion of him? Now don't make excuses for him in any way. This is a private conversation, nothing that you say will be referred to again. I want your honest opinion of him."

"He's a good boy." Mike said this without any hesitation. "I liked him from the start. But he was brought up by a woman and it's twisted his outlook. It'll take some changing."

"Why did he come here in the first place?"

"I think you'd better ask him that yourself, Sir; he can give you better answers than I can."

The old man moved from side to side in the bed. He pulled at the cover, tugged at the buttons of his nightshirt, then reached to a side-table and took a drink from a glass. When he had replaced the glass he said, "It's my money he's after, not the farm. That's small fry—it's the shipyard."

Mike's lips pursed and he shook his head. "I don't think so, Sir. He can fend for himself all right, and he's as independent as they come. No, I don't think it's that. Perhaps he's got your own complaint, perhaps that's what brought him here—loneliness, wanting to belong to somebody. He won't admit it, who would? but I think that's the real reason, I do."

"What am I going to do, Shaughnessy?"

Perhaps for the first time in his life Mike was at a loss. The old man, the old devil, was appealing to him, Mike Shaughnessy, asking him what he should do, waiting for his advice. He found himself leaning forward, and his feeling came over in his voice as he said, "Do what you want to do, Sir, in your heart. Recognize him."

This suggestion seemed to agitate the old man, and

he muttered, "But it could all be a fluke, this resemblance. He could have belonged to——" He shook his head. "Don't you think that she would have told me if she knew she was bearing my child?"

Before Mike could answer the old man pressed himself back amongst the pillows, and, raising his hand as if to check any comment, went on, "No, no, she wouldn't. She would have done it to spite me. She did it to spite me. Yes. Yes, she was capable of that." His eyes looked into Mike's now. "Women are cruel—cruel."

The room was quiet. Mr. Lord was lying now as if he was dozing, and Mike did nothing to disturb him. He felt that the old man had momentarily gone back into the past, and as the silence went on he thought: "God! what a life he's had. Give me mine any day, workhouse an' all. And I had Liz, I've got Liz, and the other one." It was strange, but he knew that in his mind he did not think of Michael, he did not think of his son, yet the old man before him had craved, he knew, all his life for a son.

He was startled by Mr. Lord's voice, and his sudden change in manner, almost an alertness, as he sat up and said, "What's he paying you?"

"Paying me?" Mike was puzzled.

"For board?"

Now Mike did smile. "I think he pays Lizzie three pounds a week."

"Three pounds! Not enough—not enough these days. I'll charge him four, perhaps five, he's got to know the value of money."

It was all Mike could do not to give vent to a roar. He wanted to put out his hand and touch the old man's shoulder. He had come into this room thinking that it was his job that would be the topic of conversation and feeling already a dismissed man, not, he had told himself, that he cared a damn, for he had already applied for two other jobs. And now the matter of his work had not been mentioned, the matter of his lapse had not been mentioned and he couldn't see even a heart attack blotting that out from the old man's mind. He stood up and said, softly, "Would you like to see him, Sir?"

"No, no!" Mr. Lord became agitated. "I don't want

to see him. I don't want him here. I was only thinking, that's all, just thinking. You're to say nothing, nothing about this whatever, do you hear? I wouldn't have brought you here. . . ."

"It's quite all right, Sir, don't worry." Mike's voice was soothing. "I won't say a word. I just thought——"

"Say nothing, nothing. I don't want to see him."

"But what if he should go, he's talking about it, Sir?"

For a moment the old man looked startled, then with a return of his old, truculent manner, he exclaimed, "Then let him go. Let him go. There's nobody stopping him." Mr. Lord now waved his hand as if in dismissal.

"Goodbye, Sir." Mike turned and made for the door, but before he opened it, Mr. Lord's voice stopped him, "Shaughnessy!" Mike turned again towards the bed.

"About the farm, and your work. The accounts, I mean. The buying and selling, I've found it too much —too much. You'll have to take that on." The pale blue eyes peered at Mike across the distance, and he demanded, "All right?"

On a great sigh of relief that Mike could hardly suppress, he nodded his head once, and said firmly, "All right, Sir." And without another word he went out, down the stairs, across the hall, through the kitchen —with a nod to Ben, and out on to the hill almost as quickly as Mary Ann had done a short time earlier. Below him the farm lay bathed in sunshine. The accounts—the buying and selling. He was manager now without a doubt. He had not, until this moment, realized just how fearful he had been of losing this job, the job on which he was merely a probationer, and now, with the few words, the old man had passed the management, the complete management, to him. Even if he acknowledged Tony to be his grandson that would make no difference—the old man was always as good as his word, give him his due. His shoulders back, he marched down the hill, across the yard and up to his house, and going into the kitchen he went straight to Lizzie and to her astonishment grabbed her with his one arm and kissed her on the lips. So fierce

195

was the kiss, yet so full of relief, that Lizzie, without a word, began to cry. Whatever had happened, everything was all right with her man.

Three weeks had passed since her da had gone to see Mr. Lord, and everything was lovely, or nearly so. Anyway, joy of joys, the farm was her da's, or as nearly so as made no odds. Her da now did all the books, he sat in the office at nights, and he went to the market and sold the cows, and if anybody came to the farm on any bausiness whatever it was to see Mr. Shaughnessy—Mr. Shaughnessy, Sir. Yes, that's how they addressed her da now, Mr. Shaughnessy, Sir. And joy on top of joy, she wasn't going back to Jarrow school. That humiliation had been lifted from her life the day after her da's visit to Mr. Lord, for her da had picked her up in his arm and pushed her on to his shoulder and galloped her round the kitchen, then had set her on the table and said, "You're going to a good school, me girl. Do you hear that?" He had pushed his finger into her chest. "And it's me that's sending you there. Do you hear that?" She had wanted to jump and yell her joy, but her ma had gone into the scullery, and she saw that she was crying. So now, in a very short time, she'd be going to this posh school. But she'd travel home every night. She had been to see it only last week, it had been closed for the holidays but had, nevertheless, been very impressive. She had told Mr. Lord all about it as he sat before the big window in his drawing-room, smothered up with rugs.

Mr. Lord was a lot better, but he was still very weak. She had tried to make him laugh, but she hadn't succeeded. Each day, as he had commanded her, she gave him an account of the doings of Tony, and she saw that all she said was to Tony's merit. But even this didn't make him ask to see Tony. She had never said to him, "Why don't you let him come in?" for, after his visit, her da had taken her aside and warned her to keep off the subject of Tony when with Mr. Lord. "Least said, soonest mended," he had said. "The old man will make his decisions in his own time. So mind, be careful what you say and don't mention his name." She hadn't told him that Tony was the only thing she talked about, and the only thing Mr. Lord wanted her to talk about; but even so she had been wise enough to refrain from saying, "Why don't you let him in?" But now things had come a cropper. Tony was saying he was going away. He had said it only that morning. She had heard her da arguing with him in the scullery, and saying, "Now, hold your horses. I'm telling you I know what I'm talking about." But Tony had said, "It's no use, Mike. I'm going before he gets on his feet and starts playing cat and mouse with me. I couldn't stand that. If he wanted to see me, he would have made a move before now."

This news had put a blight on Mary Ann's day. She knew that Mr. Lord would find it nearly impossible to send for Tony, but she also knew that he would be very sorry if Tony went away. Moreover, she was only too well aware that Tony would on no account present himself to the old man without being asked. She liked Tony. Last night she had put a question to her mother, as she tucked her up in bed. She had said, "Ma. How old must I be before I can have a lad?" Her ma had burst out laughing, then playfully smacked her bottom and said, "A good many years yet, me girl. Sixteen you'll have to be."

"Sixteen!" She had sat up in bed, all her shyness over asking the question gone, as she explained, "But Sarah Flannagan's got one . . . two!" Her mother had made a long face, then exclaimed, "Oh, has she, indeed! So that's what's put it into your head." She had been strong in her denials, saying that she didn't mind Sarah Flannagan having a lad, but anyway she couldn't understand what any lad could see in Sarah Flannagan. Yet on the other hand, if Sarah Flannagan had a lad, why couldn't she? Her mother had smacked her bottom again and said, "Sarah Flannagan's a good deal older than you."

"Sixteen," she had said from the door, nodding her head; then added, with a laugh, "Fifteen, if you grow up quickly."

Fifteen, and she was just turned nine! . . . How old was Tony? Nineteen. He was a man, yet her da always talked of him as if he was a lad. And she thought of him as a lad. But when she was nineteen Tony would be

197

twenty-nine. Would she know Tony when she was nineteen? Her quick mind told her she wouldn't if he once left the farm. Once gone, Tony would go out of her life, and out of Mr. Lord's life, and as much as she didn't want him to go out of her life it was much more necessary, she knew, that he should not go out of Mr. Lord's life. Mr. Lord needed him.

She reached the back door, passed through the kitchen, saying "Hello," to Mrs. Quigley, who was now helping out, then on through the hall and into the drawing-room. She loved the drawing-room. It was so beautiful, it almost took her breath away. Mr. Lord was by the window, but not wrapped up so much this morning. He was pushing at Ben's wavering hands, and crying, "Give over, man! You're like an old hen. You and she are a good pair."

Mary Ann knew he was referring to the nurse, and when she said, "Hello," both Ben and he answered her. "Hello," they said. Then Mr. Lord, turning on the faithful Ben as if he hated the sight of him, cried, "Go on, get out and leave me alone."

Quite unruffled, Ben finished his patting and straightening before leaving his master, and Mary Ann, taking her usual seat on a padded footstool, remarked, "It's a lovely morning."

"I don't want to hear about the morning. I can see it."

He was in a bad temper. Her da said it was a good sign when he was in a bad temper; it showed he was getting better. "Well, what have you got to say?"

"Nothing." Mary Ann looked up at him. His fierce gaze did not disturb her. Her mind was working rapidly, telling her something had to be done. She would likely, she knew, catch it from her da and ma if she carried out the hazy plan in her mind. Moreover, if Mr. Lord started to yell and got excited and brought on another heart attack she would get all the blame. But as her da said, the worse his temper the better he was. So, looking at him now, she deduced that he must be feeling pretty well this morning.

"What do you mean—nothing!"

She faced him squarely and moved her head from side to side just a little bit cheekily, as she said, "Well, you want to hear about Tony and there's nothing more to tell you, because he's going away." She saw the hand resting on the arm of the chair suddenly contract, until the knuckles became shiny.

"When?"

She did not really know when—it could be the end of the week or next week—but she felt that the greater the urgency she could give to this matter the greater its success, so she said, flatly, "The day."

"Today?"

She watched his face twitch, then his hands, then his feet. She watched them kick off the rug that Ben had placed around him, and with an effort and the aid of his stick, draw himself to this feet, then with faltering steps walk towards the open window.

He stood there for so long and so quietly that she was forced to cough to remind him that she was still there. The cough apparently did the trick, for he returned to his seat, but much to her surprise did not question her further. She wanted to say to him, "Will I fetch him?" but she knew what his answer would be. It would be a bark of "No!"

Some time elapsed before he spoke, and then it was not to her but to himself that he said, "Let him go."

Mary Ann rose and stood looking at him. Then she said softly, "I'm going. Bye-bye."

He brought his eyes to her, opened his mouth to speak, then shook his head at himself and said briefly, "Goodbye."

She went out quietly and closed the door. In the hall she stood biting at her thumb nail. He would never ask anybody to bring Tony here, and if Tony did not leave the farm and Mr. Lord met him when he got about they would surely fight like cat and dog, and then Tony would go off in a huff. It seemed as broad as it was long. Somehow, she felt that Tony had to come into this house—he had to meet Mr. Lord when he was bad, but not too bad that he would collapse, yet not too strong that he would say, "Go!" and mean it.

Suddenly she gave a little skip that was soundless on the thick carpet. She knew what she would do. She would likely get wrong off everybody, but she was always getting wrong, so once more wouldn't make any difference, would it? Two things only were in her mind now. One was that Mr. Lord was very unhappy and she wanted above all things to make him happy; the other was, she didn't want Tony to leave the farm. Outside the house she began to run, but cautioned herself when she reached the cinder track. She'd had enough of running on that to last her a lifetime, her hands and knees still had scars on them. In the farmyard she met Len leading the bull with a pole and made hastily for cover in one of the byres, from where she shouted, "Len, where's Tony?"

"Top field," replied Len, with a backward movement of his head.

When the bull was well past she ran across the yard, through a gate and over a field, and from there, in the far distance, she saw Tony. Long before reaching him she drew his attention with her voice and waving arms, and he came towards the field gate to meet her.

Her running stood her in good stead, for her gasping was the real thing as she brought out, "You're to come. . . . You're to come, he wants you."

She saw his face lose its colour, and he asked, "Who?"

She knew well enough that he knew to whom she was referring—he knew she wouldn't have run like that if her da had wanted him.

"Mr. Lord, of course."

She rested her hands on the bar of the gate and let her small chest heave like a miniature sea as she looked up at him. She could not see how the name actually affected him, for his lids covered his eyes as if he had dropped asleep while standing, and so she put her head through the bars of the gate and demanded, "What's up with you, didn't you hear me?"

"What did he say?"

For a moment she was stuck and looked across the half-mown field to where the corn stood as high as herself; and then she remarked, "He just said, 'Go and fetch him'." The lie slipped convincingly from her lips, so much so that when his eyes looked down on her through narrowed slits she did not flinch but asked, "Are you coming?"

She saw him turn away, hiding his face from her

knowing gaze, and she was aware of the conflict that was raging inside him. Also, she was not unaware of his feeling of fear which she, herself, had felt in the past when about to confront the Lord.

When he came through the gate and held out his hand to her she took it, but as he made to go down the lane and through the farm she altered his course by saying, "You could cut across by the bull's field." Then added, "The bull isn't there, Len's got him." He said nothing to this, but turned right, lifted her over some barbed wire, pressed the wire down as he flung each leg over, then taking her hand again skirted the field, and then another that led them to the back of the house.

Not until they reached the courtyard did any feeling of apprehension touch her, and then with something like panic she thought: "Eeh! What if he dies. What if he has a fit and dies." Cold feet almost forced her to give her scheme away by telling Tony the truth, but he himself prevented this by stopping. He stood staring across the yard towards the back door, his teeth pressing tightly down into his lip. The sight of him standing there dispelled her own fear, and very much as Mike would have done, she said to herself, "Well, get on with it, it's now or never." So tugging at his hand she pulled him forward.

When Ben opened the door both his astonishment and resentment were evident to Mary Ann. She had not questioned whether Ben knew about Tony, but now from his looks she knew that anything there was to know Ben was already aware of.

"What do you want?"

It was Mary Ann who said, "He's got to come in. He wants to see him." She left Ben to sort out the "he's", and with another tug on his hand drew Tony over the threshold and without hesitation, and now ignoring the snorts from Ben, passed out of the kitchen, across the hall and to the drawing-room door. Here she paused and glanced up at Tony's stiff, white face, and her mind cried at her: "Eeh! what've you done now? Eeh! you'll get into trouble. Eeh! there'll be a row. . . ." Mr. Lord would be mad. They would both be mad. And she'd not half get it from her da. Eeh! But before the last "Eeh!" had slithered over the surface of her mind, she had opened the door.

Mr. Lord was sitting staring straight ahead out of the window, and it was some seconds before he turned to find out who had entered the room. From the slow movement of his head his neck suddenly jerked to take in the pair of them standing silently just within the door. Colour like a blood-red sunset enveloped his entire face. The fit that she had feared seemed imminent. She saw his bony Adam's apple jerk up and down his scraggy neck like a piston in an engine. When it stopped for a moment he gulped and swallowed as if it was choking him. Then, as she watched, the colour faded from his face and he leaned his shoulder against the chair as if for support.

Mr. Lord had not taken his eyes from Tony for a second, and she knew Tony was all—"het up", for he was hurting her hand, crushing the fingers so much that she wanted to cry out.

Then the pain was forgotten as she received the greatest surprise of her nine years.

"Get out!"

She pulled her hand from Tony's and slowly pointing her forefinger at her breast said in astonishment, "Me?"

Mr. Lord was not looking any longer at Tony, he was looking at her, and there was not really any necessity to confirm his order, but he did.

"Get out of here, before I take my stick to you!" he cried.

Swiftly she glanced up at Tony, then back to Mr. Lord again. It was evident that Tony was not included in the dismissal. Well, that was all right, but why should he turn on her—she wanted to know what was going to happen, if they were going to be kind. Anyway, hadn't she arranged all this?

A movement from the chair and an unintelligible gabble of words, followed by a bellow, flung her round out of the door, and there she was, standing in the hall, staring at the flat, shiny surface of the drawing-room door.

It wasn't fair, it wasn't. He was a nasty, bad-tempered old thing, he was. But there was one consolation left to her: if he wouldn't let her see, he couldn't stop her from hearing.

She took a step towards the door and leant her head down to the keyhole, which unfortunately had a flap over it. No sound came to her from the room, but as she waited she heard the soft pad of footsteps on the carpet and she knew that Tony was moving forward. And then she could hardly believe her ears as Mr. Lord's voice came to her, shaky but nice, even kind, as it said, "Sit down. No, not there, sit where I can see you."

So strange was this that she felt she must see what was going on and was on the point of kneeling down before moving the keyhole flap, when for the second time in a matter of minutes she received another shock. She had no warning, heard no sound of footsteps, felt no presence, until a hand gripped her collar and she was swung up and on to her toes and pushed across the hall and into the kitchen. She was too startled for the moment to make protest. Still held at arm's length and unable to turn her head to see which one was doing this to her, her surprise was increased a thousandfold to behold Ben and Mrs. Quigley in the kitchen. She was shot past their gaping mouths, and not until she was in the yard and pulled round did she realize that the evictor was her da.

When in her transit through the kitchen she had been given proof that she was in the hands of neither Ben nor Mrs. Quigley, her old adversary, the Devil, had suggested himself as being the only other person who could do this to her. Now as she stared up at her da she saw that he had taken on the guise of Mike and she became afraid.

"What've you been up to?"

"Nothing," she whimpered. Then qualified this by adding, "I didn't mean anything."

She saw Mike stretch himself upwards and inhale deeply, then bring his lips tightly together before saying, "My God! child, if any harm comes of this. . . ." He seemed unable to go on and shook his head. Then demanded, "The old man didn't send for Tony, did he?"

"No."

203

They stared at each other. Then Mike, thrusting out his hand, pushed her roughly and said, "Go on, get home."

She turned and ran from him, her tears spurting from her eyes, and when she reached the kitchen door so great had been Mike's strides that he was close behind her.

Lizzie turned a startled face from the dresser, saying, "What is it?"

Mary Ann made straight for the armchair and throwing herself into it she buried her face in the corner and gave way to her crying. There was no restraint in her weeping now, for she bellowed loudly, while Lizzie, gazing at Mike, cried, "What is it? What's happened?"

"She's taken Tony into the old man, and he never sent for him."

"Dear God!" Lizzie's hand went to her mouth. "What if it should——" She stopped. "Mary Ann!" Her voice was angry, and Mary Ann did not lift her head but bellowed more loudly. Then once again she was whirled up and about, and she found herself across the room and standing at her mother's knee.

"You've gone too far this time, me lady. Do you know what might happen? What if Mr. Lord dies?"

For a moment Mary Ann's bellowing increased, then of a sudden it stopped, and, looking with streaming eyes at her mother, she said, "He won't."

"What makes you think that?"

"Cos—cos—" a number of sniffs—"he bellowed at me."

There was a quick exchange of glances between Mike and Lizzie, then Lizzie said, "What if they row, and he has another heart attack? Did you think of that?"

"He won't . . . they won't."

Again the swift exchange of glances, then Mike's voice demanded, "Why are you so sure of that?"

After her rough treatment Mary Ann felt disinclined to enlighten them. They deserved to be kept in the dark. She would have liked to have flounced round and sat in the chair and sulked and kept her mouth shut, but the latter being an impossibility she found herself saying, "Mr. Lord was nice to him, he asked him to sit down, where he could look at him. He was nice and kind."

After a long, thoughtful moment Mike gave a great sigh, wiped the sweat from his forehead, walked to the fire, put his forearm on the high mantelpiece and, resting his head against it, muttered, "Is there any tea going—strong?"

Lizzie rose and went out into the scullery, and Mary Ann returned to her chair, miserable and misunderstood. She hated everybody. Yes, everybody, right down from her da and ma through Mr. Lord, and Father Owen, right down to Sarah Flannagan, not forgetting their Michael, Ben and Mrs. Quigley. She watched her da drink his tea—he never even offered her a sup. She was only allowed to drink tea at breakfast and tea-time, but sometimes her da gave her a drop in his saucer, but not today. He had three big cupfuls, one after the other, with piles of sugar, yet after he had drained the last cup he did not go out, but remained in the kitchen by the table, rubbing his hand over it every now and again. Her mother, too, remained in the kitchen. She busied herself at nothing, and when this had gone on for what appeared to Mary Ann a lifetime, but which was merely half an hour, she felt she could stand it no longer, and made a move to rise, only to sit back with a plop as her da barked at her, "You stay put. Don't move out of here till I tell you."

Her lips trembled again. What was the matter with him, keeping on. You'd think she had committed a crime. He was going on nearly as bad as he did the night she came back from the convent, when all she had done was to please Mr. Lord—and she knew she had pleased him. It didn't matter what he said about not wanting to see Tony, he had wanted to see him. She knew.

The present monotony was broken by the appearance of Michael who enquired somewhat anxiously, "What's up?"

Mike answered him briefly, saying, "You'll know soon enough." But Lizzie went on to explain the situation, nodding while she did so at Mary Ann's bowed head.

When Michael, whom she knew was looking at her said, "My hat! What will she do next!" Mary Ann found great difficulty in restraining herself from barking, "Something that you wouldn't think of, anyway, you big softie." And she might have said this within the next second, but the kitchen door opened again, and the attention of them all was directed towards it.

Tony was standing there, and he wasn't looking at her da or ma or their Michael, but straight at her. He looked different somehow. She watched him come into the room, and when she realized he was making for her, she pressed herself back in the chair. Fear rushed upon her and her mind gabbled, "Eeh! what have I done. Eeh!"

Tony's face was giving nothing away, on he came until he towered over her. When his hand came out and grabbed her she let out a terrified squeak, and as she was once again lifted from the chair her cry of "Da!" turned into an astonished gulp when she felt his lips brush her cheek, and when he muttered, "You little devil you," she looked into his eyes, which were close to hers, and a little giggle started to work up from her stomach. But before it reached her lips she stopped it. Over Tony's shoulder she looked at her da's relieved face, and her own took on a primness which said plainly to him, "You see, what did I tell you? All that fuss and bother!" She wriggled from Tony's arms and walked over to the table where Lizzie was standing leaning heavily on it, her relief also evident, and she looked up at her mother and, with the injustice she had received at the hands of her family made plain in her voice, she asked, "Can I have a drop tea now?"

ANN—NO LAST, when she faced him, looking at the room. What .... Mary—Ann found great difficulty in restraining herself from bark-ing. "Something that you wouldn't think of, anyway, you big .... And she ought have said this within the ...... second, but the kitchen door opened again, and ....

12

What was the matter with everybody? Mary Ann had no way as yet of describing to herself that flat feeling that follows on too much excitement. During the past two weeks the excitement about the farm had been in-tense. People coming and going, two men all the way from London. And Mr. Lord's solicitor from New-castle came nearly every day for a week. And men from the works, all going in and out of the big house—and Tony there nearly all the time. When he wasn't there he was with her da, talking. They talked and talked and talked, her da and Tony, of things she could find no interest in at all—about herds and buying more land and building a stockyard, whatever that was.

The day following her final piece of strategy she had not of course gone to Mr. Lord at her usual time, for that, she told herself, would have been daft. She was not out to court trouble, she'd had enough of it. So instead she had gone up on to a half-levelled rick to play, only to be dragged down by her mother, her hair and clothes straightened, and yet again she was sent up the hill at a run. Yet there had been no quiet reconciliation awaiting her. When she went into the drawing-room Mr. Lord barked her head off as she knew he would, and she said to herself that it wasn't fair, he could be nice to Tony whom he had been going on about all the time, and now because she had made things right for him he was going for her! It wasn't fair. When, the unfairness getting the better of her, she began to snivel, he sud-denly became nice and pulled her to him, but be-wildered her still further by saying, in his rare and kind voice, "Don't ever let anyone change you, Mary Ann. Always act on your heart."

She could understand the first bit all right, but not the second. Whatever way she acted, she thought, she always got wrong.

Then there was the excitement of Tony moving up to the house. He hadn't really wanted to go; he had said things could go on just as they were. It was her da who had said he must go. But anyway, it hadn't made much difference, for he was always in and out of their kitchen, having scones and things. Her ma liked Tony. So did their Michael.

In some way the entire farm seemed to have changed. The Polinskis had gone and in their place was a new man, a Mr. Johnston, and there was a Mrs. Johnston and a big girl called Lorna. Lorna was sixteen and worked in Newcastle. Mary Ann didn't quite know if she liked Lorna or not. But Lorna was not sufficiently on her horizon as yet to warrant any mind searching.

Last week Mr. Lord had sat outside and watched the men make his garden. There were umpteen of them, and he had yelled at one, which proved he was a lot better. Yesterday, he was yelling at everybody, that is, everybody except Tony. This peculiar attitude of his towards Tony intrigued her. He never yelled at Tony; every time he spoke to him his voice was quiet, even, she could not believe the word herself but it seemed, gentle. With regards to Tony Mr. Lord was not acting to pattern, and she asked herself from time to time when she saw them together, "What's up with him?"

Now, after fourteen days of excitement and school looming up on Monday, life had become suddenly stale. There was nothing to talk about any more. Everybody on the farm knew everything, of course—there was no one of her own age to brag to. She had seen Sara Flannagan once in the past two days, and again with an escort, a single one this time. It was the lad who had walked with his head down. Sarah Flannagan seemed to have moved into another sphere, an enviable sphere. Although Mary Ann would have died rather than admit this, there were times now when she gave this matter much thought, for Sarah Flannagan's life seemed full of excitement compared with her own.

She had taken heart when her mother had informed her last night that she was to go to Mrs. McBride's today, taking with her a chicken already for the oven and a dozen eggs. She had seen this as an opportunity to tell Tony's story, with embellishments of course, to her friend. Moreover, while in Burton Street, there might present itself the opportunity to throw into Sarah Flannagan's face the glory of the new school. In any case, she knew that if she failed to encounter Sarah, Mrs. McBride would soon impart the news to Mrs. Flannagan and take joy in doing so.

Excitedly she had started out with the chicken and eggs and reached Mulhattans' Hall in a glow of benevolence, only to find Mrs. McBride out and her grandson in charge. The grandson's name was Corney, and she didn't like Corney very much, he was bigger than her and always pulled her hair. Yet at this meeting she found herself viewing him in a different light: was he eligible for—a lad? No. His rough, red face and moist nose turned her sensitive feelings away from such a proposition, and reluctant as she was to leave without seeing Mrs. McBride she could not risk staying in the same room with him, unless she was prepared to have a rough and tumble. And she knew who would get the better of that. So leaving her gifts and a message, she had retreated hastily from Mrs. McBride's kitchen and Mulhattans' Hall.

Burton Street was practically empty, which was very unusual. She looked across to the Flannagans' house. The windows were prim and neat as ever, but there was no sign of Sarah or Mrs. Flannagan. So, in a very depressed state, she left the neighbourhood and made her way to church, to pay a visit before embarking on the bus for home.

The church too, with everything else, had changed. The Holy Family were of little or no comfort at all. She told them all about everything, but they looked as if they couldn't care less. It was funny about them, she thought. Sometimes they were all over you and other times they didn't let on you were there.

The Holy Family having taken on the ways of the world, Mary Ann had looked about her in the hope that she would see Father Owen and have a talk with him about something—the Devil or anything, it wouldn't matter as long as she could talk. Of course, it wouldn't be any good talking to him about the affairs on the farm, for he knew as much about them as she did, if not more. He had been at the farm twice in the past week, and closeted with Mr. Lord. She hadn't known up till then that when he was a lad he had been friends with Mr. Lord, for she couldn't imagine Mr. Lord ever being a lad. Also that Father Owen had known Tony's grannie. So to talk of the business of the farm would be covering old ground. Yet at the present moment she would have willingly covered any ground just to be able to talk to him. But he wasn't to be seen. Nor did any rustling or noise come from the vestry to indicate his presence there. She did think for a moment of going and knocking at his house door, but then what excuse could she make to Miss Honeysett, because he wasn't bad or anything and had to be visited. Life was very dull, so dull that had she encountered Mrs. Flannagan and Sarah as she left the church she would have welcomed the sight of them. She thought of the morrow, the new school and strange girls. Well, they couldn't be more snooty than the girls at the convent. She had no qualms about her status in the new school. It might be posh, it was posh, and nuns taught there, but it couldn't be posher than the convent. Already she was looking down her nose a little at this new school.

She crossed the road and was walking slowly towards the bus stop when a honk-honk of a motor-horn brought her around with face abeam. And there drawing up to the kerb on the other side of the road was Mr. Lord's car, but with Tony at the wheel.

Taking no heed of the traffic, she dashed across to it, and hanging on to the window exclaimed, "Eeh! what are you doin' here?"

For answer Tony said firmly, "Don't you run across the road without looking where you're going."

As she dived round the back of the car she thought, "He's like Mr. Lord, always on." When she was seated beside him, she asked excitedly again, "What you doing here? Where you going?"

"Home, of course." He pressed his foot on the pedal.

"But what have you been in Jarrow for?"

"I just came down for some hinges for the stockyard gate."

"Oh." The stockyard gate. . . . Her da and him and Len were making a stockyard for the bullocks. They could talk of nothing else, and they wouldn't play or lark on. She was sick of the stockyard, and in less than fifteen minutes she would be home and confronted by it all again. This at the moment seemed unbearable. She wanted to go for a ride in the car—somewhere . . . anywhere.

A wonderful idea suddenly hit her. She wriggled round on the seat and said excitedly, "Me ma sent me with a chicken and some eggs to Mrs. McBride and she wasn't in and I left them there, but I've got to go back and see if she's got them. Will you take me round?"

"Where does she live?"

"Oh, it won't take you a tick. It's just four streets and a bit away, at the end of Burton Street."

"Very well." He smiled sideways at her. "But mind, I'm not staying, I've got to get back. Mike—your father's waiting for me."

She wriggled herself straight again and looked out of the window. "There won't be any need to stay, I've just got to tell her."

If Mary Ann ever harboured any doubts about endeavour having its just reward they were put to flight as the car swung into the top of Burton Street, for whereas she had left it only half an hour earlier almost deserted now it was full with people. Immediately she sensed the cause of the change—there was a row going on. Twisting herself round and kneeling quickly up on the seat she discerned in the far distance Mrs. McBride. Dressed in her outdoor things, she was standing at the top of the steps of Mulhattans' Hall, with her fists dug into her sides and her head bouncing in the direction of the road, where stood Mrs. Flannagan with Sarah behind her.

The street was alive. People were at their doors and windows, children thronged the gutter, while a group of the more courageous formed a barrier across the road to get a close-up of the scene.

"It's a row." Mary Ann passed this information to Tony without looking at him, and Tony, without much interest, asked, "Where do you want to go?"

"Right to the top, where it is—where the row's going on. It's Mrs. McBride, she's going for Mrs. Flannagan."

This information caused Tony quickly to brake the car, much to Mary Ann's consternation, and she turned round on him and demanded, "You're not going to stop here! Go on to the top."

"The road's full, I can't get up there. Anyway, you don't want to go into that row, do you?" His face and voice showed concern, and she looked at him in amazement as she said quickly, "It's Mrs. McBride. Ah, Tony." She paused a moment, then changed her tone into a coaxing wheedle as she realised that it was a chip of Mr. Lord she was dealing with and not just Tony, for the set look on his face told her that he was not going to drive into the row. "Aw! come on, take me up. Aw! come on, Tony. I won't ask you to do anything else . . . ever, honest I won't. Just this once. Aw! come on."

Tony looked at her, shook his head slowly, drew in a breath, and accelerated just the slightest. The car moved slowly up to the outskirts of the crowd, and as he shut off the engine Mrs. McBride's voice came booming to them, yelling:

"Kicked her in the shins, did he. Well, she's lucky he didn't kick her in the backside an' all! I would've done, and you an' all, me fine lady. And let me tell you, you lay a finger on him and begod! you'll wake up and find yourself a corpse. And it's me that's tellin' you."

Tony found himself with a ringside view of the fight. He saw a thin woman standing in the roadway, her face contorted with temper. He did not know her, but he did recognize the fat old woman on the steps. And so angry and flaming was her countenance that he warned Mary Ann sternly as she made to get out, "Stay where you are."

What! She turned quickly and looked at him. Stay where she was and a row going on. She sensed that he was afraid for her, and she laughed within herself at anyone being afraid of mixing up in a row, especially in Burton Street, and more especially when one of the combatants was Mrs. McBride. No harm could ever come to her if she was under the banner of Mrs. McBride.

"I've told you, you're not getting out. At least not yet." His hand was firmly holding her arm.

"Aw! man, nothing'll happen to me. It's Mrs. McBride—she's at Mrs. Flannagan. Her there." She pointed. "Mrs. McBride always beats her. Aw! Tony, leave go, it'll be over in a minute."

"It's over now. Look, she's seen you, she's coming down." He nodded to where Mrs. McBride was descending the steps, her chin up in the air, and shouting to the children as she reached the pavement, "Out of me way! Out of me way! Out of me way, the lot of you."

"You see." The look Mary Ann bestowed on Tony was not without satisfaction; it told him he deserved all he was likely to get, for now the car was encircled with children and all crying, "It's Mary Ann."

"Hullo, Mary Ann."

"Hullo, Mary Ann."

"It's Mary Ann."

"Eeh! Mary Ann. Is this your car?"

"Eeh! by, Mary Ann."

"Oo . . . ooh! Mary Ann. Ooh!"

"Out of me way." Mrs. McBride's face filled the open window, her smile breaking up her anger. "Why, hullo there, hinny. What's brought you this way?"

"Hello, Mrs. McBride." Mary Ann smiled widely back at Fanny. "I came before. I brought you a chicken from me ma and some eggs."

"A chicken did you say? and eggs. Well!"

"Did you hear that?" Fanny withdrew her head from the car, and looking over the top of it sent her piercing gaze towards her enemy, repeating, "A chicken and eggs. Did you hear that? Sent to me from me friend."

Her head popping into the window again, she now addressed Tony, nodding to him and saying, "Hullo, there, lad."

"Hello," said Tony.

Both in his manner and voice it was evident that Tony was slightly nervous and somewhat at a loss. Quantities like Mrs. McBride needed getting used to, especially when they were in their battling form.

"Aren't you coming in for a drop tea, the pair of you?"

Mary Ann looked swiftly at Tony, and her disappointment was great as he said, with some slight emphasis, "No, thank you. You see I'm on an errand." And aiming to temper his refusal, he added, "It's for Mike—some hinges."

"Oh!" The exclamation swept over the street, which Mrs. McBride now addressed, rather than Tony. "Grand news I've been hearing about Mike. Running the whole show he is now. Well, haven't I always said he had it in him? Aye, the just shall be rewarded." Her head was bouncing over the top of the car towards Mrs. Flannagan again, and the prim lady, not being able to stand any more either of her enemy or of the other thorn in her flesh, now preening herself in the car, turned away, marched through her front door and banged it after her. It was evident that she had, for the moment, forgotten about Sarah, who made no move to follow her mother but stared fascinated at the car, and at Mary Ann seated on the far side of the nice-looking young lad.

Acutely embarrassed, Tony was telling himself that he must get out of this, for now converging on the car from all sides, slowly, and somewhat tentatively but nevertheless insistently, were the neighbours, all apparently anxious to hear Mary Ann's news. So when Fanny put her head once again through the window he said quickly, "If you'll excuse us, I must get back."

"Certainly, certainly, lad. I understand. And give my very best to Mike. And——" Mrs. McBride's podgy and none too clean hand came in and grabbed at Mary Ann's, and she muttered, somewhat softly now, "And thank your ma, hinny, for me. Tell her God bless her."

"I will, Mrs. McBride." Mary Ann's face was agleam. She was the benevolent lady bestowing chickens and eggs right and left. At this moment she would have loved to have a lorry piled high with chickens and eggs, the former, of course, inert, to distribute among the entire population of Burton Street—with one exception, naturally, the Flannagans.

"Goodbye, hinny."

"Goodbye, Mrs. McBride."

As Tony started the car and was edging it forward,

Mary Ann made a plain statement. "You can't get out at the top, you'll have to turn here," she said.

With an intake of breath, he slowly turned the nose and backed, under shouted directions from Mary Ann inside the car and from Mrs. McBride outside, and he was openly sighing his relief and about to take the car swiftly forward when Mary Ann's grip on his hand almost turned the wheels into the kerb.

"What are you doing! Be careful!" He braked, looking and sounding angry as he did so.

"Stop a minute . . . oh, just a minute. Just a tick, Tony."

"Look here, Mary Ann!" He was talking to her bac'., for she was now hanging out of the window addressing a grim-faced, tallish girl.

There was no lad now with Sarah Flannagan and no mother; she stood unprotected, her face not now tranquilly lost in the throes of first love, nor yet grinning under the protection of her mother . . . she was alone —Mary Ann did not count the other children gathered on the pavement. And as once before she had addressed her enemy from out of the window of this very same car, she now repeated the process. Her tongue going twenty-five to the dozen in an effort to get it all in before he started up, she cried, "You thought I was coming back to your school, didn't you, you and your ma! Well, I'm not, see—I'm going to another posh school, a bigger one. And me da's taking me, see! Sending me on his own, see!"

This news made no impression whatever on Sarah's countenance. Her mouth remained tight, her eyes narrow, her face overall very grim. Mary Ann was naturally, therefore, forced to do something to break this indifference. So quickly she resorted to a subject that had been very much in her mind of late—lads.

"And you're not the only one who can have a lad, see!" This was accompanied by a deep bounce of her head. "I've got one, and a better one than you'll ever have, see!" Covertly, she thumbed in the direction of Tony, and not only did she indicate him with her thumb, but with her eyes, too.

Sarah's widening gaze as she took in the young man

was like a draught of heady wine to Mary Ann, and stimulated by it nothing could prevent her from going the whole hog.

"And me ma says I can go out when I'm fifteen and be married when I'm nineteen, so there!"

From its expression of amazement Sarah's face now turned to one of open scorn and disbelief, and this had a sudden dampening effect on Mary Ann. She knew she had gone beyond the bounds even of fantasy, and nothing could prove her right but a declaration from the horse's mouth itself. So quickly she turned her face to Tony. He was looking at her with very much the same expression that Sarah had been wearing, which filled her with irritation, and if she'd had time to think about it she would have thought along the lines of Mike and would have said, "He's not quick off the mark about some things." And when a person isn't quick off the mark, he has to be prompted.

"Aren't I going to be married when I'm nineteen?"

That her advanced thinking had definitely stunned Tony for the moment was plain to be seen, for he made no response, until a jab of her blocked and, therefore, quite hard toecap in his ankle brought him to his senses, and he explained over-loudly, "Yes, yes—that's so——"

The rest of his mumbled words was lost on her for she was now half-way out of the window. It seemed that she couldn't get near enough to Sarah as she spurted the remainder of the fantasy at her. "So you see. And he buys me——" she was going to say bullets, but her mind quickly rejected this as common and changed it to sweets. But even this word in a split second was discarded for something more glamorous, and she ended, "Chocolates. Big 'uns, in a box, like you have at Christmas. So there . . . you see!"

There was a sharp burr as Tony's foot struck the pedal, and her words were whipped away on a gasp as she was pulled inside the car, plumped on to the seat, and for a second held within the circle of his arm as he pressed her to his side. He was laughing now, laughing so much that she could not hear the sound of her own voice as she cried, "Give over. Aw! give over, man. What you laughing at?"

When they reached the main road Tony was still laughing, he was laughing so much that the tears were running down his face, and she was becoming a little irritated. Perhaps it had been funny, but why was he keeping on? And she said again, "Aw! give over." She didn't like being laughed at so much. She liked to make people laugh but not them to laugh at her and keep on. Now he was looking down at her, his face more bright and alive than she had ever seen it, even after the morning he had come from Mr. Lord's, and in an imitation of her own voice, he demanded, "Can't a lad laugh at his lass?"

Her head slowly drooped from his gaze, and she moved primly on the seat, trying to suppress a smile. He had said she was his lass. Suddenly, she had visions of herself being escorted back down Burton Street by him, but on their feet—cars, for the purpose she had in mind, moved too quickly—and they would be walking, of course, under the wilting gaze of Sarah Flannagan. And still with the eyes of her enemy upon her and bulging with envy, she saw herself walking up the aisle of the crowded church in her best clothes followed by her escort . . . and, finally, going to the pictures. But on this thought her reason leapt at her and said flatly, "Don't be daft. You won't be able to do that for ages and ages."

She slanted her eyes and glanced at Tony. He was still smiling, but he had returned to normal and was driving with his whole attention on the wheel. A feeling of ownership took hold of her, as strong as any feeling she'd had for Mr. Lord.

She was only nine and she had a lad!

ABOUT THE AUTHOR

CATHERINE COOKSON is one of the most widely read contemporary woman novelists. Her background, which she so vividly re-creates in many of her novels, was the north of England at Tyne Dock. Since her first book in 1950, she has been acclaimed both as a regional writer and as the author of exciting historical fiction. Two of her books have been filmed and others translated into as many as eight languages. American readers will remember her for *The Dwelling Place, The Glass Virgin, Kate Hannigan, Katie Mulholland, Feathers in the Fire, The Fifteen Streets, Fenwick Houses, Pure as the Lily, The Invisible Cord, Rooney,* her Mallen family trilogy (*The Mallen Girl, The Mallen Streak* and *The Mallen Lot*) and her "Mary Ann" series. Mrs. Cookson and her husband, a schoolmaster, now live in Hastings, England.